MORE DARK
SECRETS
OF THE TURF

MORE DARK
SECRETS
OF THE TURF

JOHN WHITE

(Former Magazine Sportswriter of the Year
and author of *The Racegoers' Encyclopedia*)

B. T. BATSFORD LTD · LONDON
Batsford Business Online: www.batsford.com

© BT Batsford 1998
First published 1998

Published by BT Batsford Ltd,
583 Fulham Road,
London SW6 5BY

Batsford Business Online: www.batsford.com

Printed by
Redwood Books
Trowbridge
Wiltshire

ISBN 0 7134 8346 6

A CIP catalogue record for this book
is available from The British Library

MORE DARK SECRETS OF THE TURF

PART ONE : SIDING WITH TRAINERS

PART TWO : SIDING WITH JOCKEYS

PART THREE : SIDING WITH OWNERS

PART FOUR : SIDING WITH HORSES

PART FIVE : SIDING WITH THE BIZARRE

ABOUT THE AUTHOR

In 1990 John White was voted Magazine Sportswriter of the Year. A past contributor to *The Sporting Life, The Observer Colour Supplement, Competition Rider, Royalty Monthly, The Lady, The Irish Post, Equestrian World, Prediction, Mensa Magazine, Writers' Monthly, The Betting Man's Contact* and to both *Racing Monthly* and *Turf and Track* as Pegasus, their systems expert, he has already written this book's companion volume – the best-selling *Dark Secrets of the Turf* – that he revised and updated to provide a 'last for ever' second edition in 1996.

He has also written *First Past the Post* (another compendium of strategies for making racing far more enjoyable and profitable), the innovative *Racing Systems with the Pocket Calculator,* as well as, for HarperCollins, *The Racegoers' Encyclopaedia* – the critically acclaimed, first, fully comprehensive A–Z of British and Irish Flat and National Hunt racing.

Happy to combine journalism with examining and tutoring in English Language and Literature, he lives at Falmouth in Cornwall.

ACKNOWLEDGEMENTS

I owe much to my daughter Nicola and to my wife as my typists, to Derrick Payne as the stimulus for several of the ideas this book contains and to the excellent journalists who contribute to the racing pages of the *Daily Telegraph*, *The Times* and the *Daily Mail*.

I have gleaned a great deal of valuable information from the daily editions of *The Racing Post* and *The Sporting Life*, as well as from the pages of many excellent *Superform* publications. Special thanks are also due to Geoff Johnson of Weatherbys and to my editor, John Winters of B. T. Batsford.

"Winning would put any man into courage."
Cymbeline, Act 2

"It never yet did hurt
To lay down likelihoods and forms of hope."
King Henry IV, Act 1

For all my family and in loving memory of my mother.

INTRODUCTION

This sequel to the original *Dark Secrets of the Turf* presents a further set of practical winner-finding strategies. Unrivalled, like its predecessor, for the sheer depth of its research, its entertaining style and thought-provoking insights, *More Dark Secrets of the Turf* has been specially written so as to appeal to both the knowledgeable and the novice racing fan. It may well become the bane of bookmakers since it provides those battling against them with some extremely powerful ammunition.

The fact that winnings from bets with bookmakers on racecourses are uneroded by tax and, whether resulting from wagers struck on or off course, need not be declared to the Inland Revenue, represents a major attraction and *raison d'étre* for what follows - an account of several ingenious and intelligent strategies for 'beating the book', each learnt the hard way over 35 years by a hard-bitten backer and racing enthusiast.

PART ONE

SIDING WITH TRAINERS

STRATEGY 1

TRAINERS FOR RACES

As someone who has regularly studied the results of particular races over an extensive period, I cannot agree with Henry Ford's declaration that 'history is bunk'. In fact, the belief that on the turf the opposite is true has led those publishing Britain's two sporting dailies, the *Racing Post* and *The Sporting Life* to respectively employ Craig Thake and Gerald Delamere to delve into the form book so they can give readers of these papers any 'history lessons' resulting from their research into the past ten runnings of certain select events.

Unfortunately, these are highly competitive (as they are invariably races of the highest class) and this means that over the years they are won by a host of different trainers.

So it is often preferable to engage in a little 'do it yourself' delving into the ten-year race records of events far too humble for Thake or Delamere to scrutinise, since these are not staged at top-class competitive race meetings, but truly local ones where races are often 'farmed' by smaller yards.

Worcester is one such track and the results of no less than four out of five races staged there at a recent evening meeting rather spectacularly vindicated the ten-year 'tell tale' approach to winner-finding that racing weeklies such as *The Sporting Life Weekender* have made a regular feature of their coverage of weekend racing.

The evening before this Worcester meeting, I settled down to do my history homework with the help of the *Evening Mail* published in nearby Birmingham. This involved monitoring the past ten runnings of the six races I was looking forward to later watching in person.

My task was not as onerous as it may sound. In the first race on the card, I noticed that the only previous successful trainers with runners were Martin Pipe and Frank Jordan. As the former had recently been more successful than the latter and was fielding a runner quoted at a shorter forecast rate of odds, I decided to make his Nordic Delight my selection and was truly delighted when it trotted up at 9-4 (a rate of odds only slightly less enticing than the 5-2 that was forecast).

Since my research pinpointed the fact that John Upson was the only previously successful trainer with a runner in the second race - the Dylan Thomas Handicap Chase, and had also won this race when it was last contested, I felt his Deep Dark Dawn might go and so it proved when this six-year-old also went in at 100-30.

In the third race Martin Pipe was seen to have by far the past best training record (with two wins in the past ten runnings) and so I again plumped for his representative which ran out a ready winner at a most acceptable 5-1!

By now I felt that with three wins to its credit, the 'ten-year trends plan' might be riding for a fall but to my amazement it continued its extremely smooth start when a six-year-old of this name sent to race by A James (as the only previously successful trainer in the Captain Cat Novices Chase) won this race at 11-1!

As no previously successful handler was fielding a runner in the fifth race, I ended my assault on the Worcester bookmakers by supporting John Jenkins's Fierce in the final race but, on this occasion, Henry Ford's view of history seemed vindicated for the horse failed to make the frame!

The past results of particular races can often show that the 'trainers for races' approach, when applied selectively, can prove lucrative.

For example, year after year, many races, both top class flat and National Hunt 'pattern' contests and far humbler events are 'farmed' by certain trainers.

Such 'farming' of formerly well-ploughed racing fields can be readily anticipated if backers purchase copies of annual guides to flat and jump racing in which detailed results extending back over ten years are given for particularly prestigious races and if, additionally, they are prepared to undertake some detailed delving into form books to discover past winners of much humbler contests.

Such delving has thrown up the outstanding 'strike rates' of some trainers in what seem to be their favourite races. In April 1996 Santillana's 6-1 win in Sandown's Thresher Classic Trial was reported on as follows in the *Daily Telegraph:*

> ' Santillana, who ran on well to give John Gosden his fourth win in the Thresher Classic Trial in the space of five years, was never entered for the Derby.
> "I always target this race (the Classic Trial)," said Gosden. "It is a good purse, and it is run on probably the best day's racing of the year. '

As for prestigious late season contests, my particular favourite is Doncaster's May Hill Stakes, run in early September. Henry Cecil's 15-2 winner in this in 1995, his triumphant 1996 representative, Reams of Verse and his Midnight Line, victorious at 3-1 in 1997, brought his tally out of the last 11 runnings to seven! Incidentally, Cecil is also fond of farming a race run slightly earlier at Doncaster - the Park Hill Stakes - which he captured three times in the first half of the present decade.

Those who might regard such repeated successes in some races as little more than coincidental might care to study this strategy's concluding report on a recent training feat by Luca Cumani.

FROM *THE INDEPENDENT*

DONCASTER

2.05: 1. LEND A HAND (J Weaver) 8-1; **2. Rabah** 12-1; **3. The Glow-Worm** 14-1; **4. Kim's Brave** 16-1. **21 ran.** 11-2 fav Monsajem (5th). 1½, 2½. (M Johnston). **Tote:** £6.30; £1.60, £3.50, £3.40, £10.30. DF: £48.20. CSF: £93.65. Tricast: £1,260.69. Trio: £324.30. NRs: Legend Of Love, Mowbray, Take A Turn.

2.35: 1. ALMUSHTARAK (R Cochrane) 25-1; **2. Decorated Hero** 9-4 jt fav; **3. Samara** 11-1. **8 ran.** 9-4 jt fav Poteen (4th). Nk, hd. (K Mahdi). **Tote:** £28.50; £4.10, £1.30, £2.70. DF: £27.50. CSF: £74.77. Trio: £99.70. NR: Centre Stalls.

3.10: 1. CANON CAN (K Fallon) 6-1; **2. Persian Punch** 13-2; **3. Further Flight** 9-2. **5 ran.** 8-13 fav Double Trigger (4th). 1¼, nk. (H Cecil). **Tote:** £5.60; £1.80, £2.30. DF: £13.00. CSF: £36.67.

3.40: 1. MIDNIGHT LINE (K Fallon) 3-1 fav; **2. Flawless** 12-1; **3. Glorosia** 100-30. **9 ran.** ½, 3. (H Cecil). **Tote:** £3.30; £1.50, £2.70, £1.60. DF: £22.60. CSF: £36.77. Trio: £33.70.

4.10: 1. AUNTY JANE (Pat Eddery) 8-1; **2. Dazzle** 100-30; **3. Miss Riviera** 12-1. **10 ran.** 11-4 fav Noisette. Hd, hd. (J Dunlop). **Tote:** £7.10; £1.70, £1.80, £2.80. DF: £10.30. CSF: £31.74. Trio: £47.40. NRs: Sally Slade, Wellspring.

4.40: 1. SAFIO (D Wright) 6-1 fav; **2. Al Muallim** 9-1; **3. Mr Teigh** 10-1; **4. Cybertechnology** 11-1. **21 ran.** ½, hd. (A Bailey). **Tote:** £5.70; £1.80, £2.00, £2.20, £2.50. DF: £19.60. CSF: £47.28. Tricast: £501.18. Trio: £72.00. NR: Sualtach.

Jackpot: Not won. Pool of £105,516.30 carried forward to Doncaster today.

Placepot: £461.70. **Quadpot:** £60.60.

Place 6: £821.83. **Place 5:** £187.30.

The trophy for this Group Three race could probably find its own way to Warren Place. Cecil has now won seven of the last 11 runnings and 11 in all, including one with Midnight Air, Midnight Line's dam.

FROM *THE DAILY TELEGRAPH*

LUCA CUMANI recorded his sixth win in the last seven runnings of the Blue Seal Stakes at Ascot yesterday when newcomer Queen's View obliged in soft ground.

They might also do well to remember that such is the soundness of the thinking behind the 'trainers for particular races' strategy that national newspapers like *The Sun* have incorporated it into their racing coverage. Indeed, this newspaper once advertised its *Trainerfax* feature as having achieved the following very impressive results!

Trainerfax produced one of its best results at Sandown's jumps meeting December 5:

■TRAINERFAX: D Elsworth won the 1.55 in 1987, '91. M Pipe won the 2.30 in 1988, '89, '91. D Nicholson won the 3.0 in 1987, '89, '91. J Gifford won the 3.30 in 1988, '91.

1.55 D Elsworth ran Big Beat (1st 4-1), 2.30 M Pipe ran Valfinet (1st 5-4), 3.0 D Nicholson ran Waterloo Boy (1st 11-4), 3.30 J Gifford ran Run Up The Flag (1st 9-4) They produced a smashing 136-1 accumulator!

One other application of the 'trainers for races' approach to winner-finding involves the penchant for success in particular British races that, over the years, has been demonstrated by handlers based in France.

Francois Doumen's predilection for success in Kempton's King George VI Steeplechase was, of course, extensively chronicled in the still available *Dark Secrets of the Turf* (ISBN 0 984035 32 3, this present book's best-selling predecessor) and, interestingly, another top Gaelic handler, Andre Fabre, also has an outstanding record of success with runners he sends to bid for top British prizes. Indeed, Fabre has such a high success rate that, season after season, a good level stake profit can be made by backing all the raiders he sends to Britain.

Moreover, this Frenchman's record in particular races is outstanding and one of these is the last major two-year-old race of the flat racing season, the Dewhurst Stakes, run at Newmarket in mid-October.

Just prior to this race's recent running on 18 October, 1997, I scrutinised the following feature in my *Daily Telegraph* in which detailed consideration was given to the past fates of horses previously sent to run in the Dewhurst by trainers also fielding contestants in 1997.

3.30 THOROUGHBRED CORPORATION
DEWHURST STKS 2YO 7f £59,477 (7)   **CH4**

401	4111	CENTRAL PARK (IRE) (80) (D) (Fahd Salman) P Cole 9 0 .... T Quinn	5
402	111	DAGGERS DRAWN (USA) (36) (D) (Cliveden Stud) H Cecil 9 0 .... K Fallon	3
403	125	DESERT PRINCE (IRE) (55) (Lucayan Stud) D Loder 9 0............................ L Dettori	6
404	211	IMPRESSIONIST (IRE) (49) (D) (Mrs J Magnier) A P O'Brien (Ire) 9 0 M J Kinane	2
405	2	PEGNITZ (USA) (20) (B H Voak) C Brittain 9 0 .... J Reid	4
406	111	TAMARISK (18)(CD) (Highclere Th'bred Racing Ltd) R Charlton 9 0........... T Sprake	7
407	1121	XAAR (28) (D) (K Abdulla) A Fabre (Fr) 9 0....................................... O Peslier	1

S.P. FORECAST: 7-4 Daggers Drawn, 15-8 Xaar, 7-2 Central Park, 7-1 Tamarisk, 12-1 Desert Prince, 25-1 Impressionist, 66-1 Pegnitz.

1996: In Command 9 0 M Hills 10-1 B Hills 8 ran.

FORM GUIDE.— Central Park was impressive when beating Docksider (rec 3lb) by 3l at Goodwood (7f). **Daggers Drawn** took a little while to get on top after having been blocked in his run when beating Docksider (rec 4lb) by ½l at Doncaster (7f). **Xaar** found a fine turn of foot to beat Charge d'Affaires in a Group One event at Longchamp (7f) by 3l. **Tamarisk** was supplemented for this race after making all to win the valuable Tattersalls Houghton Sales Stakes over this course and distance last month, when he beat Sapphire Ring by 3½l. **Desert Prince** could find no extra in the final furlong when 2l 5th of 7 to Charge d'Affaires at Deauville (6f) in August. **Impressionist** beat Fruits of Love by 1l at The Curragh (7f) and will give his stable a good line to the merits of their higher-profile juveniles. **Pegnitz** made a promising debut when 2l runner-up in Grade B event at Ascot (7f) but faces a severe task on only his second appearance.   **XAAR** is preferred to **Central Park**.

10-YEAR DEWHURST RECORD OF TRAINERS

P Cole: The West 7th of 8 (96); Green Perfume 2nd of 7 (94); River Deep 7th of 10 (93); Firm Pledge 3rd of 11 (92); Great Palm 2nd of 9 (91); Generous Won 50-1 (90).
H Cecil: Eltish 5-2F 3rd of 7 (94), Al Widyan last of 7 (94); Pursuit of Love 4th of 9 (91); Sedair last of 8 (90); Opening Verse 5th of 6 (88), Samoan last of 6 (88).
D Loder: Bahamian Bounty 7-2F 4th of 8 (96).
A O'Brien: Desert King 6th of 8 (96).
C Brittain: Air Express 3rd of 8 (96); Village Eagle 9th of 19 (94); Alanees last of 10 (93); Sueboog 4th of 11 (92); Tony San last of 11 (91); Kohinoor 7th of 8 (90); Call To Arms 2nd of 7 (89).
R Charlton: Inchinor 2nd of 11 (92).
A Fabre: Pennekamp Won 5-2JF (95), Zafonic Won 10-11F (92).

As can be seen from the above, prior to 1997, Fabre's past winners to runners ratio in the Dewhurst was 100 per cent. Moreover, since his 1997 representative, Xaar was prominent in the betting forecast and, even more crucially, the choice of the *Daily Telegraph's* Form expert, I felt that here was yet another French 'avenger of Waterloo' that might well run his English rivals ragged.

In the event Xaar was significantly backed down to 11-8 favourite and, in truly spectacular fashion, duly romped home by four lengths over the far-from-lengthy seven furlong Dewhurst race distance!

A further variation of the 'trainers for races' approach to winner-finding involves capitalising on the occasional fact that some races are named after trainers who then send runners to try to win their 'own' races. Not so long ago, for example, at Wetherby, a Roddy Armytage trained runner in a race of this name had his exertions directed by this handler's daughter, Gee, and touted by her brother Marcus, a fellow jockey and racing correspondent of the *Daily Telegraph*.

It was small wonder then that this 'family' favourite proved a worthy 11-8 market leader when winning their father's race by three-and-a-half lengths!

3.15 RODDY ARMYTAGE HANDICAP CHASE 3m 110yds £3,548 (6)

1	253P52	MERRY MASTER (26) (CD) R Armytage 10 11 11
		.... **Gee Armytage** †
2	14U3PP	HIGH PADRE (44) (CD) J FitzGerald 8 10 12 .... M Dwyer
3	FP02/04	JELUPE (23) (D) R Sandys-Clarke 12 10 5 Mr R Sandys-Clarke
4	R2P322	GLOVE PUPPET (10) (D) G Balding 9 10 3 .... B Clifford
5	0P5602	JESTERS PROSPECT (18) Mrs J Goodfellow 10 10 2 . B Storey
6	5-06562	FISH QUAY (10) (D) Mrs K Lamb 11 10 0 .... Miss S Lamb (7)

S.P. FORECAST: 7-4 Merry Master, 7-2 High Padre, 4-1 Fish Quay, 6-1 Jelupe, 8-1 Glove Puppet, 10-1 Jesters Prospect.

WETHERBY

Going: GOOD

2.05 (2m nov hdle): **GOING PUBLIC** (K Johnson, 5-2F) 1; **Otter Bush** (4-1) 2; Pimsboy (33-1) 3. 11 ran. ¾, nk. (P Cheesbrough). Tote: win £3.80; places £1.40, £1.90, £10.90. DF: £11.30. CSF: £12.17.

2.40 (2m hdle): **NOTABLE EXCEPTION** (S Mason, 9-2) 1; **Chadwick's Ginger** (12-1) 2; All Welcome (7-2) 3. 13 ran. All Greek To Me 5-2F. 2, 2. (Mrs M Reveley). Tote: win £5.80; places £2.30, £1.90, £2.40. Dual F'cast: £66.30. CSF: £53.68.

3.15 (3m 110y h'cap ch): **MERRY MASTER** (Gee Armytage, 11-8F) 1; **Glove Puppet** (5-2) 2; Jesters Prospect (5-1) 3. 6 ran. 3½, 25. (R Armytage). Tote: win £2.40; places £1.70, £1.70. DF: £2.30. CSF: £5.17.

Even more recently, on 9 August, 1997, trainer Mrs Mary Reveley sent out, not just the winner of her own race at Redcar, but achieved a double success in this by also saddling the runner-up. Both were owned by the Mary Reveley Racing Club and, astonishingly, only a neck separated them after they had raced for 14 furlongs.

In line with French practice (often adopted in relation to stablemates) I wanted to couple them in my wager and so arranged to stake varying amounts on Durgams First and Charity Crusader, so that, whichever prevailed, I would make the tidy sum I sought as my profit. The wisdom of this ploy emerged when I saw them battle out the finish and victory finally go to the more resolute of Mrs Reveley's two representatives.

3.40 **Mary Reveley Racing Club Claiming**
[OFF 3.41] **Stakes (Class F)** (1m6f19y)1m6f
For: 3yo and upwards, each claimable at their advertised claiming price 1st £2,511 2nd £696 3rd £333

1 **CHARITY CRUSADER** (6) 6 9-1b............(42) S Copp(5)
b g by Rousillon (USA)—Height of Folly (Shirley Heights)
(Mrs M Reveley) *led, quickened clear over 3f out, held on well towards finish* bets of £1,125-£500, £2,000-£1,000
[op 6/4] **9/4**

2 nk **DURGAMS FIRST (IRE)** (4) 5 9-8............(51) A Culhane
ch g by Durgam (USA)—Miromaid (Simply Great (FR))
(Mrs M Reveley) *held up, steady headway over 3f out, shaken up and challenged over 1f out, not quicken near finish* bets of even £500, £1,000-£1,100, £500-£550(x2), £5,000-£6,000, £2,000-£2,400, £1,500-£1,800, £1,000-£1,200(x3), £500-£600(x3), £800-£1,000
[op 4/5, early Evens in places, tchd 5/6] **4/5F**

3 3½ **MADDIE** (1) 5 9-7..N Day
b m by Primitive Rising (USA)—Dubavarna (Dubassoff (USA))
(W W Haigh) *tracked leaders, pushed along over 4f out, kept on same pace* [op 10/1 tchd 12/1] **11/1**

4 1¼ **FINESTATETOBEIN** (2) 4 9-1 ....(30) J F Egan
(F Watson) *outpaced 8f out, headway under pressure over 3f out, one pace* [op 16/1 tchd 25/1 in places] **20/1**

5 9 **CHANCANCOOK** (5) 4 8-13 ....(25) O Pears
(J L Eyre) *tracked winner until weakened over 2f out*
[op 25/1] **33/1**

6 3 **FOX SPARROW** (3) 7 9-4b............................(42) K Darley
(N Tinkler) *held up, effort 3f out, no response*
[op 12/1 tchd 20/1 in places] **16/1**

6 ran **TIME** 3m 07.90s (slow by 6.80s) **SP TOTAL PERCENT** 108

1st OWNER: The Mary Reveley Racing Club; BRED: Lavinia Duchess of Norfolk
TRAINER: Mrs M Reveley at Lingdale, Cleveland
2nd OWNER: The Mary Reveley Racing Club **3rd** OWNER: Mrs P Gibbon
TOTE WIN £3.90; PL: £1.70,£1.10; DF £1.10; CSF £3.66

ANALYSIS This was a poor claimer, dominated by the Mary Reveley-trained pair of **CHARITY CRUSADER** and **DURGAMS FIRST**. The latter had the higher rating, but he lacks resolution and after apparently cruising up to challenge his rival he found little. This was the third successive time he has been beaten when a short-priced favourite and he is one to treat with caution.

Only 10 days later, on 19 August, 1997, the 'Trainers for Races' approach produced yet another winner in the most prestigious of the races run at York's festival meeting. As it happened, 13 days before this race, the suitably named International Stakes, I had read this report by Chris McGrath in *The Times*:

> 'When Michael Stoute, Singspiel's trainer, arrived from Barbados it was to learn his trade at nearby Malton, and he duly has a great fondness for the Ebor meeting. Few things would give him more pleasure than to see Entrepreneur quench his Derby failure in the International, which Stoute has won previously with Ezzoud (in successive years) and Shardari.'

It so transpired that Entrepreneur did not go to post, but the Stoute-trained Singspiel proved a more than able deputy by winning the International at a very generous 4-1.

STRATEGY 2

TRAINERS BIDDING FOR SPECIAL BONUSES

As many employers and employees know only too well, one of the most effective incentives towards making a particularly determined effort is the bonus.

In racing, too, this attractive inducement is offered when, on occasion, the sponsors of certain races give owners and trainers of racehorses the chance to make even more money out of winning several of these. Such a bonus is usually paid to a horse or yard that can win a series of sponsors' races. Therefore, as this proceeds, it is worth checking to see whether any 'connections' might particularly want to win its last leg.

On a recent Wednesday in October, such monitoring revealed the distinct probability that, having just captured the prestigious Tiffany Highflier Two-year-old Stakes with Young Senor at Newmarket, local trainer Geoff Wragg would be extremely keen to capture another Group One race for first season performers - the Cheveley Park Stakes – as it carried a special bonus from horse auctioneers, Tattersalls.

This was being offered partly (and excitingly) because the 'Cheveley Park' was the sequel to the 'Highflier' on, 2 October.

After I had watched Young Senor win the former contest at 14-1, I became particularly keen on the chances of Wragg's runner in the latter race, which the form book also suggested were excellent, as it showed that this, his two-year-old bay filly, Marling, had won all of its three previous races!

I made a decent wager at what I thought was the very generous rate of 15-8 and, while I was probably not quite so thrilled as the Geoff Wragg team (whose two Tattersall-sponsored race victories netted prize money and bonuses that together totalled a tidy sum) I went away from 'Headquarters' well satisfied with the bonus I had earnt for my day's work.

In fact, I had been quite confident that I would return from Newmarket well in profit as, only about six weeks earlier, a race had been run at Yarmouth, on 21 August, that not only put some more wheat in my bin but clearly underlined the wisdom of supporting horses whose victories will bring their connections payouts handsomely augmented by bonuses.

This race, the J Medler Handicap, was the last of three identically named events that, during a recent summer, on 4 June, 13 August and 21 August, had all been staged at Yarmouth.

On the morning of 21 August, my *Daily Telegraph* carried a report indicating that, as Annabelle Royale had already won the first two legs of this three-race series of sponsored handicaps, the victory of this five-year-old would bring her owner (Mr I Farini) a £25,000 bonus.

Impressively forewarned, I entrusted a good deal of my cash to Annabelle and was delighted with the 4-1 starting price her 'expected' victory involved!

The backer should carefully read specialist racing dailies and the sports pages of daily newspapers and note down the names of any horses like Annabelle Royale that are bidding to earn such bonuses. If nothing else, such contenders will be 'trained to the minute' and one can be certain that they will be really trying.

The rationale behind the 'trainers bidding for special bonuses' strategy is as valid over jumps as it is on the flat - a fact that was rather spectacularly demonstrated at the 1996 Cheltenham Festival.

In actual fact it was at another Midlands jumping venue - the far humbler Warwick - that I read on a page in my racecard, fully a month before the big Cheltenham meeting, a headline announcing that some past Warwick winners were in line for a special bonus. This was described as worth £15,000 to the connections of any of these named Warwick winners that could then go on to win the much more prestigious Sun Alliance 'chase to be run at Cheltenham in mid-March.

As an accompaniment to the racecard article outlining this major incentive to achieve a big race success, one particular horse, Nahthen Lad, was pictured and described as 'flying the last at Warwick'. I reasoned that, given his facile success at this track and advantage in being trained by top trainer Jenny Pitman, Nahthen Lad would make a massively determined bid to add the Sun Alliance and £15,000 to this lady handler's already rich Cheltenham haul.

This is why I resolved to row in with this young jumper when he eventually took his chance at the festival meeting. Fortunately Nahthen Lad readily earnt the bonus on offer to his connections when winning the 1996 Sun Alliance by eight lengths at 7-1!

STRATEGY 3

TRAINERS IN FORM AND RUNNING INTO IT

Nothing succeeds like success is a maxim whose validity is frequently evident in many spheres of activity, one of which is horse racing. Indeed, regular scrutiny of the racing returns will indicate how stables tend to send out winner after winner during a few successive halcyon days on which their runners seem to be so on song and so full of well-being that several of them manage to see off all comers.

The recognition of this easily verifiable fact has recently led two suppliers of racing form - *The Sporting Life* and the specialist form service *Superform* - to indicate which stables have recently been in winning form.

The former publication most usefully includes a feature known as *Trainerform* in which the 'wins to runners' ratios of yards that have been the most successful in the recent past are exhaustively documented.

These particular records are so detailed that the successive columns they involve allow the detection both of yards that have been in form and yet seem to be going out of it and those that seem, like well-placed surfers, to be likely to push ahead by riding a form 'wave' that is developing and building up promisingly.

A stable that seems likely to ride along on the crest of such a form wave that looks like growing and running for some time can be spotted if it can be seen to have been out of form, save in the most recent period covered by the *Life's Trainerform* statistics.

So on any racing day I look for yards whose latest runners have been winners. Such stables are shown in a very useful Trainerform column headed 'runners since win' in which the digit 0 is obviously the one to look for.

For example, I noticed from the *Sporting Life* feature that the stables of H Cecil, R Hannon, B Hills, J Gosden, L Cumani, M H Easterby, R Charlton, P Chapple-Hyam, Lord Huntingdon, M Bell, P Walwyn, R Akehurst, G Wragg and J Hetherton had succeeded with the very last horse that each of these trainers had sent to the racecourse.

The next stage was to see (from the Trainerform column showing their 'wins to runners' ratios during the past seven days) whether the latest winning runner of any of the above trainers had been the sequel to a rather lacklustre display on the part of its stable in the very recent past.

Interestingly, the last runner of P T Walwyn and that of G Wragg and the last representative of R Akehurst had each provided the sole highlight of its stable's performance during this very recent period. In fact during this, as indicated in column two of Trainerform, Walwyn's horses had only achieved a 1 win to 6 runs ratio (16.6%), as too had the horses of Wragg and Akehurst which had each registered two wins from twelve runs.

In the belief then, that, if attracting market support, the next runners of these trainers (whose last representatives had ended very recent lean spells) might be well worth serious consideration, I scanned *The Sporting Life* that was on display on the walls of my local betting office.

I had gone there to see if any of the runners of Walwyn, Wragg and Akehurst might line up as favourites and, to my delight, this was the case as regards three horses.

I rowed in with these forecast and eventual favourites, all of which were clearly indicated by the 'developing formwave' plan. These were Wragg's Jeune, which won at 4-9, and the same trainer's Zamirah which followed up at Yarmouth at 11-4.

Only Akehurst's Pharamineux, which according to Superform was unsuited by the soft ground he encountered at Sandown, let me down by finishing last at 13-8!

STRATEGY 4

TRAINERS LANDING DOUBLES AND TREBLES

Pay Days at the Races is the title of one particular American guide to the turf and these are precisely what some very shrewd trainers rather spectacularly seek to enjoy via successes gained on one particular racing day.

It is only a handful of handlers who regularly achieve such successes (more commonly at one meeting and sometimes on an 'across the card' basis at more than one) and knowing their identities by researching past results can prove lucrative. As for the perhaps more difficult feat of sending out multiple winners at different racecourses on one racing day, one exponent of this art is a handler of performers on the flat who, interestingly and perhaps significantly, has had extensive experience of racing in America.

This is John Gosden, son of a Lewes-based handler who, since his fairly recent return to his homeland, has sent out a steady stream of winners for many prominent owners.

Americans, of course, make light of travelling long distances and perhaps his experience on freeways has given Gosden a zest for racing far and wide in his quest for 'across the card' successes. In fact, extensive research has shown that during a recent flat racing season Gosden gained five across the card doubles with horses whose identification prior to completion was facilitated by the fact that they were 1st or 2nd favourites.

Knowing of Gosden's fondness for multiple wins at different meetings, I felt the writing was really on the wall when I noticed (on a mid-April day not long ago) that, of two likely favourites, one, Hieroglyphic, had been despatched to faraway Edinburgh and the other 'down the road' to Newmarket.

Imagine my delight when Persianalli and Hieroglyphic, in both proving winning favourites at 6-4 and 8-13 (the latter was later noted by Superform as having been particularly well backed) gave me a handsome winning double. Only twelve days later, I was again able to decipher the message being provided by Hieroglyphic since I noticed that this 'scopey' son of Darshaan was again likely to start as favourite in a handicap at Leicester on the same afternoon as Man of Gold was being despatched on a longer journey to Ripon, where he seemed likely to start favourite in a race for maiden three-year-olds.

I was naturally impressed, but far from surprised, when the appropriately named 'man of gold', John Gosden, saw Sheikh Mohammed's three-year-old of this name win at 10-11, to supplement the earlier success at Leicester of Hieroglyphic at 2-1.

Astonishingly, less than a fortnight later, on the afternoon of 8 May, John Gosden again sent out two well-fancied horses to two far-distant racecourses, Chester and Salisbury.

These were Hieroglyphic (again) who went in at the former meeting at 2.15 (this time as a more generously priced 3-1 favourite) and Shah Diamond who, only 15 minutes later, landed a most impressive across-the-card-double by winning a three-year-old maiden, after being heavily backed down to 4-5.

I had less than a month to wait before I again noticed that Gosden might be about to strike on two tracks within a very short space of time. Just prior to the Derby, I saw he had booked Pat Eddery to partner the newcomer Daki in the *Taxi News* three-year-old fillies; Stakes - the 3.30 at Leicester - and had also sent Last Lion to run in the 8:15 at Edinburgh's evening meeting.

Since Daki was shown as the likely second favourite for her race, I felt another John Gosden across-the-card-double was on the cards and so it proved when Last Lion, at 10-11, added to Daki's earlier success at 3-1.

Then, when I noticed that Gosden had sent two likely favourites to Redcar - Last Lion (again) and Badawi - and had sent only one horse on a much longer journey to Ayr, I reasoned that he might be planning to land a treble involving two meetings.

This belief proved well founded when Royal Standard, his 15-2 Ayr winner nicely supplemented the previous Redcar wins of Last Lion at 8-11 and Badawi at 4-6!

Any doubts about John Gosden's fondness for landing across-the-card-doubles, were then spectacularly dispelled on two successive late June days in the same flat racing season.

On the first of these, I saw that John had sent a forecast favourite north for a likely-looking opportunity at Newcastle, while also having sent another probable market leader 'down the road' to run at Newmarket.

Since the latter contestant, Western Approach, was partnered by top jockey Pat Eddery and attracted over £30,000 in substantial on course wagers, it was not surprising that she left the stalls as a 4-6 favourite in the British Olympic Appeal Fillies Stakes, before winning this comfortably by five lengths at 5.10.

FROM *THE RACING POST*

5.10 **British Olympic Appeal Fillies**
[OFF 5.10] **Stakes** 6f July
For: three yrs old and upwards, fillies and mares only which, at starting,have not won or been placed second or third in a Pattern Race 1st £4,308 2nd £1,284 3rd £612 4th £276

1 **WESTERN APPROACH (USA)** (3) 3 8-10......**Pat Eddery**
b f by Gone West (USA)—Devon Diva (USA) (The Minstrel (CAN))
made all, shaken up approaching final furlong,
comfortably bets of even £500, £1,000-£1,100(x2), £700-£770, £500-£550, £300-£330, £454-£500, £2,500-£3,000, £1,250-£1,500, £1,000-£1,200(x2), £2,400-£3,000, £2,000-£2,500(x2), £800-£1,000, £400-£500(x4), £1,200-£1,650, £800-£1,100, £2,000-£3,000, £800-£1,200, office money [op 4/5 tchd 10/11 and evens in a place] **4/6F**

As I expected, this decisive success supplemented that gained only ten minutes earlier in the 5.00 at Doncaster by the Gosden-trained three-year-old, Brier Creek - another most worthy favourite which top-flight jockey, Ray Cochrane booted home to a two-length win at 4-7 in Newcastle's British Coal Handicap.

FROM *THE RACING POST*

5.00 **British Coal Handicap Guaranteed**
[OFF 5.01] **Sweepstakes** 1m4f
For: three yrs old and upwards-Rated 0-90 1st £3,200 2nd £950 3rd £450 4th £200

1		**BRIER CREEK (USA) (1)** 3 8-07 !4 ....R Cochrane	

b c by Blushing Groom (FR)—Savannah Dancer (USA) (Northern Dancer (CAN))
made all, ridden and kept on strongly final 2f bets of £800-£1,300(x5), £400-£650(x4), £2,000-£3,500, £600-£1,050, £400-£700(x2), office money   [op 1/2 tchd 8/13] **4/7F**

2 2 **TAYLORS PRINCE (2)** 5 8-03.....................J Quinn
ch g by Sandhurst Prince—Maiden's Dance (Hotfoot)
tracked winner, challenged over 2f out, one pace final furlong   [op 5/1 tchd 9/2] **5/1**

3 3 **SECRET SOCIETY (3)** 5 9-13.....................N Connorton
b/br h by Law Society (USA)—Shaara (FR) (Sanctus II)
held up, smooth headway over 3f out, gradually lost place final 2f   [op 7/1] **8/1**

4 10 **BIGWHEEL BILL (IRE) (4)** 3 8-03.................J Lowe
tracked winner until weakened 3f out   [op 4/1] **5/1**

4 ran   **TIME:** 2m 31.92s (fast by 2.28s)   **SP TOTAL PERCENT** 108
1st OWNER: SheikhMohammed **TRAINER:** J.H.M.Gosden (Newmarket, Suffolk) **BRED:** Allen E.Paulson
2nd OWNER: MrH.J.Collingridge **TRAINER:** H.J.Collingridge
3rd OWNER: LordMatthews **TRAINER:** M.J.Camacho
TOTE: WIN £1.50 **DF:** £1.60 **CSF:** £3.50

Amazingly, on the very next day, Gosden repeated his 'home and away' double act by gaining yet another across-the-card success that involved his local track and a Northern venue.

The first leg of this again concerned Pat Eddery who seemed to me to have an excellent chance on Toussard in the 3.35 at Newmarket.

After watching this progressive three-year-old prevail at 7-1, I was delighted, but not really surprised, when only 15 minutes later,

Gosden's runner in the £42,159 Northumberland Plate, Witness Box, came home at 6-1 to provide a near 45-1 'across-the-card' winning double.

Naturally, few racehorse handlers are capable of the very difficult training feat of mounting successful raids at different racecourses on any one racing day. Readers wanting to identify further across-the-card specialists should monitor past seasons' results or more easily search for these 'master trainers' by making a daily check on the previous day's racing results.

FROM *THE INDEPENDENT ON SUNDAY*

3.35: 1. TOUSSAUD (Pat Eddery) *1-1*; *4.* **Prince Ferdinand** 11-10 fav; **3. Casteddu** 7-2. 7 ran. ¾, nk. (J Gosden, Newmarket). **Tote:** £7.00; £2.70, £1.50. DF: £5.30, CSF: £15.21.

3.50: (2m 19yd Northumberland Plate Handicap)
1. WITNESS BOX bay horse Lyphard — Excellent Alibi .... **G Duffield 6-1**
2. Cabochon .... **Paul Eddery 8-1**
3. Satin Lover .... **R Cochrane 5-1 jt-fav**
Also ran: 5-1 jt-fav Requested, 13-2 Hawait Al Barr (**4th**), 7-1 Highflying (**5th**), 11-1 Farsi, 14-1 Star Player, Aahsayiad, Beau Quest, 16-1 Quick Ransom, 20-1 Mrs Barton, Line Drummer (**6th**).
13 ran. sht-hd, ½, 1½, ¾, ¾. (J Gosden, Newmarket, for Sheikh Mohammed). **Tote:** £6.90; £2.40, £3.50, £1.90. DF: £54.20. Trio: £120.10. CSF: £52.40. Tricast: £238.75. An objection by the second to the winner was overruled.
Time: 3min 25.48sec (0.02sec below standard).

As recently as May 1996, in two successive days towards the end of this month, John Gosden again demonstrated his expertise as an '-across-the-card specialist. In fact, the very next day after (on 27 May) his Aerleon Jane, at 6-1, had succeeded at Sandown under top jockey, Pat Eddery, two hours before stable companion Strazo had justified 1-2 favouritism at far-distant Chepstow, Gosden fielded two forecast favourites at two other far-apart racecourses. First, he sent Alreeh all the way from his Newmarket base to win Redcar's 4:45 at 2-1 and then, two hours and 35 minutes later, he sent out Shantou to win a Sandown handicap as the very heavily backed 4-5 mount of champion jockey, Frankie Dettori!

SANDOWN PARK

Going: SOFT (straight GOOD)

2.00 (5f6y): **MOONSHINE GIRL** (J Reid, 9-4) 1; **Dancing Drop** (11-2) 2; **Queen's Pageant** (20-1) 3. 6 ran. Sketch Pad 5-6F. sh hd, 1¾. (M Stoute). Tote: win £3.40; places £1.60, £2.70. Dual F'cast: £9.40. CSF: £13.79.

2.35 (7f16y h'cap): **AERLEON JANE** (Pat Eddery, 6-1) 1; **Alpine Twist** (9-1) 2; **Prends Ca** (7-2JF) 3. 7 ran. Consordino, Forest Cat 7-2JFs. 1, 2. (J Gosden). Tote: win £6.30; places £2.60, £3.70. Dual F'cast: £27.80. CSF: £49.27.

3.05 (2m78y): **DOUBLE TRIGGER** (J Weaver, 5-6F) 1; **Assessor** (6-1) 2; **Court of Honour** (15-8) 3. 5 ran. 7, ½. (M Johnston). Tote: win £1.70; places £1.30, £1.70. Dual F'cast: £2.90. CSF: £5.91. NRs: Moonax, Wannaplantatree.

3.40 (5f6y): **MIND GAMES** (J Carroll, 7-2F) 1; **Struggler** (11-2) 2; **Woodborough** (6-1) 3. 9 ran. ¾, 1. (J Berry). Tote: win £3.30; places £1.80, £1.90, £1.90. Dual F'cast: £11.80. CSF: £21.38. Trio: £35.40. NR: Lucky Lionel.

4.10 (1m14y h'cap): **BLOMBERG** (J Carroll, 20-1) 1; **Royal Philosopher** (15-2) 2; **Chief Burundi** (13-2) 3. 14 ran. Cool Edge 3F. 1¼, nk. (J Fanshawe). Tote: win £29.30; places £6.40, £2.90, £2.50. Dual F'cast: £130.10. CSF: £163.07. Tricast: £1,042.53. Trio: £318.40.

4.45 (7f16y): **FARMOST** (G Duffield, 5-2F) 1; **Brighton Road** (12-1) 2; **Menoo Hal Batal** (4-1) 3. 11 ran. 3½, ½. (M Prescott). Tote: win £3.80; places £1.70, £2.30, £2.10. Dual F'cast: £22.40. CSF: £31.37. Tricast: £109.85. Trio: £49.40.

5.20 (1m2f7y h'cap): **BAKHETA** (M Henry, 9-2) 1; **Silently** (16-1) 2; **Koathary** (16-1) 3. 13 ran. Domitia 11-4F. nk, 2½. (Miss G Kelleway). Tote: win £4.90; places £2.00, £4.80, £4.70. Dual F'cast: £86.30. CSF: £68.05. Tricast: £984.73. Trio: £232.30. NR: Sovereign Page.

JACKPOT: £13,344.80 — part won. Pool of £3,759.11 carried forward to Redcar today. QUADPOT: £19.70. PLACEPOT: £237.70. .

CHEPSTOW

Going: GOOD TO SOFT

2.00 (1m4f23y): **ROYAL COURT** (R Havlin, 3-1) 1; **Jiyush** (6-4F) 2; **Bowled Over** (9-4) 3. 6 ran. 20, ½. (P Chapple-Hyam). Tote: win £3.80; places £1.70, £1.40. Dual F'cast: £2.90. CSF: £7.70. NR: Pompier.

2.30 (1m4f23y h'cap): **ROUFONTAINE** (R Havlin, 12-1) 1; **Uncharted Waters** (8-1) 2; **Ma Petite Anglaise** (7-1) 3. 13 ran. Ashby Hill 6JF. 1, 1¾. (W Muir). Tote: win £9.80; places £2.80, £2.30, £2.80. Dual F'cast: £28.70. CSF: £95.82. Tricast: £669.22. Trio: £49.00.

3.00 (6f16y sell): **DON'T FORGET SHOKA**

4.00 (1m14y): **STRAZO** (B Thomson, 1-2F) 1; **Effectual** (13-2) 2; **Battle Spark** (7-1) 3. 7 ran. 5, 7. (J Gosden). Tote: win £1.50; places £1.30. £2.20. Dual F'cast: £2.70. CSF: £4.35

4.30 (6f16y): **PATSY GRIMES** (Aimee Cook, 15-2) 1; **Tinker Osmaston** (9-1) 2; **Rambold** (16-1) 3. 11 ran. Loose Talk 4F. 3, ½. (J Moore). Tote: win £10.60; places £3.30, £2.30, £4.40. Dual F'cast: £34.00. CSF: £68.12. Tricast: £968.18. Trio: £153.10.

QUADPOT: £10.90. PLACEPOT: £60.40.

REDCAR

Going: GOOD TO FIRM

2.15 (6f): **REUNION** (R Hills, Evens-F) 1; **Falls O'Moness** (11-8) 2; **Taome** (20-1) 3. 6 ran. nk, 1. (J Hills). Tote: win £1.70; places £1.10, £1.80. Dual F'cast: £1.50. CSF: £2.75.

2.45 (6f h'cap): **RESPECT A SECRET** (Mrs D Kettlewell, 16-1) 1; **Bowcliffe Grange** (14-1) 2; **Sallyoreally** (9-2F) 3; **Northern Clan** (25-1) 4. 18 ran. 1¼, 3½. (S Kettlewell). Tote: win £33.00; places £5.00, £4.70, £1.60, £5.30. Dual F'cast: £380.70. CSF: £202.63. Tricast: £1,086.36. Trio: £369.00.

3.15 (5f h'cap): **JUCEA** (J Weaver, 11-2) 1; **Portend** (6-1) 2; **Insider Trader** (14-1) 3. 11 ran. Ann's Pearl, Brecongill Lad, Lady Sheriff 5JF. ½, ½. (J Spearing). Tote: win £7.20; places £2.00, £3.40, £3.50. DF: £21.80. CSF: £37.76. Tc: £322.92. Trio: £63.60. NR: Celandine.

3.45 (1m1f h'cap): **ALABANG** (L Charnock, 8-1) 1; **Bold Amusement** (25-1) 2; **Habeta** (7-1) 3. 12 ran. Maradata 5-2F. 2½, 1¼. (M Camacho). Tote: win £12.30; places £3.00, £9.60, £1.60. Dual F'cast: £135.80. CSF: £167.49. Tricast: £1,368.89. Trio: £363.20.

4.15 (1m6f19y h'cap): **FORGIE** (M Birch, 4-1) 1; **Phar Closer** (20-1) 2; **What Jim Wants** (11-1) 3. 12 ran. Ship's Dancer 15-8F. ¾, 3½. (P Calver). Tote: win £4.70; places £1.10, £21.70, £2.50. DF: £108.90. CSF: £77.73. TC: £786.07. Trio: £156.00. NRs: Fortuitious, General Glow.

4.45 (1m2f): **ALREEH** (R Hills, 2-1F) 1; **Lady of Leisure** (4-1) 2; **Salty Girl** (10-1) 3. 10 ran. 1¼, 1½. (J Gosden). Tote: win £2.20; places £1.50, £1.60, £2.10. Dual F'cast: £5.50. CSF: £10.89. Trio: £19.20.

5.15 (7f): **POETRY** (P Robinson, 11-8F) 1; **Equerry** (7-1) 2; **The Stager** (100-30) 3. 7 ran. 3, nk. (M Tompkins). Tote: win £2.10; places £1.70, £3.10. Dual F'cast: £5.40. CSF: £11.70.

JACKPOT: Not won. Pool of £7,300.25 carried forward to Folkestone today. QUADPOT: £432.40. PLACEPOT: £1,270.50.

SANDOWN PARK

Going: GOOD TO SOFT

6.20 (1m14y): **EARLY PEACE** (Dane O'Neill, 16-1) 1; **Loveyoumillions** (3-1JF) 2; **Denomination** (14-1) 3. 10 ran. Te Amo 3JF. 1½, ½. (R Hannon). Tote: win £26.60; places £5.60, £1.20, £2.50. Dual F'cast: £37.80. CSF: £58.87. Trio: £184.30. Winner claimed by G Phillips for £11,000.

6.50 (1m3f91y h'cap): **ATLANTIC MIST** (G Bardwell, 7-1) 1; **Rivercare** (12-1) 2; **Soldier Mak** (14-1) 3. 10 ran. Deadline Time 5-2F. ½, 1¼. (B Millman). Tote: win £8.90; places £2.30, £2.20, £2.90. Dual F'cast: £46.60. CSF: £75.09. Tricast: £1,033.99. Trio: £220.60. NR: Get Away With It.

7.20 (1m2f7y mdn): **SHANTOU** (L Dettori, 4-5F) 1; **Rocky Oasis** (9-2) 2; **Ginger Fox** (9-1) 3. 16 ran. ¾, 6. (J Gosden). Tote: win £1.90; places £1.40, £1.70, £2.40. Dual F'cast: £3.10. CSF: £5.37. Trio: £10.60. NR: Ectomorph.

As for trainers who pull off the less difficult, but still taxing, feat of sending out more than one winner at any one meeting, some names to note for the flat are Richard Hannon, Peter Chapple-Hyam and Barry Hills and, over jumps, Mary Reveley, Gordon Richards and Andy Turnell.

Interestingly, all those named in this select list occasionally make particularly determined bids to provide multiple winners for major supporters of their yards.

R Ogden is one such leviathan owner whose multiple 'same day, same meeting' successes with horses handled by Richards, Nichols and Turnell will be discussed when Strategy 27 is later explained.

P Barber is the particular patron of the Paul Nichols National Hunt stable whose extensive support has often been repaid by several 'same meeting' successes on one particular raceday, while this major owner's counterparts, as regards the yards of Reveley and Chapple-Hyam are Peter Savill (the bane of some northern bookmakers) and Robert Sangster, respectively. Moreover, it is for Sangster that trainer Barry Hills has so often also made some particular racing days at prestigious meetings really memorable.

There is also one particular time of year when, by virtue of the fortunate fact that they are in strings of well-forward racehorses that have a fitness 'edge' over those of other handlers, some racehorses are very likely to return in triumph from the races. This is at the start of the (turf) flat racing season proper in late March and April when, because freezing conditions and temperatures can disrupt their training schedules and prevent them from thriving, many racehorses do not run within pounds of the form they showed when the sun was on their backs in the previous season, thus causing many disgruntled racegoers to feel that they might just as well throw away their form books! In 1996, as ever, the start of the flat racing season at Doncaster revealed that certain handlers were succeeding not with the ablest contenders, but the fittest ones whose sense of well-being proved very beneficial.

Knowing this was likely, I resolved, rather than stick to the accepted wisdom of 'giving the flat a month' (so its 'trappy' new season could settle into a more reliable pattern), to monitor results as they came in from the early flat meetings and to support the stablemates of horses that had already entered the winner's enclosure at these fixtures. Encouraged on the second day of the new season by trainer Gay Kelleway's two winners at 6-1 and 11-1 and, on the following (Lincoln Handicap) day by Richard Hannon's own, far from unprecedented, pair of Doncaster winners (this Eversleigh handler sent out Stone Ridge to win the new season's first big race at 33-1 and then followed up with Fire Bonnet), I was really eager on the very next racing day, 25 March to examine the flat racing card in my *Times* for Folkestone. I soon settled down to watch the Ceefax transmission of results, as they came in from this Kent meeting. Shortly after 1.50, I knew the result of the first race in time to take a betting interest, if a stablemate of its winner was due to contest the next race, the 2.20. As it happened, the day's first successful trainer was represented again by two runners, so I decided to support the runner with the higher form rating. This was the C Dwyer trained Lloc whose 10-1 success by five lengths duly followed the earlier and propitious-looking first race triumph of Jeanelle by six lengths, after she had only had a chance to race over the minimum distance of five furlongs!

1.50 HEADCORN MAIDEN AUCTION STAKES
(2-Y-O fillies: £2,381: 5f) (11 runners)

101	(2)		SYLVANIA LIGHTS (Camelot Racing) W Muir 8-3	M Henry (5)	--
102	(4)		MOLLY MUSIC (P Axon) G Margarson 8-1	M Baird (5)	--
103	(1)		MUJADIL EXPRESS (Mrs V Goodman) J Moore 8-0	J F Egan	--
104	(7)		SWIFT REFUSAL (Wheatmille Partners) M Haynes 8-0	C Rutter	--
105	(3)		CAVIAR AND CANDY (A MacGillivray) D Cosgrove 7-13	F Lynch (5)	--
106	(8)		DOZEN ROSES (Mrs A Brown) T Jones 7-13	A Whelan (3)	--
107	(9)		JENNELLE (Mrs J Cornwell) C Dwyer 7-13	J Quinn	--
108	(5)		SUMMER RISOTTO (Hargood Ltd) D ffrench Davis 7-13	C Adamson (5)	--
109	(10)		ANATOMIC (M Foy) M Channon 7-12	A Gorman	--
110	(6)		BURBERRY QUEST (S Horn) B Millman 7-12	J Fanning	--
111	(11)		FACE IT. (Facetious Partners) W G M Turner 7-12	A Daly (5)	--

BETTING: 3-1 Anatomic, 7-2 Face It, 5-1 Burberry Quest, 6-1 Mujadil Express, Jennelle, 8-1 Sylvania Lights, 10-1 others.

1995: MAGGI FOR MARGARET 8-1 C Rutter (2-1 fav) M Channon 7 ran

2.20 ROCHESTER HANDICAP (£3,343: 5f) (16 runners)

201	(5)	003304	LEIGH CROFTER 10 (B,D,F,G,S) (P Dimmock) P Cundell 7-9-12	S Whitworth	93
202	(1)	6/00500-	MARANDA 101 (V,G,S) (Binding Matters) C Dwyer 4-9-11	M Wigham	88
203	(15)	65-2443	HALBERT 46 (V,D,F) (T Barker) P Burgoyne 7-9-9	D R McCabe (3)	99
204	(1)	155280-	MALIBU MAN 158 (D,G) (Church Racing) S Mellor 4-9-3	T Sprake	98
205	(9)	000-300	ROCKCRACKER 55 (P Axon) G Margarson 4-9-2	P Robinson	90
206	(14)	360144-	THAI MORNING 150 (CD,F) (Thai Connection) P Harris 3-9-0	G Hind	97
207	(10)	030332-	LA BELLE DOMINIQUE 245 (R Withers) S Knight 4-8-13	V Slattery	91
208	(12)	10500-0	SECRET MESS 28 (D,S) (A Jones) A Jones 4-8-11	J Quinn	97
209	(3)	023463-	DOMICKSKY 147 (C,D,F,G,S) (Miss B Coyle) M Channon 8-8-11	D Sweeney (7)	98
210	(11)	000015-	FOLLOWMEGIRLS 147 (B,D,F,G,S) (Mrs A Martin) Mrs A King 7-8-8	A Garth	98
211	(16)	230000-	LLOC 154 (D,S) (Mrs S Rawson) C Dwyer 4-8-7	J Stack (3)	96
212	(6)	240000-	SONDERISE 303 (D,G,S) (Mrs D Wright) N Tinkler 7-8-3	G Carter	90
213	(8)	000056-5	NOMADIC DANCER 19 (M Saunders) M Saunders 4-8-1	N Adams	89
214	(4)	/0-0000/	TAUBER 466 (C,D,F,G,S) (Mrs C Reed) P Mitchell 12-8-0	M Fenton	--
215	(13)	114000-	MAZZARELLO 110 (D,F,G) (D Hoskyns) R Curtis 6-7-13	J F Egan	91
216	(2)	00060-0	BONNY MELODY 54 (G) (Mrs E Dawson) P Evans 5-7-11	Amanda Sanders (5)	98

BETTING: 4-1 Domicksky, 5-1 Followmegirls, 7-1 Thai Morning, 8-1 Leigh Crofter, La Belle Dominique, 10-1 Halbert, 12-1 others.

1995: NORDICO PRINCESS 4-9-12 R Cochrane (6-4 fav) G Oldroyd 8 ran

2.50 SHORNECLIFFE MEDIAN AUCTION MAIDEN STAKES
(3-Y-O: £2,381: 6f) (14 runners)

301	(13)	4064-	BELDRAY PARK 153 (Stainless Fasteners) Mrs A King 9-0	J Quinn	80
302	(4)	440-233	LANCASHIRE LEGEND 27 (B Taker & D Wilson) S Dow 9-0	T Quinn	97
303	(6)	0063-	MINDRACE 153 (D Abbott) K Ivory 9-0	D Biggs	98
304	(3)	00-	MISTER WOODSTOCK 199 (J Sims) M Jarvis 9-0	P Robinson	--
305	(11)		OLD GOLD N TAN 23 (A Osborne) J Poulton 9-0	P McCabe (3)	--
306	(2)	32-	PRIDE OF BRIXTON 179 (Voice Group) G Lewis 9-0	S Whitworth	99
307	(12)	60-	REALMS OF GLORY 167 (D Crowson) P Mitchell 9-0	A Clark	79
308	(14)	24-	SHARP STOCK 154 (Mrs M Fairbairn) B Meehan 9-0	R Hughes	96
309	(5)		WILL DO (A Smith) M Meade 9-0	V Slattery	--
310	(10)	00-2	YOUNG MAZAAD 11 (Letts Green Farm) D O'Brien 9-0	G Bardwell	85
311	(8)	00-	BLESSED SPIRIT 149 (W Stuttaford) C Wall 8-9	W Woods	95
312	(7)	4U6336-	MRS MCBADGER 140 (C Badger) B Smart 8-9	R Cochrane	98
313	(1)		PEACE HOUSE (Mrs B Speller) J Spearing 8-9	S Drowne (3)	--
314	(9)		TRIANNA (T Nakoo) Lord Huntingdon 8-9	D Harrison	--

BETTING: 3-1 Pride Of Brixton, 5-1 Lancashire Legend, 6-1 Trianna, Young Mazaad, 8-1 Sharp Stock, 10-1 Mindrace, 12-1 others.

1995: TIHEROS 9-0 T Quinn (7-2) R Hannon 6 ran

3.20 ALDINGTON RATING RELATED MAIDEN STAKES
(3-Y-O: £2,381: 6f 189yd) (9 runners)

401	(4)	06060-	GET TOUGH 19 (Gray Boys Racing) S Dow 9-0	A Daly (5)	82
402	(3)	352436-	IVORY'S GRAB HIRE 213 (D Ivory) K Ivory 9-0	C Scully (7)	76
403	(2)	0050-	LONGHILL BOY 187 (Vintage Services Ltd) B Meehan 9-0	M Tebbutt	74
404	(1)	640-	NAKHAL 154 (Fort Partners) J Murray Smith 9-0	J Weaver	--
405	(8)	300-	BASOOD 157 (M Al Maktoum) E Dunlop 8-11	J Tate	86
406	(6)	2344-	CISERANO 253 (K Dack) M Channon 8-11	T Quinn	93
407	(9)	646-234	GREEN GEM 23 (P Madeleini) S Williams 8-11	K Darley	94
408	(7)	363-	MAY QUEEN MEGAN 140 (S Harrison) Mrs A King 8-11	A Garth	87
409	(5)	0-00	VALJESS 31 (Mrs R Blake) D O'Brien 8-11	G Bardwell	--

BETTING: 3-1 Ciserano, 7-2 Basood, 4-1 Nakhal, 6-1 Green Gem, 7-1 Longhill Boy, May Queen Megan, 8-1 others.

1995: DOUBLE RUSH 9-0 J Reid (100-30) T Mills 7 ran

3.50 ALKHAM HANDICAP (£3,398: 1m 1f 149yd) (15 runners)

501	(12)	1/2-1331	EXPLOSIVE POWER 9 (D,G) (H Short) G Bravery 5-10-0	D R McCabe (3)	94
502	(11)	240150-	PISTOL 276 (CD,F,G) (Mrs B Sumner) C Horgan 6-9-7	J Weaver	87
503	(6)	010/00-0	KETABI 11 (G) (B & D Whitney) R Akehurst 5-9-7	T Quinn	--
504	(14)	1501-00	WET PATCH 74 (F,G) (P Hammond) R Hannon 4-9-6	R Hughes	94
505	(3)	02/0014-	SWINGING SIXTIES 23J (G) (A Higson) G L Moore 5-9-6	S Whitworth	86
506	(8)	000260-	BELLAS GATE BOY 198J (J Pearce) J Pearce 4-9-6	J McLaughlin	83
507	(9)	20/606/	AUDE LA BELLE 721 (F,G) (Mrs V Pladkins) S Knight 8-9-6	A McGlone	--
508	(1)	0-00306	CANARY FALCON 25 (G) (L Pipe) John Berry 5-9-4	V Smith	90
509	(13)	50200/0-	KELLY MAC 143 (D,F,G) (Mrs V O'Brien) D O'Brien 6-9-4	K Darley	--
510	(4)	04-1056	OUR TOM 23 (G) (J Berry) J Wharton 4-9-4	J Quinn	92
511	(5)	60-5154	TODD 9 (G) (J Morton) P Mitchell 5-9-1	A Clark	90
512	(10)	321060-	HARVEY WHITE 136 (F) (Harvey White Partners) J Pearce 4-9-1	G Bardwell	96
513	(7)	000060-	WARNING SHOT 18J (S) (Continental Racing) M Meade 4-9-0	J Reid	97
514	(2)	50200-0	BROWN EYED GIRL 9 (Miss L Regis) B Meehan 4-9-0	M Tebbutt	93
515	(5)	064441-	NOEPROB 268 (F,G,S) (Mrs P Bradshaw) R Hodges 6-8-3	S Drowne (3)	87

BETTING: 9-2 Pistol, 5-1 Explosive Power, 6-1 Todd, 10-1 Ketabi, Swinging Sixties, Our Tom, 12-1 others.

1995: QUEENS STROLLER 4-8-13 D Harrison (7-1) C Elsey 14 ran

4.20 LEVY BOARD HANDICAP (£3,289: 1m 189yd) (16 runners)

601	(12)	4005-60	REVERAND THICKNESS 23 (D,F,G,S) S Williams 5-10-0	R Hughes	94
602	(15)	040F25-	BATTLESHIP BRUCE 66J (G,S) (T Foreman) N Callaghan 4-9-8	J Reid	95
603	(16)	050-145	SOAKING 25 (D,F,G) (P Saunders) P Burgoyne 6-9-6	D R McCabe (3)	97
604	(4)	0/5040-	ZATOPEK 158 (A Spargo) J Cullinan 4-9-5	T Quinn	85
605	(13)	600000-	ORTHORHOMBUS 234 (B,CD,F,G) D Cosgrove 7-8-13	M Wigham	94
606	(3)	550400-6	HALLJARD 34 (G) (Nest Holt Partners) T Jones 5-8-13	A McGlone	90
607	(14)	54300-	SECRET PLEASURE 165 (Mrs S S-Phillips) R Hannon 3-8-12	Dane O'Neill (5)	90
608	(9)	510005-	ALMAPA 235 (D,G) (P Slade) R Hodges 4-8-8	S Drowne (3)	92
609	(5)	50-0505	ROCKY TWO 11 (G) (H Bennett) P Howling 5-8-6	A Cochrane	87
610	(11)	4-06006	SNEAKY SNAPS PRIDE 23 (P Cundell) P Cundell 4-8-2	J Quinn	87
611	(2)	3-53133	SEA SPOUSE 10 (G) (Seven Sears Racing) M Blanshard 5-7-13	N Adams	93
612	(6)	004004-	PRIDE OF KASHMIR 140 (New Recruits) P Harris 3-7-13	F Norton	89
613	(1)	0000-	GEE GEE TEE 140 (J Trickett) J Akehurst 3-7-12	Dale Gibson	87
614	(7)	000-	SHARP 'N' SHADY 126 (W Wallics) C Wall 3-7-11	W Lord	84
615	(8)	0/00-330	PALACEGATE GOLD 11 (B,C,F,G,S) (R Hodgers) R Hodges 7-7-10	N Carlisle	82
616	(10)	030600-	TITANIUM HONDA 196 (D,G) (Mrs V Costello) D O'Brien 5-7-10	G Bardwell	87

Long handicap: Titanium Honda 6-13.

BETTING: 9-2 Battleship Bruce, 5-1 Secret Pleasure, 6-1 Soaking, 8-1 Pride Of Kashmir, 10-1 Reverand Thickness, Sea Spouse, 12-1 others.

1995: ORTHORHOMBUS 6-9-4 M Rimmer (20-1) D Cosgrove 16 ran

4.50 KINGSNORTH HANDICAP (3-Y-O: £3,371: 1m 4f) (17 runners)

1	(6)	300-121	NIKITA'S STAR 23 (D,G) (Nikita's Partners) D Murray Smith 9-7	J Weaver	95
2	(10)	0-41216	MONTECRISTO 23 (D,G) (Matthews Racing) R Guest 9-5	F Lynch (5)	98
3	(17)	50-0430	ASKING FOR KINGS 36 (Mrs G Smith) S Dow 9-5	A Daly (5)	80
4	(16)	060-	JUMP THE LIGHTS 171 (R Crawley) S Woods 9-2	W Woods	--
5	(15)	040-	MINNISAM 151 (Mrs C Forrester) J Dunlop 8-11	T Quinn	84
6	(2)	000-6	RIVERCARE 10 (P Stoner) M Polglase 8-11	M Henry (5)	--
7	(12)	541-0	KISSING GATE 76 (G) (The Queen) R Charlton 8-10	S Sanders	90
8	(8)	50204-0	AUTOBABBLE 23 (B) (B Adams) R Hannon 8-9	J Reid	98
9	(4)	3000-	ATLANTIC MIST 177 (Wardour Partners) B Millman 8-6	S Drowne (3)	88
10	(11)	60000-0	INFLUENCE PEDLER 28 (C Brittain) C Brittain 8-5	K Darley	94
11	(13)	443	HIGHLIGHTS 40 (Bloomsbury Stud) D Morris 8-4	R Cochrane	90
12	(1)	000-	SIEGE PERILOUS 175 (S Demanuele) S Williams 8-1	J Tate	--
13	(9)	0000-	SHAMAND 188 (J McCarthy) B Meehan 8-1	J F Egan	--
14	(3)	00500-	FORLIANDO 160 (N & M Pike & Sons) M Saunders 7-12	F Norton	95
15	(7)	0000-	HADADABBLE 122 (Fun Managers) Pat Mitchell 7-10	J Quinn	80
16	(14)	6-60	NATIVE SONG 25 (B) (Invicta Bloodstock) M Haynes 7-10	M Baird (5)	83
17	(5)	000-004	TARTAN EXPRESS 25 (Mrs E Nield) B Pearce 7-10	A Clark	--

Long handicap: Hadedabble 7-9, Native Song 7-4, Tartan Express 6-13

BETTING: 7-2 Nikita's Star, 9-2 Highlights, 6-1 Montecristo, 8-1 Asking For Kings, Minnisam, 12-1 Jump The Lights, Kissing Gate, 14-1 others.

Although at the very same Folkestone meeting trainer Anabel King's success with a well-forward member of her Warwickshire string in the third race at 33-1 was not followed by the success of a stable mate in the fourth race, the handler who succeeded in winning this event - S Williams - was seen to be fielding another two runners at Folkestone; Reverand Thickness in the 4.20 and Siege Perilous in the last race. This time, as I had no pair of form ratings to help me differentiate between these two strategy qualifiers, I decided to support both and thus was mightily relieved when, after the prayers of Reverand Thickness fell on deaf ears, Siege Perilous was rewarded for the risk-taking onslaught of his enterprising jockey with a 14-1 success!

Incidentally, the 'Reverand' won next time out at 9-1.

FROM *THE TIMES*

Folkestone

Going: good to soft

1.50 (5f) 1, **Jennelle** (J Quinn, 5-2 fav); 2, Swift Refusal (11-4); 3, Caviar And Candy (25-1). 9 ran. NR: Mujadil Express. 6l, ¾l. C Dwyer. Tote: £2.40; £1.10, £1.40, £4.80. DF: £4.70. Trio: £107.90. CSF: £8.71. Sylvania Lights (12-1) was withdrawn, not unders orders — rule 4 applies to all bets, deduction 5p in pound.

2.20 (5f) 1, **Lloc** (J Stack, 10-1); 2, Malibu Man (10-1); 3, Bonny Melody (33-1); 4, Sonderise (13-2). Thai Morning 9-2 fav. 16 ran. 5l, ¾l. C Dwyer. Tote: £14.90; £4.70, £2.90, £8.50, £1.30. DF: £93.70. Trio: £348.00 (part won; pool of £196.08 carried forward to 4.00 at Huntingdon today). CSF: £99.17. Tricast: £2,983.76.

2.50 (6f) 1, **Beldray Park** (J Quinn, 25-1); 2, Blessed Spirit (5-1); 3, Pride Of Brixton (13-8 fav). 14 ran. ¾l, 1¾l. Mrs A King. Tote: £55.10; £11.40, £2.30, £1.20. DF: £198.90. Trio: £132.80. CSF: £156.88.

3.20 (6f 189yd) 1, **Green Gem** (K Darley, 7-1); 2, Basood (11-2); 3, Nakhal (100-30). Ciserano 3-1 fav. 9 ran. 2½l, 2½l. S Williams. Tote: £7.40; £2.60, £2.40, £2.00. DF: £11.00. Trio: £25.80. CSF: £42.33.

3.50 (1m 1f 149yd) 1, **Swinging Sixties** (S Whitworth, 6-1 jt-fav); 2, Bellas Gate Boy (25-1); 3, Wet Patch (6-1). Explosive Power 6-1 jt-fav. 15 ran. Sh hd, 5l. G L Moore. Tote: £10.30; £2.70, £9.80, £3.00. DF: £129.90. Trio: £302.00 (part won; pool of £106.34 carried forward to 4.00 at Huntingdon today). CSF: £130.55. Tricast: £874.19.

4.20 (6f 189yd) 1, **Sea Spouse** (N Adams, 6-1: **Private Handicapper's top rating**); 2, Pride Of Kashmir (13-2); 3, Zatopek (16-1); 4, Battleship Bruce (13-2). Reverand Thickness 5-1 fav. 16 ran. Hd, ½l. M Blanshard. Tote: £7.10; £1.40, £1.60, £2.80, £2.60. DF: £21.70. Trio: £284.00. CSF: £44.92. Tricast: £412.20.

4.50 (1m 4f) 1, **Siege Perilous** (J Tate, 14-1); 2, Minnisam (7-1); 3, Montecristo (8-1); 4, Atlantic Mist (16-1). Kissing Gate 7-2 fav. 17 ran. 1½l, 5l. S Williams. Tote: £25.70; £4.20, £1.80, £2.70, £2.90. DF: £311.80. Trio: £781.30. CSF: £117.13. Tricast: £802.88.

Jackpot: not won (pool of £124,991.56 carried forward to Huntingdon today).
Placepot: £299.60.
Quadpot: £34.30.

STRATEGY 5

TRAINERS FIELDING MANY REPRESENTATIVES

Some handlers train in such a small way that when a horsebox full of their runners travels to a racecourse it contains nearly all of their stable's occupants.

This was certainly the case when one January E. M. Caine, who trains in a very modest way at High Crossett at Chopgate in Cleveland, sent all of his stable's runners to Catterick in an attempt to start off the new year in fine style!

The problem, of course, was deciding which of the many runners would bring home the bacon for pig farmer Caine and this I solved by seeing if any of these had come to the notice of either a private handicapper or watch-holder.

FROM *THE SPORTING LIFE*

STOP WATCH RATINGS

1.20: Feeling Rosey 43f (-), Bonanza 28s (-).
1.55: Cavalier Crossett 40y (-), Midland Express 38g (-), Barkisland 33g (-).
2.30: Ainsty Fox 21g (-).

Since Stopwatch of *The Sporting Life* made Cavalier Crossett his selection for Catterick's 1:55, I reasoned that, of his string, this Caine representative was the one to be on, especially as the *Life* also showed he had, exactly twelve months before, won a race over the distance at the same Catterick meeting.

Thus I waded in at 33-1 - a rate of odds that did not deter me as the above-mentioned win had involved odds of 25-1.

I was delighted when, ably ridden by Mr P McLoughlin, this seasoned campaigner gave 'Red' Caine a red letter, first day of the new year.

'Red' even made the following declaration to the press: "All being well, if he eats up, he'll go for a race tomorrow".

When only hours later, Cavalier Crossett duly lined up for a handicap chase that he had won over course and distance, a year and a day previously, I needed no encouragement to play up my winnings on him as a truly 'race fit' runner.

Most gratifyingly, he won by 12 lengths at 4-1 to put yet more wheat in farmer Caine's bin.

FROM *THE DAILY TELEGRAPH*

> Cavalier Crossett, a 25-1 winner of the Zetland Chase on the corresponding day last year, was up to his old tricks at Catterick Bridge yesterday, winning the Stand Novice Hurdle at 33-1. His trainer "Red" Caine, a Billsdale pig farmer, was getting off the mark for the season, but is not allowing Cavalier Crossett to rest on his laurels.
> He explained: "All being well, if he eats up, he'll go for a race here tomorrow."

Much more commonly, a really large raid is organised by a trainer with a string which, although much larger than that of 'Red' Caine, is not of the massive size of that of a handler like Henry Cecil or Martin Pipe.

Micky Hammond is the name to note as regards a well-known, but hardly leviathan trainer, who occasionally decides to send so many of his charges 'over the top' that many of them are bound to cover themselves with glory.

Hammond certainly made headlines on 24 February 1996, when careful scrutiny of northern racecards would have revealed that a large number of his horseboxes were being despatched to Musselburgh,

Doncaster and Haydock.

As it happens, on any racing day, one should always take note of any trainer who sends runners to three, or sometimes even more, meetings, as the sheer expense, the trouble and the travelling involved may well suggest that the horses concerned are not going to race meetings just to breathe in the air!

When, as with Hammond's horseboxes, a single such conveyance can be seen to be especially well loaded (he sent seven out of his 11 raiders to lowly Musselburgh on his February 1996 raid), it is probably best if the backer concentrates attention on what is the heaviest of several equine consignments. This I certainly did on 24 February 1996 and was rewarded with two Musselburgh seconds at 16-1 and 9-4, as well as with three winners at 16-1, 2-1 and 5-2! Indeed, had Hammond had a runner in the second race, he might well have landed the Musselburgh place pot with his stable's representatives!

While I was cashing in on his success in Scotland, Hammond's second most heavily loaded horsebox, containing three horses sent to Haydock, was yielding two winners at 7-1 and 9-1, while this Middleham maestro's sole representative at Doncaster ran a disappointing second at 6-1, to at least suggest that nothing succeeds like success in the case of large numbers of stablemates sent to the races by a trainer who on a single race day casts a large net far and wide.

STRATEGY 6

TRAINERS AND FUTURE RACES

In the first, now revised, updated and re-issued 'companion' edition of this book, considerable attention was paid to the often lucrative procedure of monitoring trainers' entries and mention was made of 'Futureform' of 82 Girton Road, Cambridge, whose purchasable offerings are solely devoted to this strategy.

As it happens, one convenient, cheap and rapidly performed variation of this sound approach (of assessing impending prospects by seeing whether a future entry in a more valuable race suggests a horse is really well thought of) can sometimes be performed if one studies bookmakers' ante-post betting shows, as appearing in racing dailies, that involve important future races. If in these one then finds the names of horses (about which some high hopes and great expectations are clearly entertained) that are listed in one's racing daily as due to line up in far less prestigious and valuable impending races, then one indeed may have really found something to bet on, since such a runner is clearly facing a far less onerous task than that which awaits it in future.

For example, in the *Racing Post* of 2 September 1995, a leading bookmaker offered ante-post odds on 18 horses entered for the Tote Sunday Handicap, due to be contested 22 days later at Ascot. Of these 18, only two - Burooj, quoted at 16/1 for this new race and Inquisitor with an ante-post quotation of 20-1, were due to contest separate, much less valuable, races on the very day these prices were advertised. Rather significantly, and not unacceptably, these runners, like big fish placed in ponds that were far too small for them, easily devoured the small bait on offer to them. Ironically Burooj, with a lower ante-post quote than Inquisitor, won at 8-1, while the latter went in at 3-1, to underline the value of monitoring ante-post betting shows on future events for clues to present day winners.

STRATEGY 7

TRAINERS SIDE-STEPPING FUTURE RACES

Getting a horse fit to race is rather different from getting it fit to win and this latter proceeding is always a matter of fine tuning and precise timing - so much so that some trainers set great store by propitious blood counts just prior to racecourse outings.

This is for the very good reason that, when entries have to be made, potential winners are many days away from the condition of fitness they need to attain. Many trainers enter their charges in several races that are due to be run around the time they anticipate these runners will be 'cherry ripe'.

As for the juiciest cherries on the racing tree, many of these only appear on Saturdays, which is why, using my *Racing Post,* I always look for runners that, are declining to run in alternative contests on the following Monday, Tuesday or Wednesday.

Such horses can be readily identified if a regular *Racing Post* Saturday feature entitled Entries Index is consulted (see example overleaf):

RACING POST

ENTRIES INDEX

Abingdon Flyer	Wdr 7.30 M
	Eps 6.30 W
Able Lassie	Pon 5.15 M
Abso	Chp 3.00 Tu
Absolutely Right	Wdr 7.30 M
	Chp 5.00 Tu
Across The Bay	Eps 9.10 W
Actinella	Wdr 7.00 M
	Wol 2.30 M
Aegean Lady	Cat 8.30 W
Affirmed's Destiny	Yar 5.15 W
Afore Jane	Pon 5.15 M
After The Last	Fol 2.15 Tu
	Eps 7.00 W
Agil's Pet	Wdr 7.00 M
Agincourt Song	Wdr 9.00 M
Aide Memoire	Pon 5.15 M
Akura	Ham 7.45 M
Alasib	Pon 2.15 M
Albert	Wol 2.00 M
	Fol 4.45 Tu
Aldahe	Chp 3.00 Tu
Alhamad	Wdr 9.00 M
Alkarif	War 5.00 W
Al Karnak	Wdr 9.00 M
Allez Bianco	Eps 7.00 W
All Promises	Fol 3.15 Tu
Alpha Helix	Ham 9.15 M
Alternation	War 4.30 W
Amaze	Wdr 9.00 M
Ambassador Royale	
	Wdr 7.30 M
Anchorage	Wol 4.00 M
Anguish	Ham 9.15 M
Anil Amit	Wol 3.00 M
Anna of Saxony	Eps 7.35 W
Annie Rose	Cat 7.00 W
April Shadow	Cat 9.00 W
Arabellajill	Wdr 8.30 M
Aragon Court	Wdr 6.35 M
	Yar 3.45 W
Arc Lamp	Pon 3.15 M
Arley	Wdr 9.00 M
	Yar 4.15 W
Arighi Boy	Yar 2.45 W
Arrogant Daughter	Yar 2.45 W
Ashtina	Eps 8.05 W
Asian Punter	Yar 4.15 W
Aspirant	Chp 4.30 Tu
Assignment	Eps 8.05 W
Atbar	Fol 4.45 Tu
Athene Noctua	Pon 5.15 M
Atherton Green	Pon 4.15 M
Aughfad	Eps 8.05 W
Avril Etoile	Fol 2.15 Tu
Badawiah	Wdr 8.30 M
Ballad Dancer	Ham 7.15 M
Balustrade Boy	War 3.30 W
Banana Cufflinks	Cat 8.00 W
Banbury Flyer	War 4.00 W
Barbara's Cutie	Wol 4.30 M
E.,rkston Singer	Yar 3.45 W
	Yar 4.45 W
Barmbrack	War 5.00 W
Barniemeboy	Wdr 8.00 M
Barnsview	Cat 8.30 W
Bar Three	Chp 4.00 Tu
Bartolomeo	Cat 7.30 W
Bashamah	Yar 5.15 W
Battling Bella	Fol 1.45 Tu
Bear With Me	Wol 3.30 M
	Fol 1.45 Tu
Bee Dee Ell	Ham 7.45 M
	Ham 8.15 M
	Ham 8.45 M
Behaanis	Yar 3.15 W
Belated	Wdr 8.30 M
	Fol 2.45 Tu
	Cat 6.30 W
Bel Baraka	Eps 7.35 W
Belfort Ruler	Eps 9.10 W
Bella Bettina	Wol 5.00 M
Bella's Match	Wol 3.30 M
Bellatrix	Chp 3.00 Tu
Bells of Longwick	Wol 5.00 M
Be My Habitat	Yar 3.45 W
Benefact	Pon 2.45 M
Beneficial	Yar 3.15 W
Bengal Tiger	Wdr 6.35 M
Bentico	Wdr 7.30 M
Bernie Silvers	Yar 2.45 W
Betrayed	Cat 7.00 W
Beyond The Moon	Wdr 8.30 M
Bichette	Eps 7.00 W
Bid For Six	Eps 7.35 W
Big Easy	Wdr 9.00 M
Bighayir	Chp 5.00 Tu
Big Pat	Pon 2.45 M
Bilberry	Cat 7.30 W
Bill Moon	Yar 3.45 W
Bird Hunter	War 3.30 W
Bit of A Lark	Chp 3.30 Tu
Bluebella	Cat 7.00 W
Blue Drifter	Fol 2.45 Tu
Blue Grit	Ham 8.15 M
Blue Sea	Chp 4.00 Tu
Blushing Belle	Chp 4.30 Tu
Blyostka	Fol 2.45 Tu
	Cat 6.30 W
Bohemian Queen	Chp 2.00 Tu
	War 3.30 W
Bo Knows Best	Wdr 6.35 M
Bold Boss	Pon 3.45 M
	Eps 7.35 W
Bold Face	Fol 2.15 Tu
Bold Habit	Pon 3.15 M
Bonita Bee	Wdr 8.00 M
Boring	Cat 7.30 W
Bourbon Jack	War 3.30 W
Brambleberry	Pon 3.45 M
Brambles Way	Cat 8.30 W
Brave Bidder	Wdr 8.00 M
Breezy Sailor	Yar 4.15 W
Bridle Talk	Wol 5.00 M
Brier Creek	Eps 6.30 W
Brigadore Gold	Fol 2.15 Tu
Briggscare	Yar 5.15 W
Briggs Lad	Wdr 7.30 M
	Wol 4.00 M
	Cat 7.30 W
Briggsmaid	Yar 5.15 W
Brilliant Disguise	Ham 7.45 M
Bronze Runner	Pon 4.45 M
Broughton Blues	Fol 4.45 Tu
Broughton's Gold	Pon 5.15 M
	Wdr 7.30 M
Broughton's Tango	Wdr 6.35 M
Brush Wolf	Wdr 6.35 M
Brusque	Ham 9.15 M
Buddy	War 5.00 W
Bustinetta	Wdr 9.00 M
Buzzards Crest	Fol 4.45 Tu
Caithness Rock	Cat 7.30 W
	Cat 8.00 W
Calachuchi	Cat 8.00 W
Calenick Lass	Wol 3.00 M
Calisar	Chp 2.00 Tu
	War 3.30 W
Cal's Boy	War 2.30 W
Camino A Ronda	Wol 5.00 M
Candle King	Yar 3.45 W
Canon Kyle	Cat 9.00 W
Cantanta	Fol 3.45 Tu
	Yar 5.15 W
Cape Pigeon	Chp 2.30 Tu
Capital Idea	Wol 5.00 M
Cr'ingford	Ham 9.15 M
Carabrea Snip	War 5.30 W
Caroles Clown	Fol 3.45 Tu
Caroles Express	Eps 9.10 W
Carpentier	Eps 7.35 W
Cashable	Fol 2.15 Tu
	Yar 3.15 W
Cashtal Queen	War 4.00 W
Casienne	Chp 5.00 Tu
Castle Maid	Chp 3.00 Tu
Castoret	Eps 6.30 W
Catel Ring	Wdr 6.35 M
Cathos	Eps 6.30 W
Cee-En-Cee	Eps 9.10 W
Chaff	Yar 3.45 W
Chain Dance	Wdr 7.00 M
Champenoise	Chp 5.00 Tu
Chantry Bellini	Cat 7.30 W
Charity Express	Wdr 7.00 M
Charmed Knave	Chp 3.00 Tu
Charming Gift	Yar 3.45 W
Chateau Nord	Ham 7.15 M
Cheshire Annie	Wol 5.00 M
Chiparopai	Cat 8.00 W
Christian Flight	Wol 3.30 M
	Fol 1.45 Tu
	Fol 2.45 Tu
Christian Spirit	Eps 7.00 W
Christian Warrior	Fol 4.45 Tu
Cinders Girl	Wdr 7.00 M
	Wdr 8.00 M
	War 5.30 W
Citiqueen	Pon 5.15 M
City Line	Chp 4.00 Tu
Clair Soleil	Pon 3.45 M
Classical Charmer	War 5.00 W
Classic Exhibit	Yar 2.45 W
Classic Storm	Chp 2.00 Tu
Clear Honey	Wol 2.30 M
Clifton Charlie	Chp 3.30 Tu
Clifton Chase	Cat 7.30 W
Club Verge	Ham 6.45 M
Cobblers Hill	Ham 7.45 M
	Wdr 6.35 M
Cold Shower	Pon 2.45 M
	Pon 4.45 M
Come On My Girl	Ham 7.15 M
	Ham 8.15 M
Comtec's Legend	Wol 3.00 M
Cool Parade	Pon 4.45 M
Copper Trader	Pon 2.45 M
Coral Flutter	Yar 3.45 W
Corinthian God	Eps 7.35 W
Cottage Gallery	Ham 7.15 M
Countercheck	Fol 1.45 Tu
Courageous Knight	Eps 9.10 W
Court Minstrel	Fol 1.45 Tu
Court Rise	Fol 3.45 Tu
	War 4.30 W
	Yar 5.15 W
Cov Tel Lady	Cat 7.30 W
Cradle Days	Chp 3.30 Tu
	Eps 8.05 W
Cradle of Love	Yar 4.45 W
Cranfield Comet	Wdr 8.30 M
Creagmhor	Ham 6.45 M
Creego	Yar 2.45 W
	Yar 3.45 W
Crept Out	Cat 8.30 W
	Cat 9.00 W
Crown Reserve	Yar 3.45 W
Crystado	Wdr 9.00 M
	War 2.30 W
Crystal Cross	Eps 6.30 W
Cumbrian Classic	Ham 7.45 M
	Ham 8.45 M
Dame Helene	Pon 2.45 M
Dancing Tudor	Pon 4.45 M
Danza Heights	Ham 9.15 M
Dare To Dream	Fol 3.45 Tu
	Yar 5.15 W
Dayflower	Wol 2.30 M
Dazla	Wol 2.00 M
	Yar 3.45 W
Deb's Ball	Pon 5.15 M
Debsy Do	Pon 3.15 M
Debt Swap	Wdr 9.00 M
Densben	Pon 3.15 M
Desert Mist	Pon 2.45 M
	Cat 7.30 W
	War 4.30 W
Desert Splendour	Chp 2.30 Tu
Dexter Chief	Pon 3.45 M
	Chp 4.00 Tu
	Eps 7.35 W
Doc Spot	Wol 3.00 M
Dollar Wine	Wdr 6.35 M
	Fol 4.45 Tu
Dolly Madison	Cat 7.30 W
Domiana	Wdr 6.35 M
	Chp 3.00 Tu
Don't Jump	Fol 2.15 Tu
Don't Run Me Over	Cat 8.30 W
Dordogne	Fol 3.45 Tu
	Fol 4.15 Tu
Do The Business	Wdr 6.35 M
	Yar 4.15 W
Dots Dee	Pon 2.45 M
Dotty's Walker	Wdr 7.00 M
Doulab's Image	Yar 4.45 W
Dovale	Eps 6.30 W
Dreams Eyes	Yar 2.45 W
	Yar 3.45 W
Dress Sense	Wdr 9.00 M
Drum Sergeant	Pon 3.15 M
Dublin Dream	Wol 5.00 M
Dune River	War 5.00 W
Dunnington	Cat 7.00 W
Durneltor	Eps 9.10 W
Dynavour House	Wol 3.00 M
Eastern Whisper	Fol 3.45 Tu
Eastleigh	War 5.00 W
Easy Access	Fol 2.15 Tu
Echo-Logical	Chp 3.30 Tu
Edgeaway	Wol 3.30 M
	War 2.30 W
	War 5.00 W
Edgewise	Cat 8.00 W
	Yar 3.45 W
	Yar 5.15 W
Educated Pet	Pon 3.15 M
	Chp 3.30 Tu
Efra	Fol 2.45 Tu
Eid	Yar 4.45 W
Elite Reg	War 4.30 W
Eliafitzetty	War 4.30 W
Elsharh	Pon 2.45 M
Enfant du Paradis	Yar 5.15 W
Escape Talk	Pon 4.45 M
	Pon 5.15 M
Etiquette	Wdr 9.00 M
Eurotwist	Ham 9.15 M
	Cat 7.30 W
Everglades	War 4.00 W
Express Signmaker	War 4.30 W
Fair Dare	Pon 5.15 M
Fair Flyer	Ham 7.45 M
	Ham 9.15 M
Fairspear	Chp 4.30 Tu
Famous Beauty	Pon 5.15 M
Farmer's Pet	Yar 5.15 W
Fayre Find	War 3.30 W
Felt Lucky	Wdr 8.00 M
Fern Heights	Wol 2.00 M
Field of Vision	Ham 6.45 M
Fierro	Wdr 8.00 M
Final Frontier	Fol 2.15 Tu
Finjan	Pon 3.15 M
First Bid	Pon 4.45 M
First Century	Eps 8.40 W
First Option	Cat 7.00 W
Fitzcarraldo	Yar 3.15 W
Fiveofive	Wol 2.30 M
Fivesevenfiveo	Chp 3.30 Tu
Flashy's Son	Yar 2.45 W
Fleur Power	Wol 2.30 M
Floating Line	Pon 4.45 M
Floodlight	Chp 2.00 Tu
Florac	War 5.30 W
Fly For Gold	Pon 5.15 M
Flying Amy	Eps 7.00 W
Flying Down To Rio	
	Ham 8.15 M
Flying Promise	Wdr 6.35 M
Foolish Heart	Wol 2.30 M
Foreign Assignment	
	Wdr 6.35 M
Forest Fairy	War 4.00 W
Formal Invitation	Fol 4.15 Tu
Fort Derry	Ham 8.45 M
Fortune Cay	Wdr 8.00 M
Free Mover	Wdr 9.00 M
	Chp 4.00 Tu
Freephone	Eps 8.40 W
	Yar 3.45 W
Friendly House	Wdr 9.00 M
Full Exposure	Wol 2.30 M
	Yar 3.15 W
Full Sight	War 4.30 W
Galactic Fury	Wol 3.00 M
Galejade	Wol 2.30 M
Gallant Hope	Chp 3.30 Tu
	Eps 8.05 W
Ganeshaya	Cat 8.30 W
	War 4.00 W
Gangleader	Ham 6.45 M
	Wdr 8.00 M
Garden District	Fol 3.45 Tu
	Yar 5.15 W
Garden of Heaven	Wdr 9.00 M
	Chp 4.00 Tu
Garnock Valley	Ham 6.45 M
Gay Ming	Pon 2.45 M
Gaynor Goodman	Fol 3.15 Tu
General Chase	Wol 2.30 M
General Dixie	Chp 4.00 Tu
Generally	Fol 3.15 Tu
Genesis Four	Fol 3.15 Tu
George Henry	Ham 7.45 M
George Roper	War 3.30 W
Gerish	Yar 4.15 W
Ghostly Glow	War 4.30 W
Ghurrah	War 5.00 W
Gibbet	Fol 4.45 Tu
Girl Next Door	Fol 2.15 Tu
Glenfield Greta	War 4.00 W
Glenstal Princess	Pon 3.15 M
Glowing Dancer	Eps 7.00 W
	War 3.30 W
Glowing Jade	Wdr 7.00 M
Golden Beau	Pon 4.45 M
Good As Gold	Wol 3.30 M
Goodbye Millie	Pon 2.15 M
Grand Dancer	Wdr 8.00 M
Gran Senorum	Fol 2.15 Tu
Great Lord	Ham 8.15 M
Green Dollar	Pon 3.15 M
Green's Stubbs	Chp 5.00 Tu
Green Sword	War 3.30 W
Grey Illusions	Yar 3.45 W
Grouse-N-Heather	Cat 8.00 W
Gypsy Legend	Wol 3.00 M
Hallplace	Chp 2.00 Tu
	Eps 7.00 W
Hanjessdan	Chp 4.30 Tu
Hard To Figure	Eps 9.10 W
Harlequin Girl	Wdr 6.35 M
Harry's Coming	War 4.00 W
Harry's Lady	Wol 2.00 M
Hataal	Wol 3.30 M
Have A Nightcap	Wdr 6.35 M
	Yar 2.45 W
	Yar 3.45 W
Hawaii Star	Fol 2.15 Tu
Hawke Bay	Chp 2.00 Tu
Heart Flutter	Pon 2.45 M
Heathyards Gem	Wol 2.30 M
Heavyweight	Wdr 9.00 M
Here Comes A Star	
	Ham 7.15 M
Her Honour	Chp 4.00 Tu
Hideyoshi	Eps 7.35 W
High Beacon	Eps 6.30 W
High Principles	Wol 5.00 M
Hightown-Princess	Wol 2.00 M
	Yar 3.45 W
Hinari Hi Fi	Wol 4.30 M
Hinari Video	Ham 7.15 M
Hiram B Birdbath	Yar 4.15 W
Hizeem	Ham 8.15 M
Holly Brown	Wdr 7.30 M
Homemaker	Wol 3.00 M
Honeymoon Dawn	Pon 2.15 M
Horizon	Wdr 7.30 M
How's Yer Father	Chp 2.30 Tu
Humour	Pon 4.45 M
	Wdr 9.00 M
	Wol 3.30 M
I Do Care	War 5.30 W
Ima Red Neck	Wdr 9.00 M
Impeccable Charm	Eps 7.35 W
Impressive Lad	Chp 5.00 Tu
	Fol 4.45 Tu
Imshi	Fol 3.15 Tu
Incola	Wdr 7.30 M
	Fol 4.15 Tu
Indian Flash	Wol 2.30 M
	Yar 3.15 W
Indian Style	Wol 3.30 M
Injaka Boy	Wol 5.00 M
Inseyab	Yar 2.45 W
Internal Affair	Wdr 6.35 M
	Yar 2.45 W
	Yar 3.45 W
In The Print	Chp 4.30 Tu
Intrepid Lass	Fol 3.45 Tu
Invigilate	Cat 8.30 W
Irish Groom	Wol 2.00 M
Iron King	Chp 3.30 Tu
Jaldi	Chp 2.30 Tu
Jarras	Chp 5.00 Tu
Jazilah	Pon 4.45 M
Jigsaw Boy	Wdr 8.30 M
Jocks Joker	Cat 7.00 W
John Shaw	Cat 8.00 W
Jokist	Yar 4.45 W
Jolizal	Wdr 6.35 M
Jovial Man	Eps 7.35 W
Jumeira Shark	Wdr 9.00 M
Kahhal	Chp 4.30 Tu
Kajaani	Chp 4.00 Tu
	Eps 7.35 W
Kalar	Cat 8.30 W
Kaloochi	Chp 2.00 Tu
Kandy Secret	Eps 8.40 W
Karinska	Chp 2.00 Tu
Kasikci	Wol 4.00 M
Kateb	Yar 4.45 W
Kathy Fair	Wdr 6.35 M
Kayartis	Cat 7.30 W
Kay Beeyou	Wol 3.30 M
Kaytak	Eps 6.30 W
Kelly's Kite	Wdr 6.35 M
	Yar 3.45 W
Kentucky Starlet	Wol 3.30 M
	Chp 3.00 Tu
	Fol 1.45 Tu

Kertale ... Yar 2.45 W
Killick ... Fol 4.45 Tu
Kindred Cameo ... Eps 8.40 W
Kingchip Boy ... Yar 3.45 W
Kingsfold Pet ... Eps 7.35 W
Kirriemuir ... War 4.00 W
Knayton Lodger ... Wol 3.00 M
Lady Dundee ... Pon 5.15 M
... Wdr 7.30 M
Lady Lacey ... Wol 2.00 M
Lady Lawn ... Cat 7.00 M
Lady of Sardinia (BEL)
... Wdr 9.00 M
Lady of Shadows ... Fol 3.15 Tu
Lady of The Fen ... Wol 4.30 M
Lady Risk Me ... Yar 3.45 W
La Kermesse ... Cat 9.00 W
Lamastre ... Wdr 6.35 M
Lancaster Pilot ... Pon 4.15 M
Last Orders ... Eps 8.40 W
Lawnswood Prince ... Fol 1.45 Tu
Les Amis ... Wol 2.00 M
Let's Get Lost ... Wdr 9.00 M
... Chp 4.00 Tu
... Eps 7.35 W
Libra Legend ... Yar 2.45 W
Lifetime Fame ... Wdr 8.30 M
Liffey River ... Yar 2.45 W
Lift Boy ... Cat 6.30 W
... Cat 8.30 W
Lincoln Imp ... Wdr 8.00 M
... Fol 2.15 Tu
Lincstone Boy ... Ham 7.15 M
Lindeman ... Eps 8.40 W
Lisalee ... Ham 9.15 M
... Pon 5.15 M
Litho Bold Flasher ... Yar 4.15 W
Little Bang ... Chp 4.30 Tu
Littledale ... Fol 4.45 Tu
Little Ivor ... Pon 2.45 M
... Cat 7.30 W
Loki ... Eps 6.30 W
Lord Advocate ... Cat 8.00 W
Lord Belmonte ... Wdr 6.35 M
Lord Leitrim ... Wdr 6.35 M
... Yar 2.45 W
Lord Neptune ... Cat 6.30 W
... War 3.00 W
Lord's Final ... Chp 3.00 Tu
Lots of Luck ... Fol 4.45 Tu
Lucayan Treasure ... War 3.30 W
Luks Akura ... Ham 9.15 M
... Eps 6.30 W
Lycian Moon ... Chp 4.00 Tu
Lyn's Return ... Eps 8.40 W
Lyphantastic ... Eps 6.30 W
Ma Bella Luna ... Wol 3.30 M
Magirika ... Wdr 8.00 M
Mahfil ... Eps 6.30 W
Mahrajan ... Wdr 7.30 M
Maji ... Cat 7.30 W
Major Ivor ... Yar 3.45 W
Make Mine A Double
... Pon 4.15 M
Maligned ... Wdr 9.00 M
... Eps 7.35 W
Mamalama ... Fol 4.15 Tu
Manbas ... Wol 3.30 M
Manolender ... Cat 8.30 W
... Cat 9.00 W
Manulife ... Ham 8.15 M
Many A Quest ... Pon 3.45 M
Marabou ... Chp 4.00 Tu
Mardior ... Wdr 6.35 M
Margaret's Gift ... Pon 2.15 M
Marillette ... Wol 2.30 M
Marjons Boy ... Wol 2.00 M
Maroof ... Wdr 8.00 M
Marpatann ... War 4.30 W
Martina ... Chp 3.30 Tu
Martini Executive ... Ham 8.15 M
... Yar 4.45 W
Mashakel ... Cat 8.00 W
Masrur ... Wdr 8.30 M
... Fol 1.45 Tu
... War 3.00 W
Master Copy ... Cat 7.30 W
Master's Crown ... Yar 4.15 W
MCA Below The Line
... Cat 8.00 W
... Yar 2.45 W
Mere Chants ... Eps 7.35 W
Merino Wish ... Chp 2.30 Tu
Metal Boys ... Wol 4.30 M
Milagro ... Eps 8.05 W

Millyel ... Ham 9.15 M
Minshaar ... Pon 2.15 M
Miss Bluebird ... Fol 2.45 Tu
Miss Doody ... Chp 4.30 Tu
Missed The Boat ... Ham 6.45 M
Miss Feyruz ... Fol 2.15 Tu
Miss Grosse Nez ... Cat 8.30 M
... Cat 9.00 M
Miss Haggis ... Wol 3.30 M
Miss Hyde ... Pon 4.45 M
Miss Magenta ... Wdr 6.35 M
... Yar 3.45 W
Miss Parkes ... Ham 8.45 M
Miss Siham ... Wol 5.00 M
Miss Witch ... Chp 5.00 Tu
Missy-S ... Wol 3.30 M
... Fol 4.45 Tu
Mistertopopigo ... Wol 3.00 M
Misty Goddess ... Chp 4.30 Tu
Mizyan ... Fol 4.15 Tu
Monarda ... Fol 4.15 Tu
Monorose ... Chp 4.30 Tu
Moot Point ... Fol 3.45 Tu
... Yar 5.15 W
Morsun ... Fol 1.45 Tu
... War 5.00 W
Mr News ... Cat 7.30 W
Mr Tate ... Fol 1.45 Tu
Mr Wellright ... Wol 3.00 M
Mu-Arrik ... Chp 3.00 Tu
... Eps 9.10 W
Murray's Mazda ... Cat 8.30 W
Musket Boat ... Ham 8.15 M
Mustahil ... Chp 2.30 Tu
Muzo ... Chp 5.00 Tu
My Ballyboy ... Wol 3.00 M
My Czech Mate ... Wol 6.35 M
My Ducats ... Wol 6.35 M
My Gadson ... Cat 7.00 W
My Grain ... Wol 3.30 M
My Ruby Ring ... War 4.00 W
Mystery Lad ... Ham 7.45 M
... Pon 2.45 M
Mystic Panther ... Chp 4.30 Tu
Naseem Elbarr ... Yar 5.15 W
Naseer ... Yar 5.15 W
Natral Exchange ... Cat 8.00 W
Navaresque ... Chp 3.00 Tu
Negative Pledge ... Pon 3.45 M
Nellie Dean ... War 5.00 W
Neptune's Pet ... Wol 2.00 M
Never Late ... Cat 8.30 W
Nigals Friend ... Wol 4.30 M
Noble Pet ... War 3.00 W
... War 5.00 W
No Comebacks ... Wol 3.00 M
No Extras ... Fol 3.15 Tu
Noggings ... Ham 7.45 M
Nominator ... Pon 4.15 M
Norfolkisc ... Eps 9.10 W
Norman Warrior ... Yar 4.45 W
North of Watford ... Ham 7.15 M
Notable Exception ... Pon 2.45 M
... Cat 8.00 W
... War 4.30 W
Nut Bush ... Wol 3.00 M
... Wol 3.30 M
Oak Apple ... Pon 5.15 M
Odeon ... Pon 3.45 M
Ombre Danme ... Wol 3.00 M
One Dollar More ... Wdr 6.35 M
Oratel Flyer ... Ham 7.15 M
Orchard Bay ... Yar 2.45 W
Orchid Valley ... Cat 6.30 W
Oriental Song ... Pon 3.45 M
... War 2.30 W
Our Amber ... Ham 7.15 M
Our Eddie ... Eps 8.40 W
Overpower ... Fol 4.45 Tu
Oyston's Life ... Ham 8.15 M
Paddy Chalk ... Chp 3.30 Tu
Pageboy ... Pon 3.15 M
Palacegate Gold ... Wdr 8.30 M
Palacegate Prince ... Cat 7.00 W
Paley Prince ... Chp 3.30 Tu
Paper Craft ... Pon 4.45 M
... Cat 8.00 W
Paradise Forum ... Wdr 8.30 M
Patience Please ... Cat 6.30 W
Perfect Light ... Pon 4.45 M
Perforate ... Cat 7.30 W
... War 4.30 W

Perspicacity ... Ham 8.15 M
Petiole ... Wdr 7.00 M
Petite Epaulette ... Wdr 7.00 M
Petite Lass ... Fol 3.15 Tu
Petite Loule ... Wol 2.30 M
Pettesse ... War 4.00 W
Phargold ... Pon 2.45 M
Pickles ... Yar 3.45 W
Pie Hatch ... Pon 2.45 M
... Cat 7.30 W
Pine Glen Pepper ... Wol 4.30 M
Pink's Black ... Yar 2.45 W
Pippin Park ... Chp 4.00 Tu
Plain Fact ... Wol 4.30 M
Please Please Me ... Wdr 6.35 M
Podrida ... Fol 3.45 Tu
Poker Chip ... Pon 2.15 M
Polonez Prima ... Eps 9.10 W
... Yar 4.45 W
Pompion ... Wdr 9.00 M
Poppet Plume ... Cat 7.00 W
Pop To Stans ... Wdr 8.30 M
Port In A Storm ... Pon 3.45 M
Premier Dance ... Chp 5.00 Tu
Premier Venues ... Ham 9.15 M
... Pon 4.45 M
Prenonamess ... Eps 9.10 W
Pretonic ... Ham 7.15 M
... Pon 3.15 M
Primo Pageant ... Pon 3.45 M
Prima Prince ... Wol 3.00 M
Prince Manki ... Fol 3.15 Tu
Prince of Darkness ... Pon 3.45 M
Princess Nebia ... Fol 2.15 Tu
... Eps 7.00 W
Princess of Alar ... Wol 3.00 M
Princess Tara ... Chp 2.30 Tu
Prolific ... Eps 8.05 W
Profit A Prendre ... Chp 3.00 Tu
QanMzak Idol ... Wol 3.30 M
Quantity Surveyor ... Ham 7.45 M
Quarrington Hill ... War 3.00 W
Quip ... Ham 9.15 M
Rabbit's Fool ... Fol 4.15 Tu
Racing Telegraph ... Eps 7.00 W
R A Express ... Wol 4.30 M
Raging Thunder ... Fol 2.15 Tu
Rain Splash ... Wdr 7.00 M
Rapid Lad ... Pon 4.45 M
Rapid Mover ... Ham 9.15 M
Rarfy's Dream ... Fol 4.15 Tu
Rasco ... Pon 3.45 M
Reach For Glory ... Pon 2.45 M
Red Rosein ... Eps 8.05 W
Reef of Tulloch ... Pon 4.45 M
Reflecting ... Pon 3.45 M
Rellion ... Cat 9.00 W
Respectable Jones ... War 4.00 W
Rich Pickings ... Wdr 8.30 M
Rinoroe ... Chp 4.00 Tu
Right Win ... Eps 7.00 W
Rio Trusty ... Fol 4.45 Tu
Ripsnorter ... War 5.00 W
... Yar 3.45 W
Rising Tempo ... Wdr 7.30 M
Risky Number ... Wol 3.00 M
... War 3.30 W
Roar On Tour ... Wdr 5.00 W
Rock The Boat ... Wdr 7.00 M
Rocky Waters ... Eps 9.10 W
Roger Rabbit ... Yar 3.45 W
Romola Nijinsky ... Wol 4.30 M
Rose Cot ... Yar 4.15 W
Rose Gem ... Yar 3.45 W
... Yar 4.45 W
Rosina Mae ... Chp 4.00 Tu
Rostands Hero ... Pon 2.45 M
Roucellist Bay ... Ham 9.15 M
Roxy Music ... Yar 2.45 W
... Yar 3.45 W
Royal Dartmouth ... Eps 9.10 W
Rumbelow ... Yar 3.45 W
Running Glimpse ... Eps 8.05 W
... Eps 9.10 W
Rushluan ... Chp 5.00 Tu
Russia With Love ... Wdr 7.00 M
Ryewater Dream ... Chp 5.00 Tu
Sahara Shield ... Pon 4.45 M
Sally Fay ... Wol 2.00 M
Salu ... Cat 7.30 W
... Cat 8.00 W
Samain ... Wol 2.00 M
Sanawi ... Yar 3.45 W

Sandmoor Satin ... Pon 2.15 M
Sandro ... Fol 4.15 Tu
Santarem ... Yar 4.15 W
Sapphirine ... Pon 5.15 M
Sarah-Clare ... Wdr 7.30 M
Savash ... Eps 7.35 W
Sciacca ... Yar 3.45 W
Screech ... Fol 3.15 Tu
Scultore ... War 4.30 W
Seal Indigo ... Eps 6.30 W
Sea Prodigy ... Fol 1.45 Tu
Sea Syrah ... Fol 2.15 Tu
Second Colours ... Chp 2.00 Tu
... War 3.30 W
Secret Fantasy ... Wdr 7.00 M
Seflo ... Fol 3.15 Tu
Shades of Croft ... Wol 3.00 M
Shades of Jade ... Chp 3.30 Tu
Shaddown ... Ham 9.15 M
Shadow Bird ... Pon 5.15 M
Shafayil ... Pon 2.45 M
Shakreen ... Pon 3.45 M
Shalubia ... Pon 3.45 M
Shamshom Al Arab ... Wrl 2.00 M
Share Holder ... Fol 2.45 Tu
Shar Emblem ... Fol 4.45 Tu
Sharp Dance ... Wol 3.30 M
Sharp Imp ... Eps 7.00 W
Sharp Top ... Pon 5.15 M
... Yar 5.15 W
Shayna Maidel ... Wol 3.30 M
Sheila's Secret ... Wdr 8.00 M
Sheriffmuir ... Wol 4.00 M
Shining Jewel ... Yar 4.45 W
Shrewd Girl ... Wdr 6.35 M
... Chp 4.30 Tu
Silica ... Wol 3.30 M
Silver Haze ... Ham 8.15 M
Simon Ellis ... Chp 4.30 Tu
Simonov ... Wdr 7.30 M
Singers Image ... War 5.00 W
Sintafari ... Yar 4.45 W
Sizzling Affair ... Wdr 8.30 M
Slanderinthestrand ... Eps 8.40 W
Slip-A-Solo ... Wol 4.30 M
Slumber Thyme ... Wol 3.30 M
Sly Prospect ... Wol 4.30 M
Smiling Chief ... Wdr 7.30 M
Snow Blizzard ... Fol 4.15 Tu
So Beguiling ... War 4.30 W
Solid Steel ... Fol 3.45 Tu
Solstice ... Ham 7.45 M
Son of Schula ... Pon 3.45 M
Souson ... Cat 8.00 W
Southwold Air ... War 5.00 W
Sovereign Rock ... Wol 8.30 M
Spanish Glory ... Yar 3.45 W
Spanish Performer ... Yar 3.45 W
Spanish Thread ... Pon 2.15 M
Special Risk ... Fol 2.15 Tu
Spectacular Dawn ... Eps 6.30 W
Speedo Movement ... Pon 5.15 M
Spencer's Revenge ... War 2.00 W
Spirit Sam ... Fol 4.45 Tu
Splendent ... Pon 4.15 M
... Wdr 8.00 M
Stardust Express ... Wol 3.30 M
St Athans Lad ... Pon 4.45 M
Statte ... Pon 4.45 M
Sterling Princess ... Fol 3.15 Tu
Steven's Dream ... Ham 6.45 M
... Fol 3.15 Tu
Stevie's Wonder ... Fol 2.15 Tu
Strong Suit ... Eps 9.10 W
Suanax ... Chp 4.30 Tu
Summit Fever ... Wdr 7.00 M
Super Serenade ... War 3.00 W
Sure Risk ... Chp 2.00 Tu
... Fol 3.15 Tu
Surrey Racing ... Yar 2.45 W
Swan Heights ... Wol 4.00 M
... Chp 4.00 Tu
Sweet Mignonette ... Ham 8.15 M
Sweet Request ... Yar 5.15 W
Swell Time ... Wol 2.00 M
Swift Silver ... Pon 4.45 M
... Wdr 7.30 M
Sylvan Breeze ... Fol 2.45 Tu
Systematic ... Eps 8.40 W
Tafsir ... Yar 4.15 W
Tajigrey ... Fol 1.45 Tu
Talent ... Chp 2.30 Tu
Tales of Wisdom ... Ham 7.45 M
Talish ... Ham 8.15 M

Tancred Grange ... Cat 7.30 W
Tate Dancer ... Pon 3.15 M
Taunting ... Wol 2.00 M
Taylors Prince ... Wdr 7.30 M
Teanarco ... Chp 3.00 Tu
Tee-Emm ... Fol 3.15 Tu
... Cat 7.00 W
Tempelhof ... Cat 7.30 W
Tempering ... Ham 8.15 M
Temple Knight ... Wdr 9.00 M
Tendresse ... Yar 3.45 W
The Dominant Gene ... Yar 3.45 W
The Fed ... War 5.30 W
The Institute Boy ... Eps 7.00 W
The Karaoke King ... Yar 4.15 W
Thomaam ... War 3.00 W
The Noble Oak ... Wol 3.00 M
The Right Time ... Ham 7.15 M
... Wol 4.30 M
The Rover's ... Wol 3.00 M
Thewaarf ... Fol 1.45 Tu
The Yomper ... Fol 4.15 Tu
Thimbalina ... Pon 5.15 M
... Fol 4.15 Tu
Tiger Shoot ... Wdr 7.30 M
Times Are Hard ... Yar 3.45 W
Tino Tere ... Wol 4.30 M
Tommy Tempest ... Wol 5.00 M
Top Scale ... Pon 4.45 M
Top Song ... Wol 3.30 M
... Fol 1.45 Tu
Top Table ... Pon 5.15 M
Tour Leader ... Ham 7.45 M
... Cat 8.00 W
Treasure Time ... Ham 8.45 M
Trosllan Owl ... Chp 4.30 Tu
Trial Times ... War 5.00 W
Trieg Park ... Fol 3.45 Tu
Trooping ... Pon 3.45 M
Tropical Tie ... Fol 3.15 Tu
True Contender ... War 4.30 W
True Story ... Chp 2.00 Tu
Try Leguard ... Eps 9.10 W
Tulapol ... Fol 1.45 Tu
... Eps 8.40 W
Turgenov ... Wol 4.00 M
Turning Heads ... Pon 2.45 M
Tuscan Dawn ... Wdr 8.00 M
Twice As Much ... Chp 4.00 Tu
... Eps 7.35 W
Tylers Wood ... Eps 8.05 W
Ukam's Lady ... Wol 3.00 M
Uppence ... Ham 7.15 M
Up The Punjab ... Fol 4.45 Tu
... Eps 8.40 W
Vallance ... Pon 4.45 M
... Chp 5.00 Tu
Valley of Time ... Ham 8.15 M
Victorian Star ... Fol 3.15 Tu
Village Pet ... Wdr 6.35 M
... Wol 4.30 M
Virginia Cottage ... Wol 5.00 M
Waaza ... Pon 3.45 M
Walk In The Park ... Wol 4.30 M
Walkonthemoon ... Wol 3.30 M
Walnut Burt ... Eps 7.00 W
Waseela ... Wol 3.30 M
Wealthywoo ... War 3.30 W
We Are Doomed ... Fol 2.15 Tu
Wilco ... Wol 5.00 M
Will of Steel ... War 3.00 W
Windpower ... Pon 3.15 M
Winged Whisper ... Wdr 7.30 M
Wishing Cap ... Chp 2.00 Tu
Witches Coven ... Cat 7.30 W
Workingforpeanuts ... Wol 3.00 M
Yfool ... Wol 2.30 M
Young Ern ... Fol 2.15 Tu
Zany Zanna ... Chp 3.15 Tu
Zinbaq ... Chp 3.00 Tu
Zinger ... Yar 2.45 W
Zuno Warrior ... Wdr 8.00 M

FROM *THE INDEPENDENT ON SUNDAY*

NEWCASTLE

2.15: (6f claiming stakes, 2yo)
1. **CAPTAIN LE SAUX** bay colt Persian Heights – Casting Couch ...... **W R Swinburn evens fav**
2. **Daytona Beach** .... **K Darley 6-1**
3. **Shadow Jury** .... **G Baxter 5-1**

Also ran: 17-2 Grand Dancer **(4th)**, 9-1 Contract Elite **(6th)**, 10-1 Bold Seven **(5th)**, 50-1 Free Market.

7 ran. 2, hd, nk, 8, 10. (Trained by M Bell, at Newmarket, for P A Philipps). **Tote:** £2.00; £1.40, £2.00. Dual Forecast: £4.10. Computer Straight Forecast: £7.11. Non Runner: Blue Radiance.
Time: 1min 13.58sec (2.08sec above standard).

2.45: (1m Earsdon Stakes)
1. **LEAD THE DANCE** bay colt Lead On Time – Malyaasah .... **W Ryan 13-8**
2. **Ernestan** .... **M Birch 6-4 fav**
3. **Badawi** .... **R Cochrane 9-4**

3 ran. 1, 2. (H Cecil, Newmarket, for Sheikh Mohammed). **Tote:** £1.80. DF: £1.70. CSF: £3.98.
Time: 1min 41.90sec (2.90sec above standard).

3.15: (7f handicap)
1. **SUPERBRAVE** bay horse Superlative – Tribal Feast .... **J Carroll 7-1**
2. **Nordic Brave** .... **K Darley 16-1**
3. **Duckington** .... **S Maloney 7-1**

Also ran: 2-1 fav Rocton North, 6-1 Northern Rainbow **(5th)**, 13-2 Sharpalto **(4th)**, 7-1 Parliament Piece **(6th)**, 8-1 Halston Prince, 16-1 Tusky, 25-1 Letsbeonestaboutit.

10 ran. ½, ¾, 5, 4, hd. (W Jarvis, Newmarket, for W Robertson). **Tote:** £9.90; £2.50, £5.70, £2.10. DF: £53.80. CSF: £100.36. Tricast: £749.03.
Time: 1min 24.88sec (0.58sec above standard).

3.50: (2m 19yd Northumberland Plate Handicap)
1. **WITNESS BOX** bay horse Lyphard – Excellent Alibi .... **G Duffield 6-1**
2. **Cabochon** .... **Paul Eddery 8-1**
3. **Satin Lover** .... **R Cochrane 5-1 jt-fav**

Also ran: 5-1 jt-fav Requested, 13-2 Hawait Al Barr **(4th)**, 7-1 Highflying **(5th)**, 11-1 Farsi, 14-1 Star Player, Aahsaylad, Beau Quest, 16-1 Quick Ransom, 20-1 Mrs Barton, Line Drummer **(6th)**.

13 ran. sht-hd, ½, 1½, ¾, ¾. (J Gosden, Newmarket, for Sheikh Mohammed). **Tote:** £6.90; £2.40, £3.50, £1.90. DF: £54.20. Trio: £120.10. CSF: £52.40. Tricast: £238.75. An objection by the second to the winner was overruled.
Time: 3min 25.48sec (0.02sec below standard).

4.20: (6f handicap, 3yo)
1. **BIG HAND** bay gelding Tate Gallery – Clonsella Lady .... **J Lowe 9-1**
2. **Venture Capitalist** .... **N Carlisle 9-1**
3. **Tanfan Blu** .... **Dean McKeown 9-4 fav**

Also ran: 100-30 Orthorhombus, 4-1 Heather Bank **(5th)**, 5-1 Ponsardin **(4th)**, 12-1 Devon Dancer **(6th)**.

7 ran. 3½, 1½, 1, ¾, nk. (J W Watts, Richmond, for Mrs M M Haggas). **Tote:** £9.30; £3.00, £3.40. DF: £27.70. CSF: £74.12.
Time: 1min 12.72sec (1.22sec above standard).

4.50: (5f maiden stakes, 2yo)
1. **MISTERTOPOGIGO** bay colt Thatching – Decadence .... **D Nicholls 6-1**
2. **The Sharp Bidder** .... **Paul Eddery 6-1**
3. **Hawaymyson** .... **K Fallon 8-1**

Also ran: 3-1 fav Dancing Domino, 4-1 Indian Secret, Press The Bell **(4th)**, 6-1 Doc Cottrill, 17-2 Gussie Fink-Nottle **(6th)**, 12-1 First Slice **(5th)**, 33-1 Cracker Jack.

10 ran. 1½, 4, 1½, 1½, ¾. (B Beasley, Hambleton, for Giovanni Alessi). **Tote:** £16.60; £3.50, £2.00, £2.20. Dual Forecast: £100.40. Computer Straight Forecast: £46.00.
Time: 1min 1.24sec (sec above standard).

5.20: (1m 2f 32yd handicap, 3yo)
1. **DRUMMER HICKS** bay colt Seymour Hicks – Musical Princess ...... **W R Swinburn 4-1 fav**
2. **Tahitian** .... **G Baxter 13-2**
3. **Nicely Thanks** .... **Alex Greaves 8-1**

Also ran: 9-2 Very Evident, 7-1 Charioteer **(5th)**, 8-1 Philgun, Mindomica, Dramatic Pass **(6th)**, 11-1 Tales Of Wisdom **(4th)**, 12-1 Doyce, 33-1 Haut-Brion.

11 ran. 3½, 2½, hd, 3, 2. (E Weymes, Middleham, for Mrs N Napier). **Tote:** £4.60; £2.30, £2.90, £3.00. DF: £23.30. CSF: £30.37. Tricast: £188.92.
Time: 2min 9.89sec (3.19sec above standard).
Placepot: £1,775.90.

CHEPSTOW

2.20: 1. ALDERNEY PRINCE (C Rutter) 1-2 fav; **2. Kinfwyn** 11-1; **3. Hotel California** 9-4. **4 ran.** 1½, sht-hd. (P Cole, Whatcombe). **Tote:** £1.50. Dual Forecast: £2.30. Computer Straight Forecast: £5.32.

2.50: 1. BUDDY'S FRIEND (A Clark) 11-2; **2. Sooty Tern** 3-1 fav; **3. Lord's Final** 7-1. **9 ran.** 3, 2½. (R Williams, Newmarket). **Tote:** £4.30; £1.30, £1.10, £3.10. DF: £6.00. CSF: £21.39. Tricast: £106.73.

3.20: 1. ECHO-LOGICAL (G Carter) evens fav; **2. Walk In The Park** 7-1; **3. Vallmont** 6-5. **3 ran.** ½, 3½. (J Berry, Cockerham). **Tote:** £1.70. DF: £2.80. CSF: £5.31.

3.55: 1. BEATLE SONG (T Sprake) 5-1; **2. Charmed Knave** 3-1 fav; **3. Asterix** 9-1. **12 ran.** 1½, ½. (R Hodges, Somerton). **Tote:** £6.20; £2.10, £1.50, £2.60. DF: £7.40. CSF: £20.20. Tricast: £124.73. Non Runner: Bright Sea.

4.25: 1. WINTER LIGHTNING (R Fox) 14-1; **2. Smilingatstrangers** 16-1; **3. Natral Exchange** 5-1. **9 ran.** 7-2 fav Patroclus (5th). hd, 1½. (P Walwyn, Lambourn). **Tote:** £22.70; £5.00, £4.80, £1.40. DF: £254.70. CSF: £166.55. Tricast: £1,041.58. NR: Abbotsham.

5.00: 1. RAJAI (A Clark) 2-1 fav; **2. Sadler's Way** 3-1; **3. Dawn Flight** 6-1. **7 ran.** 4, ¾. (J Dunlop, Arundel). **Tote:** £2.40; £1.60, £1.30. DF: £2.80. CSF: £8.02.

5.30: 1. SAMURAI GOLD (A Mackay) 7-2; **2. Pusey Street Boy** 33-1; **3. Premier Dance** 11-2. **11 ran.** 2-1 fav Long Furlong. hd, 1½. (P Walwyn, Lambourn). **Tote:** £3.70; £1.30, £6.50, £2.20. DF: £304.50. CSF: £89.09. Tricast: £574.83.
Placepot: £39.70.

NEWMARKET

2.00: 1. WAVE HILL (Pat Eddery) 1-2 fav; **2. Kertale** 40-1; **3. Lonesome Train** 16-1. **9 ran.** ½, 5. (H Cecil, Newmarket). **Tote:** £1.60; £1.10, £3.30, £2.60. Dual Forecast: £18.20. Computer Straight Forecast: £20.12.

2.30: 1. PREVENE (L Dettori) 5-2; **2. Double Bass** 8-11 fav; **3. Friendly Brave** 11-1. **7 ran.** 1½, 1½. (P Cole, Whatcombe). **Tote:** £3.90; £1.70, £1.20. DF: £2.40. CSF: £4.85.

3.05: 1. JAHAFIL (W Carson) 10-1; **2. Shambo** 100-30; **3. Tetradonna** 10-1. **6 ran.** 2-1 fav Torchon (6th). 3, 1½. (W R Hern, Lambourn). **Tote:** £10.90; £3.50, £2.20. DF: £22.20. CSF: £39.68.

3.35: 1. TOUSSAUD (Pat Eddery) 7-1; **2. Prince Ferdinand** 11-10 fav; **3. Casteddu** 7-2. **7 ran.** ¾, nk. (J Gosden, Newmarket). **Tote:** £7.00; £2.70, £1.50. DF: £5.30. CSF: £15.21.

4.05: 1. SPEAKER'S HOUSE (Pat Eddery) 5-1; **2. Red Kite** 4-1; **3. Main Bid** 7-1. **7 ran.** 11-4 fav Robingo (5th). 1½, hd. (P Cole, Whatcombe). **Tote:** £6.10; £2.20, £2.10. DF: £12.10. CSF: £23.22.

4.35: 1. IVANKA (M Roberts) 3-1; **2. Greenlet** 8-13 fav; **3. Holly Golightly** 13-2. **5 ran.** 1½, nk. (C Brittain, Newmarket). **Tote:** £4.70; £2.00, £1.10. DF: £2.70. CSF: £5.46.

5.10: 1. HIDDEN LIGHT (K Rutter) 6-4 fav; **2. Santarem** 10-1; **3. Bar Billiards** 13-2. **8 ran.** 2½, 4. (M Jarvis, Newmarket). **Tote:** £2.50; £1.40, £2.20, £1.80. DF: £10.10. CSF: £15.98.
Jackpot: not won. Pool of £4,708.35 carried forward to Sandown on Friday.
Placepot: £47.60.

DONCASTER

6.15: 1. MISS PIN UP (D Biggs) 11-4; **2. Elsa** 9-1; **3. Thakawah** 1-2 fav. **4 ran.** 2½, 2. (Pat Mitchell, Newmarket). **Tote:** £2.90. DF: £6.80. CSF: £17.08.

6.45: 1. DALALAH (R Hills) 5-1; **2. Magication** 5-2; **3. Jade Runner** 11-1. **5 ran.** 8-11 fav Dayflower. sht-hd, 7. (H Thomson Jones, Newmarket). **Tote:** £6.40; £2.60, £1.20. DF: £6.00. CSF: £16.69. NR: Go Orange.

7.15: 1. NED'S BONANZA (J Lowe) 11-2; **2. Hi-Tech Honda** 9-4 fav; **3. Super Rocky** 9-2. **7 ran.** hd, hd. (M Dods, Darlington). **Tote:** £6.40; £2.20, £1.80. DF: £5.30. CSF: £14.50. Tricast: £38.67. Creche (7-1) withdrawn not under orders. Rule 4 applies to all bets, deduct 10p in £.

7.45: 1. SILENT EXPRESSION (M Tebbutt) 7-1; **2. Eightofus** 4-1; **3. Good Image** 3-1 fav. **13 ran.** 10, ½. (D Morris, Newmarket). **Tote:** £9.50; £3.20, £1.80, £1.90. DF: £22.30. CSF: £38.63.

8.15: 1. MERTON MILL (Paul Eddery) 3-1; **2. Cost Effective** 6-1; **3. Nikatino** 7-4 fav. **7 ran.** 1½, 1. (D Morley, Newmarket). **Tote:** £4.00; £2.30, £2.30. DF: £11.80. CSF: £19.83. Tricast: £36.19. NRs: Shooting Lodge, Dari Sound.

8.45: 1. IMPERIAL BALLET (W Ryan) 11-10 fav; **2. Big Blue** 5-4; **3. Zaire** 16-1. **4 ran.** 10, 2½. (H Cecil, Newmarket). **Tote:** £2.10. DF: £1.50. CSF: £2.75.

9.15: 1. CHARMING GIFT (K Darley) 5-1 fav; **2. Buzzards Bellbuoy** 20-1; **3. Sandmoor Denim** 7-1; **4. Douraj** 11-2. **17 ran.** ¾, 1½. (R Williams, Newmarket). **Tote:** £7.00; £1.80, £3.40, £1.10. DF: £77.00. CSF: £95.34. Tricast: £659.80.
Placepot: £139.30.

LINGFIELD

6.00: 1. CONFRONTER (J D Smith) 10-11 fav; **2. Taylor Quigley** 11-10; **3. Lamore Ritorna** 11-1. **5 ran.** 5, 5. (P Cole, Whatcombe). **Tote:** £2.10; £1.10, £1.20. DF: £1.50. CSF: £2.23.

6.30: 1. TARA'S DELIGHT (Emma O'Gorman) 5-2; **2. Hubbers Favourite** 11-2; **3. Pearl Ransom** 50-1. **9 ran.** 6-4 fav Dazzle The Crowd. sht-hd, hd. (W O'Gorman, Newmarket). **Tote:** £3.30; £1.30, £2.00, £5.00. DF: £7.30. CSF: £16.48.

7.00: 1. RAVEN RUNNER (J Reid) 5-6 fav; **2. Sharptino** 6-1; **3. Wandering Stranger** 11-2. **8 ran.** 7, 1½. (I Balding, Kingsclere). **Tote:** £2.20; £1.30, £1.90, £1.30. DF: £3.90. CSF: £6.71. Non Runner: Fisianna.

7.30: 1. STORM DOVE (M Hills) 4-5 fav; **2. La Dama Bonita** 4-1; **3. Running Glimpse** 11-1. **5 ran.** 3½, 2. (R Charlton, Beckhampton). **Tote:** £1.70; £1.40, £2.00. DF: £2.30. CSF: £4.36.

8.00: 1. NEVER SO SURE (P Bowe) 5-1 co-fav; **2. Idir Linn** 5-1 co-fav; **3. The Shanahan Bay** 6-1. **12 ran.** 5-1 co-fav Young Shadowfax (4th). 4, 1½. (A Bailey, Newmarket). **Tote:** £11.10; £3.30, £1.80, £2.40. DF: £30.30. CSF: £29.94. Tricast: £144.69.

8.30: 1. HOLIDAY ISLAND (M Hills) 2-1 fav; **2. Sandro** 13-2; **3. Smiling Chief** 4-1. **7 ran.** 2½, 1. (C Brittain, Newmarket). **Tote:** £2.90; £2.10, £3.10. DF: £10.60. CSF: £15.39.
Placepot: £18.40.

WARWICK

6.30: 1. STORM CROSSING (Pat Eddery) evens fav; **2. Receptionist** 6-1; **3. Desert Peace** 7-4. **4 ran.** 3, ¾. (G Harwood, Pulborough). **Tote:** £2.50. DF: £4.30.

7.00: 1. DRESS SENSE (L Dettori) 4-7 fav; **2. Bilateral** 6-4. **2 ran.** ¾. (L Cumani, Newmarket). **Tote:** £1.50.

7.30: 1. ALKARIF (W Carson) 10-11 fav; **2. Morocco** 5-4; **3. A Nymph Too Far** 8-1. **3 ran.** 2½, 10. (A Scott, Newmarket). **Tote:** £1.70. DF: £1.20. CSF: £2.25.

8.00: 1. ROCK SONG (T Quinn) 11-2; **2. Honey Vision** 14-1; **3. MCA Below The Line** 11-4 fav. **11 ran.** 3, 2½. (P Cole, Whatcombe). **Tote:** £6.70; £2.30, £3.50, £2.20. DF: £30.00. CSF: £75.63.

8.30: 1. BROOM ISLE (F Norton) 7-4; **2. Belafonte** 11-10 fav; **3. Merry Marigold** 3-1. **3 ran.** 7, nk. (Mrs A Knight, Cullompton). **Tote:** £2.60. DF: £1.80. CSF: £3.76.

9.00: 1. SAMSON-AGONISTES (T Quinn) 2-1 fav; **2. Arc Lamp** 7-1; **3. Rays Mead** 5-1. **6 ran.** 1½, ¾. (B McMahon, Tamworth). **Tote:** £2.90; £1.80, £2.70. DF: £12.90. CSF: £15.23.
Placepot: £112.80

Armed with this list, I often make more than my weekly wages by checking to see if any horse mentioned in it starts favourite in a race run on Saturday afternoon or evening.

For example, of the runners listed in the example in the Entries Index (as can be seen from the race results supplied) Echological won the 3.20 at Chepstow at evens, Charmed Knave was second at 3-1 in the 3.55 at this same meeting, Dayflower ran unplaced in the 6.45 at Doncaster, Dress Sense won the 7.00 at Warwick at 4-7, Alkarif the 7.30 at 10-11 and MCA Below the Line ran third at 11-4 at this same Midlands track. Finally, Charming Gift at 5-1, in winning the 9.15 at Doncaster, helped to demonstrate that, of seven Saturday favourites declining alternative engagements in the first half of the following racing week, four won and two were placed.

FROM *THE SPORTING LIFE*

Type of Bet	Select -tions	Singles	Doubles	Trebles	4 Fold	5 Fold	6 Fold	7 Fold	Total Bets
TRIXIE	3	--	3	1	--	--	--	--	4
PATENT	3	3	3	1	--	--	--	--	7
YANKEE	4	--	6	4	1	--	--	--	11
CANADIAN	5	--	10	10	5	1	--	--	26
HEINZ	6	--	15	20	15	6	1	--	57
"S" HEINZ	7	--	21	35	35	21	7	1	120

Since I had 'permed' the seven extensively engaged horses concerned in a Super Heinz (see table for details) I had made a total of 120 wagers involving them and received a handsome payout as a result of their impressive performances.

My Saturday accumulator involving horses with impending engagements that start as clear (not joint) favourites always involves smallish stakes.

This is why I also narrow down any qualifiers I include in my small stakes accumulator to a 'Saturday nap' by allotting each of them a point

9.15 George Woolston Handicap.
Winner £2,198
1m Rnd

£2,500 added **For** three yrs old and upwards–Rated 0-70 **Minimum Weight 7-7 Penalties** after June 20th, a winner 5lb **Weight-for-age** 3 from 4yo+ 10lb **Entries** 27 pay £25 **Penalty Value 1st** £2,198 **2nd** £610 **3rd** £293
POSTMARK

1 (13)	6-17162 **HABETA (USA)**[14] CD		J W Watts 6 10-00	**G Duffield** (82)
	R D Bickenson black, red epaulettes, grey sleeves, red cap			
2 (14)	070-004 **CARTEL**[14] D BF		J L Harris 5 9-00	**Paul Eddery** (81)
	G W Pykett light blue, black chevron, yellow sleeves, light blue seams, black cap			
3 (5)	308-002 **DOURAJ (IRE)**[7]		C E Brittain 3 8-11	**M Roberts** (82)
	Mohamed Obaida royal blue, red epaulets, red and royal blue striped cap			
4 (10)	645028- **SKY CAT**[302]		C Tinkler 8 8-10	**M Birch** (80)
	Gymcrak Thoroughbred Racing IV Plc pink, grey seams and sleeves, pink cap			
5 (3)	/20-009 **PARR (IRE)**[19]		J Mackie 4 8-09	**G Hind** (84)
	The Parrtnership black, white chevrons, halved sleeves, yellow cap			
6 (8)	449135 **CHARMING GIFT**[16] D		R J R Williams 5 8-08	**K Darley** (86)
	Colin G R Booth wht, r blue diamond, red slvs, r blue and wht qtdcap.			
7 (6)	-444650 **BUZZARDS BELLBUOY**[25]		H J Collingridge 3 8-08	**J Quinn** (82)
	N H Gardner pale blue, yellow cross-belts, yellow cap, red spots.			
8 (15)	166/800 **BOLD AMBITION**[8]		T Kersey 5 8-08	**K Fallon**
	T Kersey orange, royal blue hoop and armlets, royal blue and white quartered cap.			
9 (1)	555114 **SANDMOOR DENIM**[7] CD		S R Bowring 5 8-08	**S Webster** (84)
	E H Lunness pink, black diamond and diamond on cap.			
10 (11)	/0-0001 **DEPUTY TIM**[14] D		R Bastiman 9 8-05	**Dean McKeown** (85)
	Mrs P Bastiman orange, purple hooped sleeves, white cap.			
11 (4)	693-198 **FUTURES GIFT (IRE)**[23] D		A W Potts 3 8-03	**A Proud** (81)
	T Marshall orange, black stars, armlets and cap			
12 (9)	35755-7 **NOBLE CAUSE (IRE)**[24]		R Earnshaw 3 8-02	**J Carroll** (78)
	Mrs D A Earnshaw black, white diamonds on sleeves, red cap.			
13 (12)	-008530 †**QUEEN'S TICKLE**[1]		A P Jarvis 3 8-01	**S Maloney (5)** (85)
	Miss S E Jarvis black, emerald green seams, emerald green cap			
14 (17)	005-0 **PREMIER MAJOR (IRE)**[29]		B Beasley 3 7-10	**L Charnock**
	Premier Properties Plc royal blue, yellow stars and cap			
15 (7)	4-60246 **CHANCE REPORT**[7]		F H Lee 4 7-09	**N Kennedy (5)** (85)
	F H Lee wht, red stripe, r blue and wht hooped slvs, wht cap, r blue spots.			
16 (16)	32-0509 **COLONEL FAIRFAX**[15]		J W Watts 4 7-07	**J K Fanning (3)** (81)
	James Westoll light blue, pink hooped sleeves, yellow cap.			
17 (2)	709806 **TREASURE BEACH**[17]		M Brittain 3 7-07	**J Lowe** (74)
	Mel Brittain maroon and yellow check, maroon sleeves, yellow cap.			

LONG HANDICAP:Colonel Fairfax **7-05** Treasure Beach **7-02**
† Unplaced in the 3.50 at Doncaster yesterday

LAST YEAR: **SANDMOOR DENIM**   S R Bowring 4 8 04   S Webster

BETTING FORECAST: 9-2 Habeta, 5 Douraj, Cartel, 13-2 Deputy Tim, 7 Charming Gift, 9 Sandmoor Denim, 12 Queen's Tickle, 16 Futures Gift, Chance Report, Buzzards Bellbuoy, Parr, Noble Cause, Treasure Beach, Sky Cat, 20 bar

☰ SPOTLIGHT ☰

CHARMING GIFT might be worth a speculative interest in a wide-open finale.

This mare, suited by a strongly-run mile (which she should get here), was an easy winner of a celebrity riders race at Newmarket in May (only 4lb higher) and she has run creditably in defeat since. She just holds course-and-distance winner **Habeta** on their running behind American Hero over course and distance a month ago, and last time she was a respectable fifth to Camden's Ran-

som at Newbury.

Habeta ties in with several of these and it should be tight between them. He has a 2lb pull (ignoring apprentice claims) for a length with **Deputy Tim** on recent Nottingham running, when market springer **Cartel** (2lb pull with Habeta) was 1¾l away fourth.

Clive Brittain saddled maiden 3-y-o Ler Cru to win a similar event to this at Lingfield yesterday so front-running Warwick second **Douraj** also comes into it, as does course-and-distance winner **Sandmoor Denim**.

MEL CULLINAN

| **DIOMED** Charming Gift | **TOPSPEED** Charming Gift |

if I see from my *Racing Post* that it is the selection of Topspeed, Postmark, Diomed or Spotlight. In this way a maximum score of four points can be gained.

Interestingly, such was the situation on a June Saturday regarding Charming Gift, since this five-year-old mare was the selection of all of these four experts - two private handicappers (working on time and form) and two racing correspondents (working on less objective criteria).

Thus Charming Gift became a confident nap and carried a sizeable stake of mine to victory in Doncaster's last race which she won by three-quarters of a length at a most acceptable 5-1.

As it happens, the 'side-stepping' of future, originally targeted, races by the trainers of some racehorses provided a pointer to the winner of the 1996 Grand National (also indicated by Strategy 37 as described on later pages in this book). The following report from *The Times,* published nine days before the big Aintree steeplechase, should make this clear. What it made clear to me on 21 March 1996 was that Rough Quest was likely to win the world's best-known and most widely-watched horse race!

FROM *THE TIMES*

Rethink on Rough Quest

ROUGH QUEST may after all run in the Martell Grand National a week on Saturday. The gelding was initially ruled out of the race after finishing second to Imperial Call in the Gold Cup last week, but may now take his chance at Aintree.

He has been reinstated as 4-1 favourite by Ladbrokes for Aintree, in which he has been allocated just 9st 12lb.

"We are now considering the Grand National for Rough Quest," his trainer, Terry Casey, said yesterday.

"I cantered him yesterday and he felt really well and in great form. So I phoned his owner, Andrew Wates, in the evening and he came down and cantered him this morning.

"We then had a discussion and have made a joint decision to consider the National. We will make a final decision at the weekend and not keep people hanging on."

The Irish National had been the originally announced target for Rough Quest but Casey said: "The Grand National looks a very good opportunity for him. He will have lumps of weight in the Irish National and he is better going left-handed."

Casey is confident that regular jockey Mick Fitzgerald will be able to resume his partnership with Rough Quest at Aintree.

STRATEGY 8

TRAINERS SCORING AFTER FREEZE-UPS

As was again the case during the winter of 1995/6, a racing season can suffer the loss of many fixtures during prolonged or repeated cold spells after which, understandably, since it has been rendered historic and involves many no longer fully-fit animals, form tends to work out none too well.

Indeed, the aftermath of a protracted spate of meetings cancelled through inclement weather is a part of the racing season that is rather akin to the 'blank sheet' situation that often applies at the start of a new flat racing campaign on turf in March since, prior to this, flat performers have also lost their fitness through having been off the track for a while. Interestingly, the decided, and often crucial, 'edge' gained by horses that have been able to keep moving and to thrive in warm temperatures, when many of their rivals have had their training, exercise and development curtailed or precluded by bad weather, has, of late, been spectacularly demonstrated by the success of Sheikh Mohammed's Godolphin training experiment. This involves wintering horses in sunny Dubai, before running them in top-class European races during the following spring and summer. Of course, most home-based handlers, except if working for Godolphin and thus being able to ship their horses out to the desert sun during the British winter, cannot do very much to protect their charges from the threat to their fitness that a bad British winter can pose.

However, one particular, very prominent and far from indigent National Hunt trainer (who is, anyway, based in fairly temperate Somerset) has made his training complex far less subject to frozen ground than have many of his less foresighted and prosperous rivals. This is Martin Pipe who has taken out effective insurance against snow and frost by installing a woodchip gallop.

As many readers may well recall, Christmas 1995 and the New Year period in 1996 saw the cancellation of many meetings before racing on turf later resumed.

Significantly, when it did so, of the first 10 races staged over jumps, no less than five were won by Martin Pipe trained runners! If one is aware of which trainers, like Pipe, have such 'weatherproof' training facilities - some of these even feature sandy beaches near stables - then one can ensure that the turf performers one supports after a protracted spell of cancelled racing will at least strip fit when they line up on a racecourse. That was certainly the case on 3 January 1996, when on Lingfield's turf track, made sodden by thawing snow, the Pipe trained Valiant Toski and Teraq won at 3-1 and 7-1 respectively.

MARTIN PIPE once again demonstrated the benefit of having been able to keep his horses on the move during the cold snap when landing a 31-1 double at Lingfield Park yesterday.

The Wellington trainer, fresh from his Exeter hat-trick on Monday, struck with Valiant Toski in the Godstone Selling Hurdle and Terao in the Rock Saint Challenge Trophy Handicap Chase — making it five wins out of the first 10 races run over jumps this year.

"The secret of why our horses are so fit is the woodchip gallop which we put down some years ago. That strip has turned out a few winners," said Pipe, adding, "We can work even if we have to box the horses up and drive them down to it."

David Bridgwater was on both Pipe winners and seen at his best on Valiant Toski (3-1), who beat Lixos by a length in a strength-sapping finish.

Terao (7-1) took it up coming down the hill and galloped on strongly to win by three and a half lengths from Mad Thyme.

STRATEGY 9

TRAINERS KEEN TO WIN MEMORIAL RACES

When I took a photograph of the runners and riders' board at Plumpton in 1971, I had no idea that this rather distinctive study of such a prominent racecourse feature would (more than 20 years later) lead me to yet another winning method.

That this was so was the happy outcome of what initially was the rather sad experience of realising that one of the jockeys whose name appeared on this ageing photograph had been Doug Barrott who, not long after it was taken, was so tragically killed in a racecourse riding accident.

Fortunately, such supreme sacrifices on the part of jockeys are rare and so are not easily forgotten - thanks in part to the memorial races that so appropriately they can produce.

As for Doug Barrott, I had long known of his association with trainer, Josh Gifford, and thus felt that the latter, if fielding a runner for the race (run at Sandown in late November in memory of his much-missed friend) would be very keen to see it triumph.

Imagine my excitement when, on a murky late November afternoon, I noticed that in the 2 mile, 5 furlong and 75 yard Doug Barrott Handicap Hurdle, Gifford had a very live contender.

My discovery from the details given in *The Sporting Life* that the challenge cup for this race had been presented by the friends of the jockey it commemorated, only strengthened my conviction that Gifford's The Widget Man, as the winner of four of its last six races, would make a very lively bid to defeat the likely favourite and top weight The Illywhacker.

He did so in splendid style at 5-1!

FROM *THE SPORTING LIFE*

3.30 | **Doug Barrott Handicap Hurdle   2m 5f 75y**

£5500 added to stakes **for 4-y-o and up** £40 to enter Pen, after Nov 23, a winner of a hurdle 4lb A perpetual Challenge Cup, presented by friends of the late Doug Barrott, to be held by the winning owner until Nov 1st, 1992 Closed on Nov 25
Penalty value £4,211; 2nd £1,268, 3rd £644, 4th £287
Weights raised 12lb TOPWEIGHT OFFICIALLY RATED 129

1 5/J343-4 **THE ILLYWHACKER**(14)
(b g Dawn Review - Trucken Queen)
(J Hitchins)
Mrs J Pitman   6 11 10 ....M Pitman ★

2 10110-1 **THE WIDGET MAN**(22)
(b g Callernish - Le Tricolore Token)
(A Ilsley)
J T Gifford   5 11 7 ....D Murphy

3 121214- **GO SOUTH**(22F)(268)
(b g Thatching - Run To The Sun)
--bf hcp h- (Rex Joachim)
J R Jenkins   7 10 13 ....M Ahern ★

4 610/126 **TAKE ISSUE**(17)
(b g Absalom - Abstract)
(R M Flower)
J Sutcliffe   6 10 9 ....R Dunwoody

5 1F-005F **LIGHT DANCER**(15)
(ch g Niniski (USA) - Foudre)
(R Owen)
L J Codd   5 10 9 .... A Maguire (3)

6 11642- **LEGAL BEAGLE**(214)
(b g Law Society (USA) - Calandra (USA))
--bf hcp h- (Ron Miller)
G Harwood   4 10 6 .... M Perrett

7 P50/3P-0 **INDIAN BABA**(7)
(b g Indian King (USA) - Norfolk Bonnet)
--cse 2m h- (E Benfield)
G P Enright   6 10 0 ....E Murphy

8 0500/1P/ **TRUST THE IRISH**(661)
(b g Ile de Bourbon (USA) - Trusted Maiden)
(M Telford Turner)
S Woodman   10 10 0 ....J Osborne

9 FP411/5 **FOODBROKER FLYER (NZ)**(28)
(b g In The Purple (Fr) - Disguise (NZ))
(Food Brokers Ltd)
R Akehurst   7 10 0 ....L Harvey
Nine runners

Adjusted long handicap weights: Trust The Irish 9-13 and Foodbroker Flyer 9-9.

FORECAST: 11-4 The Illywhacker, **7-2** The Widget Man, **9-2** Legal Beagle, **6** Light Dancer, **8** Foodbroker Flyer, **10** Take Issue, Go South, **14** Trust The Irish, **20** Indian Baba.

Last Year: CATCH THE CROSS, 4-10-4, M Foster, 5-2 fav, (M Pipe). 16 ran.

FROM *THE RACING POST*

> **3.30** (2m6f h'cap hdle): **RUN UP THE**
> **FLAG** (D Murphy, 9-4JF) 1; **Petosku**
> (9-4JF) 2; **Sir Crusty** (14-1) 3. 7 ran. 5, 20.
> (J Gifford). Tote: win £2.60; places £1.70,
> £1.90. Dual F'cast: £3.30. CSF: £7.46. Tricast:
> £47.93. NR: Top Javalin.

1.25 DOUG BARROTT HANDICAP HURDLE 2m 6f £7,230 (6)

1 11/31P2-	**BOKARO (FR) (245)** (Dr A O'Reilly) C Brooks 9 12 0	G Bradley
2 11136-0	**ANZUM (28)** (The Old Foresters Partnership) D Nicholson 4 10 10	R Dunwoody
3 0/113B4-	**ROBERTY LEA (239) (CD)** (Wentdale Const Ltd) Mrs M Reveley 7 10 7	P Niven
4 11400-1	**REDEEMYOURSELF (IRE) (17)** (Mrs T Brown) J Gifford 6 10 3	A P McCoy
5 11606-1	**NAHTHEN LAD (IRE) (11)** (J Shaw) Mrs J Pitman 6 10 0	W Marston
6 114P3-0	**KINGSFOLD PET (15)** (G Nye) M Haynes 6 10 0	D Skyrme

S.P. FORECAST: 7-4 Nahthen Lad, 3-1 Redeemyourself, 5-1 Bokaro, 11-2 Roberty Lea, 6-1 Anzum, 14-1 Kingsfold Pet.

Should any readers of The Widget Man saga imagine that victories in memorial races are merely coincidental or flashes in the pan, they might care to ponder the fact that, exactly 12 months after this five-year-old's success at Sandown in the Doug Barrott, Gifford's Run Up The Flag also triumphed. Indeed, when this runner was made the favourite for what is clearly one of his handler's dearest races, I saw him as virtually 'nailed on', and so it proved when this five-year-old powered home at 9-4!

As it happens, Gifford has had a runner in the Doug Barrott since Run Up The Flag signalled the soundness of the rationale underpinning the 'certain races for certain trainers' plan. This was Redeem yourself, successful in 1995!

However, that this highly-skilled handler sets great store by his memories - one of which concerns the triumph of ex-cancer patient Bob Champion on Aldiniti in the 1981 Grand National - has been further demonstrated by his success in yet another memorial race whose existence concerns the loss of someone else who was very dear to him.

Josh, like so many in the racing world, was devastated by the loss of his jockey brother, Macer, to motor neurone disease in 1985. Understandably then (as *The Sporting Life* put it in the winter of 1994) "there are few races that Josh would rather win more" than the

'Macer', run at Huntingdon in early November in memory of his late brother.

Knowing of this and that a trainer's vested emotional interest is winning a particular race is something that one should try to capitalise on, I paid particular attention to Jumbeau, the runner that Josh had sent to contest his brother's race in November 1994. When Jumbeau, rather significantly like Run Up The Flag, was made the favourite, I took the hint and as much of the 4-1 as I could find on course.

FROM *THE RACING POST*

1.45 MACER GIFFORD HANDICAP CHASE
2m 4f 110yds £3,626 (8)

1 11/654- CUDDY DALE (240) (C) (D) G Hubbard 11 12 0.... G Bazin (7)
2 312-11P BOBBY SOCKS (43) (CD) R Lee 8 11 7 .... S Wynne (3)
3 1F125-P JUMBEAU (20) (CD) J Gifford 9 11 4.................... P Hide (3)
4 0F116-P CANOSCAN (11) (D) Lady Herries 9 11 2............... E Murphy
5 13145-P ARDCRONEY CHIEF (21) (CD) D Gandolfo 8 11 1.... P Holley
6 513-112 PHILIP'S WOODY (24) (D) (BF) N Henderson 6 10 7
.... J R Kavanagh
7 F122P-4 NICKLUP (14) T Forster 7 10 5.................. M A Fitzgerald
8 P312P-3 RAMSTAR (17) (D) C Mann 6 10 3..................... J Railton

S.P. FORECAST: 4-1 Philip's Woody, 9-2 Bobby Socks, 5-1 Ardcroney Chief.
Jumbeau, 6-1 Ramstar, 7-1 Cuddy Dale, 8-1 Canoscan, Nicklup.

3.30 Macer Gifford Handicap Chase
[OFF 3.31] **(Class C)** 16 fences (2m4f110y)2m4½f
For: 5yo+ Rated 0-130 1st £4,532.50 2nd £1,360 3rd £655 4th £302.50

1   KILFINNY CROSS (IRE) 7 10-8 ....(105) P Hide
     ch g by Mister Lord (USA)—Anvil Chorus (Levanter)
     (J Pearce) *chased leader, led 5th, hit 7th, mistake 8th, all out*
     bets of even £500, even £400, even £300, £500-£550(x2),
     £800-£1,000(x3), £400-£500(x4), including office money
                                        [op 4/5 tchd Evens] **8/11F**
2 *shd* DRUMSTICK 9 10-13 ....(110) A Maguire
     ch g by Henbit (USA)—Salustrina (Sallust)
     (K C Bailey) *held up, headway 9th, chased winner 2 out,*
     every chance when hit last, hard ridden flat, ran on bet of
     £750-£300   [op 2/1] **5/2**
3   4 YOUNG POKEY 10 12-0 ....(125) J A McCarthy
     b g by Uncle Pokey—Young Romance (King's Troop)
     (O Sherwood) *prominent, chased winner 8th, ridden*
     approaching 2 out, stayed on same pace
                                        [op 3/1 tchd 5/1 in a place] **9/2**
4 *dist* ELLTEE-ESS 10 10-0 87b...................(97) P J McLoughlin
     (R J Weaver) *led, not jump well, headed 5th, behind from*
     9th, tailed off   [op 33/1 tchd 66/1 in a place] **50/1**
P   VODKA FIZZ 10 10-2 82 82 ....(99) D O'Sullivan
     (R Rowe) *mistake 4th, always in rear, tailed off when pulled*
     up before 2 out   [op 10/1 tchd 12/1] **8/1**

5 ran   TIME 5m 01.10s (fast by 2.30s)   SP TOTAL PERCENT 118
1st OWNER: A J Thompson; BRED: J W O'Brien
TRAINER: J Pearce at Newmarket, Suffolk
2nd OWNER: Sarah Lady Allendale, E Hawkings, M Harris 3rd
OWNER: O M C Sherwood
TOTE WIN £2.00; PL £1.60,£1.80; DF £2.90; CSF £3.21

FROM *THE DAILY TELEGRAPH*

> **4.15: FRENCHIE NICHOLSON CONDITIONAL**
> **JOCKEYS H'CAP HDLE 2m 5f110y**
> **£1,970**
>
> 1 20F52-6 **THE LIGHTER SIDE (38)** B Preece 5 11 10 .... Judy Davies (5)
> 2 3214F-3 **RELIEF MAP (19)** K Bishop 4 11 5 .... R Greene
> 3 P043P-1 **CHASMARELLA (26)** A Davison 6 11 0 .... J Kavanagh
> 4 1236/0-5 **BRAVO STAR (USA) (7)** P Rodford 6 10 13 ..... M A Fitzgerald
> 5 6313-23 **WATERMEAD (12)** (D) D Nicholson 6 10 11 ..... D Bridgwater
>
> **5 declared**
>
> **S.P. FORECAST:** 11-8 Chasmarella, 5-2 Relief Map, 3-1 Watermead, 8-1
> The Lighter Side, 20-1 Bravo Star.

As so often happens in racing, victory had to be hard won as the claiming jockey on Jumbeau had to ride his heart out to prevail by a short head to bring his 'guvnor' a much coveted, if nail-biting, success and sequel to the 1993 victory of Champagne Lad!

Understandably, some stable jockeys can also make particularly determined bids to win the occasional races that, rather than provide posthumous tributes to trainers who have departed from the racecourse scene, celebrate their skills whilst they are very much alive and kicking!

Some seasons ago, for example, when now lady trainer Anabel King was a trainee at the Gloucestershire jockeys' academy of 'Frenchie' Nicholson, she managed to boot home a 40-1 winner of the Cheltenham race that still bears his name.

> **2.15** **FRENCHIE NICHOLSON**
> **CONDITIONAL JOCKEYS' HANDICAP**
> **HURDLE (E) 2m 110yds £2,290 (6)**
>
> 1 11-234 **NORDIC BREEZE (IRE) (11)** (D) M Pipe 5 11 10 ... G Supple $
> 2 05-R12 **ALBEMINE (USA) (8)** (BF) P Eccles 8 11 7 .... G Hogan
> 3 1P-441 **CRANDON BOULEVARD (10)** Mrs J Pitman 4 11 5
>   .... R Garrard (7)
> 4 14-112 **NISHAMIRA (24)** (D) (BF) D Nicholson 5 11 2 ... R Thornton
> 5 03-FF1 **NOBLE COLOURS (24)** (D) S Griffiths 4 10 8 ... D J Kavanagh
> 6 20-122 **SKRAM (17)** R Dickin 4 10 1 .... X Aizpuru
>
> **S.P. FORECAST:** 5-2 Crandon Boulevard, 3-1 Nishamira, 7-2 Noble Colours.
> 5-1 Nordic Breeze, 6-1 Skram, 14-1 Albemine.

> ## CHELTENHAM
> **Going: GOOD (good to firm in places)**
>
> **1.40** (2m110y nov hdle): **IRSAL** (A P McCoy,
> 1-2F) 1; **Southern Chief** (16-1) 2; **Prairie
> Minstrel** (7-1) 3. 7 ran. 3½, 7. (M Pipe). Tote:
> win £1.60; places £1.20, £5.30. Dual F'cast:
> £13.20. CSF: £10.17.
> **2.15** (2m110y h'cap hdle): **NISHAMIRA** (R
> Thornton, 11-8F) 1; **Skram** (13-2) 2; **Noble
> Colours** (9-2) 3. 6 ran. 4, 1¼. (D Nicholson).
> Tote: win £1.90; places £1.20, £2.70. Dual F'cast:
> £5.60. CSF: £9.59.

In its most recent runnings this contest has done this as a posthumous tribute since, sadly, 'Frenchie' has gone to the great unsaddling enclosure in the sky and, not long ago, I noticed that 'Frenchie's' son, David, (himself now a most successful trainer of both horses and jockeys) had sent Watermead, the bottom weight, in this very race - the 'Frenchie' Nicholson Conditional Jockeys' Handicap Hurdle–to run at a late October Cheltenham meeting, I felt that the 'memorial plan' might again produce a handsome dividend and so it proved when Nicholson's runner won at a very acceptable price.

Any reader who might imagine that Watermead's success was merely co-incidental might care to consider the fate of another Nicholson-trained runner in an even more recent running of his father's race. This took place in late October 1997 and concerned the five-year-old, Nishamira, whose success as a significant 11-8 favourite made David Nicholson's day at Cheltenham races a particularly poignant one, as my next day's *Daily Telegraph* duly revealed.

> The victory proved even more poignant for Nicholson as his mother Diana is seriously ill at present in Cheltenham General Hospital.
>
> "I only hope my mother has seen the result. It's a matter of hours not days for her but I will be going to see her this evening," said the trainer.
>
> Nicholson Senior was always a prime developer of riding talent and Pat Eddery, Paul Cook and the late Tony Murray will all be remembered as star graduates of his often-harsh regime.
>
> Fittingly, Frenchie's race is restricted to conditional jockeys and in Robert Thornton, victory went to a high-class prospect.

STRATEGY 10

TRAINERS' BIRTHDAY WINNERS

In 1991, long-distance runner, Liz McColgan confounded claims that she had returned to racing too soon after the birth of her daughter Eilish by winning a gold medal in the World Athletics Championships in Tokyo.

Such an achievement may not have surprised those who have realised that the prelude and sequel to giving birth can see many a female engaging in prodigious and most energetic feats! Indeed, many mares have won races when in foal and some lady racehorse trainers have even given birth on the same day as a horse with which they are connected has entered the winner's enclosure.

Having once had the pleasure of interviewing lady trainer Anabel King, I am well aware of her penchant for publicity and fondness for causing a stir - she is literally the 'lady in red' as far as her racecourse outfits are concerned which ensures that no-one misses her during a TV outside broadcast.

When I noticed that, despite her confinement through very advanced pregnancy, Anabel had sent Riva's Touch from her Warwickshire base at Wilmcote to run at rather distant Fontwell and had specially booked jockey Richard Dunwoody (who was also once connected with the Nicholson stable where Anabel had served her apprenticeship during which she rode a 40-1 winner), I felt that the stork might be telling me about a horse to side with.

In the event Riva's Touch flew in faster than any stork on Fontwell's figure-of-eight track and so set king-sized celebrations under way that continued when, only hours later, in the Midlands the trainer of this winning jumper gave birth to her son, Oliver Jack, who 'weighed in' at 8 lb, (and not stones as was actually reported in the following news item!).

FROM *THE RACING POST*

Little prince

TRAINER Anabel King is the proud mother of a son, Oliver Jack, who weighed in at 8st on Wednesday evening after the trainer's Riva's Touch had set celebrations under-way by winning at Fontwell in the afternoon.

'Birthday winners' seldom materialise in quite such a kingly, spectacular or biologically appropriate form, but many are 'sentimentally' sent out by racehorse trainers in the course of a season.

Those wishing to exploit the possibility that horses may be making very determined bids to give particular racehorse handlers, owners or jockeys further reasons for celebrating their birthdays are advised to consult the *Directory of the Turf* in which these particular dates are given.

Alternatively, they can consult the *Racing Post* in which the birthdays, not just of these key individuals but of others involved in racing, are given on a daily basis.

Such a ploy is my daily practice and it very often proves profitable, as was the case when I noticed that another lady trainer might well be giving a very clear signal regarding her intention of having a birthday winner.

This was Henrietta Knight whose desertion of school teaching and entry into racehorse training was encouraged by many masters of the latter craft.

On 15 December 1994, my interest was aroused by the fact that, partly in appreciation of her talents that had brought her the highest trainer's strike rate at their racecourse, the directors of Exeter racecourse were staging the Henrietta Knight Birthday Handicap Hurdle. I knew from my *Directory of the Turf* that, because of the exigencies of the fixture list, that they were in fact doing this on the day before Henrietta was due to blow out her birthday candles.

Intrigued and alerted by this discovery, I gave not just Henrietta's runner in her own birthday race extremely close scrutiny, but also accorded this to two other runners she had also sent to race at Exeter.

Of course, I decided that my main wager would be on Grouseman, Henrietta's 'birthday race' runner, especially as I noticed that, when this event had obviously carried a different name a year previously, she had sent out Edimbourg to win it as an 11-10 favourite. However, I also resolved to place small amounts on the two horses that had shared Grouseman's horsebox ride to Devon.

This proved a strategy whose wisdom seemed the greater when I noticed from my racecard that Edimbourg's previous course win had not only led the Exeter management to call their 1.50 race the 'Edimbourg Novice Chase' but that this very horse and classy steeplechaser was due to contest the 1.20 event.

Edimbourg duly won this by a very easy three lengths as a worthy 1-2 favourite which augured extremely well for my 'nap' - Grouseman - in the 'birthday' race which, 90 minutes later, he won by an even longer margin of six lengths, carrying 10 stones 13 lb and my sizeable stake.

FROM *THE RACING POST*

EXETER TOP TRAINERS

WITH RUNNERS TODAY Jumps 1990/91+	WINS-RUNS	£1 STAKE	NH FLAT & HURDLES WINS-RUNS		CHASES WINS-RUNS		COURSE RUNS SINCE WIN
M C Pipe	81-260	31%	−31.06	65-201	32%	16-59	27%	5
P J Hobbs	24-113	21%	+5.66	10-69	14%	14-44	32%	3
G B Balding	14-69	20%	−1.71	9-43	21%	5-26	19%	1
Miss H C Knight	10-31	32%	+26.88	8-19	42%	2-12	17%	1
R J Baker	9-60	15%	−6.42	8-53	15%	1-7	14%	10
R J Hodges	7-105	7%	−74.95	5-67	7%	2-38	5%	10
R G Frost	6-107	6%	−81.84	0-54	0%	6-53	11%	55
A J K Dunn	5-22	23%	−4.08	1-9	11%	4-13	31%	6
G F Edwards	5-29	17%	+19.00	4-21	19%	1-8	13%	1
P Leach	5-41	12%	−11.30	5-37	14%	0-4	0%	14
A Barrow	5-43	12%	+16.33	3-25	12%	2-18	11%	17
O Sherwood	4-15	27%	−1.37	3-8	38%	1-7	14%	0
W G M Turner	4-56	7%	−35.00	4-48	8%	0-8	0%	3
P G Murphy	3-11	27%	+33.50	2-6	33%	1-5	20%	5
A P Jones	3-18	17%	+0.50	1-15	7%	2-3	67%	3
B R Millman	3-20	15%	+9.00	2-15	13%	1-5	20%	2
R H Alner	3-25	12%	−5.50	2-10	20%	1-15	7%	15
N R Mitchell	3-36	8%	−3.50	1-23	4%	2-13	15%	4
D Burchell	2-10	20%	+6.50	1-8	13%	1-2	50%	4
N A Twiston-Davies	2-22	9%	−13.90	1-16	6%	1-6	17%	1

2.50 **Henrietta Knight Birthday Handicap**
[OFF 2.50] **Hurdle** 2m2f
For: 5yo Rated 0-115 1st £2,910.50 2nd £808.00 3rd £387.50

1		GROUSEMAN 8 10-13b............................M A Fitzgerald

gr g by Buckskin (FR)——Fortina's General (General Ironside)
made all, ridden clear from 2 out, ran on well [op 6/1 tchd
8/1] **15/2**

2 6 JUST ROSIE 5 10-8.................................S McNeill
b m by Sula Bula——Rosa Ruler (Gambling Debt)
*held up, headway 5th, chased winner from 2 out, effort
approaching last, one pace* [op 8/1] **12/1**

3 4 CHIAROSCURO 8 10-0.............................R Bellamy
b g by Idiot's Delight——Lampshade (Hot Brandy)
tracked leaders, effort approaching 2 out, one pace [op 12/1
tchd 14/1 in a place] **10/1**

4 4 CHICKABIDDY 6 10-4..............................A P McCoy (3)
held up, headway and effort approaching 2 out, one pace [op
5/1 tchd 15/2 in a place] **7/1**

5 5 BANKONIT (IRE) 6 10-0.........................I Lawrence
*mid-division, reminders 2nd, lost place next, one pace from 2
out* [op 10/1 tchd 14/1] **12/1**

6 8 CHAPEL OF BARRAS (IRE) 5 11-5...............Peter Hobbs
*pulled hard, held up behind leaders, blundered 3 out and 2 out,
soon weakened* [op 7/1 tchd 9/1] **8/1**

7 12 MUSICAL MONARCH (NZ) 8 11-10................J Osborne
*chased winner, mistakes 3 out and 2 out, soon ridden and
weakened* bet of £1,000-£400[op 5/2 tchd 11/4 in a place and
2/1] **9/4F**

8 1¼ GREEN ISLAND (USA) 8 11-0.....................J Frost
*tracked leaders, lost place after 3rd, rallied approaching 2 out,
soon weakened* [op 25/1 tchd 50/1 in a place] **40/1**

P SPREAD YOUR WINGS (IRE) 6 11-0.................G Bradley
*chased leaders from 2nd, weakened quickly after 3 out, tailed
off when pulled up before next* [op 9/2 after 5/1 in a
place] **7/2**

P TANFIRION BAY (IRE) 6 10-4......................M Richards
always behind, tailed off when pulled up before 2 out [op
25/1] **50/1**

10 ran **TIME:** 4m 23.40s (slow by 13.80s) **SP TOTAL PERCENT** 117
Non runner: Singing Forever
1st OWNER: Aquarius TRAINER: Miss H C Knight (Lockinge, Oxon) BRED:
Michael Doran
2nd OWNER: Plough Racing TRAINER: A P Jones
3rd OWNER: Clive Price TRAINER: C G Price
TOTE: WIN £8.40 PL £2.70,£3.10,£2.10 DF: £59.90 CSF: £81.52
TRICAST : £817.54
TOTE TRIO £238.60 - 2.01 winning units, pool £675.68

Incredibly, Henrietta rounded off her marvellous 46th 'birthday'
by sending out Exclusive Edition, her third and final runner at the
meeting to win the last race at Exeter by 13 lengths at 9-4! The
wisdom of following birthday horses sent out by female trainers had
been spectacularly demonstrated!

Treble makes Knight's day

HENRIETTA KNIGHT'S 48th birthday celebrations got into swing a day early at Exeter yesterday, courtesy of a 40-1 treble with Edimbourg, Grouseman and Exclusive Edition.

But the Lockinge trainer confessed to missing Edimbourg's easy victory over Jailbreaker in the Westcountry Television Handicap Chase, his fourth around the Haldon Hill circuit.

She said: "My nerves got the better of me. He's one of my favourite horses and I couldn't bear to watch. I fed him at 5.30 this morning and I thought to myself I just hope you are back here tomorrow."

However, she need not have worried as — apart from diving violently left at the open ditch — he was foot-perfect under Jamie Osborne, having three lengths to spare over the runner-up.

Grouseman's pillar-to-post romp for Mick Fitzgerald in the Henrietta Knight Birthday Handicap Hurdle, framed to wish the trainer many happy returns, was sweet to savour as the Buckskin gelding has had problems since taking a crashing fall over fences at Ludlow two years ago.

Osborne doubled up after Exclusive Edition made it a memorable day for Miss Knight as he cruised away with the Bristol Evening Post Novice Handicap Hurdle when unleashed past Beatson two out, to give the trainer the second treble of her career. Course chairman Percy Browne presented her with a glass decanter.

Finally, readers who might imagine that it is only lady trainers who try for 'birthday' winners should note the name of Richard Hannon whose liking for the sweet life extends to trying to provide this by way of a winner at an evening meeting run close to London on the last Monday evening in May for one of his principal patrons, Lord Caernarvon, on or as close as possible to Lady Caernarvon's birthday of 19 April. This Hannon has achieved of late via Lemon Souffle at 3-1, and two other debutantes, Niche and Lyric Fantasy (which won at 8-1 and 3-1) on the night my own *Racegoers' Encyclopaedia* was launched at Windsor races. Most recently of all, another newcomer, Arethusa, gave this magnanimous and shrewd handler another 'birthday' winner - and the wife of the Queen's racing manager whose maiden name was Wallop - a further reason for a champagne celebration, when it won at Kempton's first evening meeting of 1996!

STRATEGY 11

TRAINERS' LONG-DISTANCE RAIDS

Such is the extent of jingoistic patriotism on the part of British bookmakers and backers that when classy raiders from France, Ireland and, sometimes, even America, line up in races run in this country they are often allowed to go off at starting prices that are generously unreflective of their often excellent prospects.

Indeed, the small number of runners that French trainer Francois Doumen has sent to race on British jumping tracks has spectacularly demonstrated the fact that foreign raiders sent on long-distance raids often return to their home stables in triumph, having also enriched their connections on account of the attractive odds at which they've been supported.

For example, sentiment for, and hero worship of, the nation's long-time favourite chaser Desert Orchid, no doubt did much to ensure that in 1987 a classy French rival was able to defeat him in his favourite race, the Boxing Day spectacular, the King George VI Chase. Nupsala, in fact, was allowed to go to post at a ridiculously generous 25-1. As for Doumen, he went on record as saying he could hardly believe the prices on offer at Kempton which must have meant that he had a very Bonne Noel.

Amazingly, he repeated this very same trick in the very same race, to once again vindicate the belief that foreign raiders often have excellent chances and start at 'value' odds. This was with The Fellow who, in 1991, again represented Doumen in the King George VI Chase at Kempton.

The field for this again included Desert Orchid who was bidding for a record fifth victory in his favourite race. No doubt because of this, The Fellow started at 10-1 - a ridiculously long price, since he had the previous March failed by only a short head to win the Cheltenham Gold Cup! In winning, doing handsprings, by one-and-a-half lengths he clipped 1.2 seconds off the course record time and was so convincing his jockey reported he could have 'gone round again'.

Like fellow French trainer Andre Fabre, Doumen is a past master at scoring with his raiders, especially those contesting prestigious races, as he further proved in 1992, when The Fellow again captured the King George. Even more impressively, by the time his 'second string', Algan, lined up for the 1994 running of this peerless race at Kempton, I had taken due heed of the following press report that appeared a few days before this Christmas highlight was due to be staged and so, as well as The Fellow, supported this younger French raider, before he then sprang another Gaelic surprise. This he did by then winning at 16-1 to give trainer Doumen his fourth win in Kempton's best known steeplechase in eight years!

FROM *THE SPORTING LIFE & THE DAILY TELEGRAPH*

Algan value

ALGAN was all the rage with the Big Three yesterday as punters searched for seasonal each-way value in the King George VI Tripleprint Chase at Kempton on Monday.

By ANDREW SIM

The Fellow's stablemate – yet to race in Britain – was backed from 20-1 to 12-1 with Corals and Hills.

Ladbrokes, who stuck at 14-1, also reported good money for Algan, including one bet of £1,000 each-way.

Even more recently the 'trainers long-distance raids' strategy alerted me to an even more extensive journey than those undertaken by Doumen's horses that raid Britain from France.

What happened was that, on 12 December 1995, the classy winner of the Maryland Cup, America's steeplechasing Blue Riband, was sent all the way to contest a 'chase at Sandown and yet was allowed to start at ridiculously lengthy odds, given his highly impressive form credentials of 13 wins and seven places and only one fall from his previous 21 runs and the fact that he was partnered by his trainer's daughter, the reigning American champion jump jockey, Blythe Miller who, before she took the ride on Lonesome Glory at Sandown, had received tuition from top British jockey, Graham Bradley.

As it happened, if I needed any further persuasion that jingoistic patriotism and chauvinism on the part of British bookmakers were blinding them to the outstanding claims of Lonesome Glory, then this was provided on the morning of his race by John De Moraville in a *Daily Express* column. Readers of this were reminded that, since, in 1992 at Cheltenham, Lonesome Glory had won a hurdle race, here was a contender with winning experience of English obstacles. De Moraville also passed on reports that to knowledgeable locals at Lambourn Lonesome Glory 'looked a picture and was a real athlete with the class of a good horse'.

I needed no further encouragement and wasn't really surprised when Lonesome Glory lived up to his name when almost finishing alone at Sandown!

DAILY EXPRESS Friday December 1 1995

Lonesome hits chasing's Gold Cup glory trail

By JOHN de MORAVILLE

Lonesome Glory's jump career record shows 13 wins and seven placings from 21 starts (he fell in the other). He was the country's leading jumper in '92 and '93 too.

Victories—the powerfully built chestnut has earned more than $200,000 in prize money this year alone—have included the Breeders' Cup Chase and a brace of Colonial Cups.

And, with Blythe on board, he made his mark at Cheltenham landing an historic hurdles success three years ago, in a leg of the Anglo-American Sport of Kings Challenge.

Since then, Lonesome Glory has gone from strength to strength,

Much more frequently raiders are sent on long journeys within the shores of this country and, ironically, some of them travel longer distances than do Doumen's French raiders!

One trainer who recoups more than the cost of the many gallons of petrol he gets through to get his raiders to racecourses remote from his Dorset yard is W G M Turner.

I happen to know of Turner's skill with early two-year-olds and of his ability to 'bring back the bacon' from very northern racecourses and so when, on 4 April 1996, I noticed that he had sent a two-year-old filly all the way to Musselburgh to contest a humble five furlong event, I decided to join in the action.   Not surprisingly, Sweet Emmaline ran out a very acceptable 4-1 winner by five lengths - a most impressive achievement on her first run over racing's minimum distance!

Musselburgh

Going: good

2.20 (5f) 1, **Sweet Emmaline** (T Sprake, 4-1); 2, Swino (3-1 jt-fav); 3, Tribal Mischief (7-1). Bolero Boy 3-1 jt-fav, 9 ran. 5l, ¾l. W Turner. Tote: £6.80; £2.20, £1.10, £5.80. DF: £7.90. Trio: £36.90. CSF: £17.52.

Very sensibly, many backers pay particular attention if only one occupant of a horsebox is sent well over 200 miles to race for a very minor prize. The idea here is that its connections may well have to land sizeable bets to recoup more than their extensive travel costs and so make their long trip really worthwhile. *The Daily Mail* and *The Independent* both show horses sent really long distances to racecourses and if you notice (as I did recently from the latter newspaper) that a horsebox with a lone raider in it has been sent a really long distance to bid for a modest prize, then you may well have found something to bet on, if it is also the selection of the private handicapper in your newspaper. This was certainly the case with Fiveleigh Builds - sent on what I saw as much more than a petrol retrieving mission on 22 July 1997 by Lucinda Russell from her stable at Kinross in Scotland to race at faraway Worcester. This ten-year-old chaser's over 700 mile round trip looked as if it would really pay off and I regarded the fact that this handicapper was made the 13-8 clear favourite as highly significant. In the event, I was delighted, but not surprised, to see this raider come from over the border and score by 20 lengths!

FROM *THE DAILY MAIL*

WORCESTER Gd to firm

2.00 (2m 4f Hdle) — **RED NECK** (R Johnson) 12-1 1; **Northern Fleet** (R Dunwoody) **5-4 JtFav** 2; **Topaglow** (B Fenton) 5-4 JtFav 3. **10 ran.** (P Bowen, Haverfordwest, Dyfed). 3, 14. **Tote:** £8.90; £1.60, £1.30, £1.30. DF: £11.70. CSF: £25.82.

2.30 (3m Hdle) — **ARCTIC TRI-UMPH** (G Bradley) **33-1** 1; **Final Pride** (R Johnson) **4-7 Fav** 2; **Beck And Call** (N Williamson) 11-1 3. 10 ran. (M Bradstock, Wantage). nk, 11. **Tote:** £23.40; £2.10, £1.20, £1.80. DF: £21.40. CSF: £49.78.

3.00 (2m 7f 110yds Hcap Ch) — **FIVELEIGH BUILDS** (A Thornton) **13-8 JtFav** 1; **Iffeee** (R Johnson) **13-8 JtFav** 2; **Smith Too** (R Farrant) **9-4** 3. **3 ran.**

STRATEGY 12

TRAINERS PRE- AND POST-RACE COMMENTS

Trainers pre- and post-race comments on their charges, as reported by racing journalists, are often well worth noting which is perhaps why so many non-journalists can be seen 'earwigging' what is said to the press in unsaddling enclosures and elsewhere on racecourses. Expert lip-readers have even been employed in attempts to eavesdrop on trainers' conversations!

Indeed, it is always my habit to note down any handlers' comments that are reported in the racing press, as entries, arranged alphabetically by trainer, in a special index I keep for this purpose.

Sometimes the giving of what is privileged information stems from a philanthropic intention on the part of a trainer. Indeed, when miners went on strike in his home area of Stainforth, sporting trainer Ron Thompson made a suitable fraternal gesture to them by tipping Kindred as a certainty for a selling hurdle. It won, of course, and helped me, and doubtless several miners, to get in some groceries, if not some coal.

Those who wish to act on the soundly-based belief that trainers flushed by success can, in their euphoria, divulge many of their future plans for their latest winners, should scrutinise the detailed reports of racing at the previous day's meetings, as provided by the on course correspondents who produce the *Racing Post's* innovative Race Analysis feature. This is full of potentially lucrative indications of trainers' future intentions which I not only record in my A-Z index of trainers but enter into the advance diary planner that adorns the wall of my study.

One of these entries once concerned the straight-talking Jack Berry whose exclusive column in the *Star* newspaper is well worth reading.

Indeed, I found myself doing this with interest on a recent April Saturday when Jack, writing under the enticing headline of 'House Warmer', revealed that Paris House, his stout-hearted runner in Haydock Park's Beamish Irish Stout Field Marshall Stakes, was 'jumping out of its skin and raring to go'.

FROM *THE DAILY STAR*

> First thoughts were to wait until Guineas time with Paris House and have a crack at the Palace House Stakes at Headquarters but he's jumping out of his skin and raring to go so it would be wrong not to run him.
>
> I need hardly tell you how highly I regard him and it would be wonderful for owners Peter Chandler and his brother, who bought out the other two shareholders during the winter, if Paris House repaid their faith in him immediately.

When Jack further enthused with: 'I need hardly tell you how highly I regard him', I felt that these words were coming virtually straight from 'the horse's mouth'.

I didn't, as the saying in racing goes, 'put my house' on the subject of all Jack's excitement but was certainly able to afford a trip to the French capital when it won, just as Jack had virtually promised, at a most acceptable 3-1.

Perhaps in National Hunt racing Jack Berry's counterpart for candour is trainer David Nicholson and readers of the *Racing Post* are fortunate in that each winter Saturday he reports candidly on his impending runners.

Thus, when on a recent November Saturday, I read that David considered his Viking Flagship to be in 'fine form' and 'working better than ever before' - so well, in fact, as to obviate the need for a racecourse gallop prior to the Tingle Creek Chase to be run at

Sandown a week later - I made a note of what I felt was privileged, potentially gilt-edged, information.

FROM *THE RACING POST*

FEATURES

Flagship in fine form

VIKING FLAGSHIP is coming on well in preparation for next week's Tingle Creek Chase at Sandown.

He'll no doubt be better for the run, but he's in great form and working better than ever before at this stage of the season. So much so, in fact, that I no longer feel it's necessary to give him a racecourse gallop beforehand.

DAVID NICHOLSON

Eventually, when my 'day of race' handicap ratings placed Viking Flagship well ahead of his rivals for his race at Sandown, I decided that Nicholson's comments of a week earlier were sufficient to allay my fears that his charge might not be able to score on his seasonal debut.

The wisdom of this decision was vindicated when Viking Flagship ran out a fluent three lengths winner at 9-2.

As it happened, this was the second time that day that I had profited from the pre-race comments of David Nicholson, since his regular *Racing Post* column, that appeared a few hours before Viking Flagship was due to race, carried the headline 'Relkeel should win at the weights'.

My own private handicap ratings suggested this was a well-founded claim and happily, half an hour before Viking Flagship won the 1994 'Tingle Creek', Relkeel came home by three and a half lengths at 4-4.

At the start of every new (turf) flat and National Hunt season *The Sun* newspaper publishes very informative budget-priced guides to the coming action which always include the gleanings and fruits of 'fact and fancy' finding tours of leading stables. The claim that 'you'll back hundreds of winners with the Sun's Stable Tour' is no idle boast. Indeed, in the spring of 1996, I recouped far more than the £3.99 cost of my *Sun Guide to the Flat* by heeding what trainer Richard Hannon had to say about his runner in the season's first big race.

When about Stone Ridge I read Hannon's comment that 'he's in the Lincoln and is a really good mile handicapper', I felt here was a potentially lucrative piece of information and so it proved when this game performer easily won at Doncaster at 33-1!

My re-reading of *The Sun's* 'Stable Tour' feature a few weeks later led me to take note of what top trainer Luca Cumani had reported about one of his best hopes for the 1996 season.

I felt that the sometimes tight-lipped Cumani's bullish appraisal of the prospects of Lucky Di had been highlighted by the editor of my *Sun* annual for a very good reason and so it proved when, first time out in 1996, at Kempton in April, this three-year-old prevailed by three lengths at 11-2!

STRATEGY 13

TRAINERS CHASING TITLES

Such is the kudos attached to the title of 'champion trainer' that, if a race for this develops towards the close of a racing season, horses sent out by the contending handlers concerned should be given serious attention, but only if they are also top-rated on form.

Interestingly, at the end of the 1996 flat racing season, a battle royal for the championship developed between trainers Saeed Bin Suroor and Henry Cecil and the fact that a year earlier the latter had parted company with Sheikh Mohammed, the former's employer, only served to increase the intensity of the titanic struggle between these two leviathans of the training craft. What made their rivalry even more personal was that Bin Suroor had been handed some of Cecil's best ammunition by the Sheikh and, during the 1996 flat campaign and had used it against his rival with a vengeance.

All this meant that, as this campaign neared its autumnal close, the press made much of the exciting duel that had developed between two men whose reputations seemed so firmly on the line. Headlines such as 'Cecil rallies troops for a final assault' began to appear; indeed, I read those particular words in my *Times* of 11 September 1996 and under them the further comment of Julian Muscat that 'Saeed Bin Suroor, at present heading the trainers' championship, takes a narrow advantage over Henry Cecil into the St Leger meeting at Doncaster today. So tight are the margins that the lead could change twice during the afternoon.'

I reasoned that, if ever there was to be a day on which two trainers would be making Herculean efforts to win then it had surely arrived!

Rapid and rather feverish scrutiny of the Doncaster card in my *Times* soon revealed that the horses concerned in the continuing, and now knife-edge, struggle for the trainers' championship were Out West (Cecil) in the 1.30, Corradini (Cecil) in the 2.00 and both Eva Luna (Cecil) and Russian Snows (Bin Suroor) in the 3.10.

3.10 STONES BITTER PARK HILL STAKES C4
(Group III: Fillies: £21,044: 1m 6f 132yd) (6 runners)

401	(2)	2211-26	RUSSIAN SNOWS 21 (F,S) (Godolphin) S bin Suroor 4-9-8	L Dettori	95
402	(1)	411412	BEAUCHAMP JADE 21 (C,F,G) (E Penser) H Candy 4-9-3	G Carter	90
403	(3)	2/11-002	BEYOND DOUBT 46 (F,G) (The Queen) Lord Huntingdon 4-9-3	W R Swinburn	88
404	(5)	11	EVA LUNA 20 (F) (K Abdulla) H Cecil 4-9-3	Pat Eddery	99
405	(6)	315444	ALZABELLA 15 (G) (M Wauchope) J Hills 3-8-5	M Hills	88
406	(4)	0-2122	TIME ALLOWED 20 (F) (R Barnett) M Stoute 3-8-5	J Reid	98

BETTING: 2-1 Eva Luna, 11-4 Time Allowed, 4-1 Beauchamp Jade, 9-2 Russian Snows, 8-1 others.

1995: NOBLE ROSE 4-9-3 L Dettori (11-4 fav) L Cumani 8 ran

After some reflection, I felt that, given the fact that only one of these extremely 'live' contenders - Eva Luna - was top-rated on form by the private handicapper of my *Times,* then this should be by only selection and banker bet. Fortunately, this proved a wise choice, as Eva Luna duly gave Cecil the outcome he desired, nicely augmented my bank balance, allowed jockey Pat Eddery to reach the 150 winner mark and vindicated the thinking behind the 'trainers chasing titles' strategy.

So too did Cecil's Reams of Verse on the following day at Doncaster when, as the only 'title contender' top-rated on form according to the dispassionately numerical calculations of the private handicapper of *The Times,* she won the May Hill Stakes. As it happened, I had an even heavier interest in this two-year-old since, for running in a race her trainer had already won eight times previously, she was also a Strategy 1 selection!

3.10 MAY HILL STAKES C4
(Group III: 2-Y-O fillies: £16,280: 1m rnd) (12 runners)

301	(9)	61	CATWALK 33 (F) (M Brower) W Haggas 8-12	M Hills	88
302	(4)		ATTITRE (R Pledger) C Brittain 8-9	K Fallon	--
303	(12)	2	BINT BALADEE 20 (Godolphin) Saeed bin Suroor 8-9	L Dettori	98
304	(2)	21220	DAME LAURA 65 (F) (A Morrison) P Cole 8-9	T Quinn	93
305	(8)	11022	FERNANDA 18 (B,F,G) (Sultan Al Kabeer) J Dunlop 8-9	W Carson	93
306	(10)	16	GRETEL 49 (S) (Sheikh Mohammed) M Stoute 8-9	W R Swinburn	87
307	(7)	43	MRS MINIVER 43 (L Hurley) P Kelleway 8-9	O Peslier	79
308	(6)	31	QUINTELLINA 42 (F) (M Dawson) L Cumani 8-9	K Darley	89
309	(1)	4213	RAINDANCING 47 (F) (N Hayes) R Hannon 8-9	J Reid	88
310	(11)	21	REAMS OF VERSE 20 (S) (K Abdulla) H Cecil 8-9	Pat Eddery	99
311	(5)	1	THE IN-LAWS 23 (F) (G Waters) M Prescott 8-9	G Duffield	70
312	(3)	3413	VAGABOND CHANTEUSE 17 (G) (W Green) T Etherington 8-9	L Charnock	86

BETTING: 3-1 Reams Of Verse, 7-2 Bint Baladee, 6-1 Fernanda, 7-1 Catwalk, 8-1 Dame Laura, Quintellina, 10-1 Raindancing, 12-1 others.

1995: SOLAR CRYSTAL 8-9 W Ryan (15-2) H Cecil 11 ran

Trainer & Jockeys Record - Winners/Places/Rides

L Charnock 1-1-8
M Baird 1-1-7
R Cochrane 1-2-9
T Ives 1-2-6

W S CUNNINGHAM
A McGlone 1-0-1
D R McCabe 1-2-5
J Stack 1-0-1
K Darley 1-0-3

B J CURLEY
W Ryan 1-0-2

R CURTIS
M Baird 2-0-3
R Hughes 1-1-2
S Lanigan 1-1-4

C A CYZER
T Ives 6-1-15
D Biggs 5-22-72
K Darley 2-3-7
A Clark 1-0-1
D R McCabe 1-2-7
K Fallon 1-2-9
M Baird 1-0-1

P T DALTON
J F Egan 1-0-2
P McCabe 1-1-3

M DODS
J Weaver 4-4-18
J Carroll 2-0-14
A Clark 1-0-1
C Webb 1-1-5
Dale Gibson 1-4-27
Dean McKeown 1-1-7
Mr S Swiers 1-0-1
S Whitworth 1-2-4
W Woods 1-2-9

T W DONNELLY
C Rutter 1-1-4
Mr R Johnson 1-0-1

S DOW
A Daly 11-23-96
M Roberts 4-6-26
T Quinn 4-6-35
Mr T Cuff 2-2-11
Stephen Davies 2-8-31
D Harrison 1-3-13
F Norton 1-0-10
G Duffield 1-3-15
Mr T McCarthy 1-2-4
R Hughes 1-2-12
S Sanders 1-0-10

MISS JACQUELINE S DOYLE
A Whelan 1-0-4
J Quinn 1-1-2

C J DREWE
R Hughes 1-0-3

E A L DUNLOP
W R Swinburn 5-11-52
R Hills 3-4-15
J Stack 2-2-6
W Ryan 2-1-6
J Tate 1-12-41
J Weaver 1-3-6
K Darley 1-0-3
Paul Eddery 1-6-19
S Whitworth 1-1-3

J L DUNLOP
W Carson 50-64-210
G Carter 12-17-54
J Reid 12-10-48
Pat Eddery 11-12-38
K Darley 9-18-37
T Quinn 6-8-34
J Weaver 4-8-24
Paul Eddery 3-3-17
R Cochrane 3-3-14
F Jovine 2-2-5
G Duffield 2-6-22
L Dettori 2-7-12
M J Kinane 2-4-10
R Hills 2-4-21
T Sprake 2-0-6
D R McCabe 1-0-1
G Forte 1-1-3
M Tellini 1-0-1
Miss E Johnson Houghton 1-0-1
Mr J Durkan 1-0-1
Mr K Santana 1-0-2
N Connorton 1-1-4
W Newnes 1-1-10
W R Swinburn 1-1-4
W Ryan 1-5-15

C A DWYER
C Dwyer 2-4-21
J Stack 2-0-6
D Harrison 1-0-2
N Varley 1-1-9

T DYER
J Quinn 2-0-3
J Fanning 1-4-9
J Fortune 1-1-6

M H EASTERBY
M Birch 10-26-145
S Maloney 8-15-110
G Faulkner 1-0-1
J Carroll 1-1-4
J Lowe 1-2-8

M W EASTERBY
Ruth Coulter 3-4-39
G Carter 2-2-5
L Charnock 2-12-81
S Maloney 2-4-17
W Carson 2-0-7
C Teague 1-0-1
G Bardwell 1-1-6
J Fanning 1-2-9

L Newton 1-1-5
M Birch 1-6-36
M J Dwyer 1-1-3
M J Kinane 1-1-3
N Varley 1-0-3
P Fessey 1-2-20
T Williams 1-0-3

C R EGERTON
B Thomson 2-2-16
G Bardwell 1-0-3
M Roberts 1-0-5
T Ives 1-0-2
T Quinn 1-0-2

B ELLISON
N Kennedy 2-0-12
S Whitworth 1-0-2

C C ELSEY
D Harrison 3-1-13
C Rutter 1-2-16
M Hills 1-0-4
Miss A Elsey 1-0-6

C W C ELSEY
N Kennedy 2-3-16
P Fessey 1-4-14

D R C ELSWORTH
A Procter 5-7-33
M Roberts 3-4-15
T Quinn 3-3-14
Pat Eddery 2-3-12
Paul Eddery 2-0-7
J Williams 1-4-24

R W EMERY
J Williams 1-0-6

T J ETHERINGTON
A Culhane 5-5-16
K Darley 2-1-11
G Carter 1-0-2
W Carson 1-0-1

J M P EUSTACE
R Cochrane 7-7-39
J Tate 2-0-7
M Tebbutt 2-5-27
M Hills 1-0-3

P D EVANS
Amanda Sanders 6-4-34
G Hind 6-9-46
J Fortune 4-7-24
K Fallon 3-1-8
L Dettori 3-4-12
S Sanders 3-4-21
G Mitchell 1-0-2
Jo Hunnam 1-1-3
K Darley 1-0-6
Paul Eddery 1-3-12
T Ives 1-4-6
T Quinn 1-0-4

J L EYRE
R Lappin 14-25-135
S D Williams 4-7-27
J Stack 2-0-3
Miss Diana Jones 2-3-12
N Varley 2-8-32
D Griffiths 1-0-7
D Sweeney 1-0-1
D Wright 1-0-3
G MacDonald 1-1-7
J Fanning 1-1-10
J Fortune 1-6-31
J Tate 1-2-11
L Charnock 1-0-3
Mrs D Kettlewell 1-0-1
T Ives 1-2-7

R A FAHEY
A Culhane 4-8-29
J Quinn 1-1-4
L Charnock 1-2-4
S Maloney 1-2-7

C W FAIRHURST
R Cochrane 4-5-21
Dean McKeown 2-0-14
J Tate 2-5-13
N Kennedy 2-6-25
J Fanning 1-2-21
L Dettori 1-0-1
Mrs S Bosley 1-1-10
Paul Eddery 1-1-3

J R FANSHAWE
D Harrison 20-53-157
N Varley 5-11-42
L Dettori 2-0-4
T Quinn 1-2-6
W R Swinburn 1-1-6

P J FEILDEN
Miss J Feilden 1-0-1

P S FELGATE
A Mackay 2-0-11
D Wright 2-2-8
W Ryan 2-1-6
G Hind 1-1-11
K Darley 1-1-5
P McCabe 1-5-22

M J FETHERSTON GODLEY
W R Swinburn 3-3-11
D Holland 2-0-3
J Reid 2-3-10
F Norton 1-0-22
W Newnes 1-0-1

J FFITCH HEYES
M Henry 2-0-4
G Duffield 1-1-8

R F FISHER
K Fallon 1-1-3
N Connorton 1-0-4

STRATEGY 14

TRAINERS BOOKING TOP JOCKEYS

I have long been an admirer of the well-named Superform, whose form books are an indispensable part of my racing armoury, and thus it came as no surprise to me that this Shoreham-based form assessment concern, in the spring of 1996, in launching an innovative A-Z of past equine performances, arranged, not by race, but by racehorse, had included in its 1,276 pages detailed and up-to-date statistics regarding the bookings of jockeys by flat race trainers.

Admittedly, some of these bookings reflected the arrangements whereby some jockeys are retained by particular stables, but this was not the case with several of those indicated as having been the most successful for certain handlers.

My daily practice is to check to see if any rider has again been - perhaps especially booked (outside of any regular retaining arrangements) by a particular trainer who has previously demonstrated this particular development has often had a winning outcome. For example, I knew from page 1,278 of *Superform's Flat Racehorses A-Z 1996 edition* that jockey J Stack had the best previous (30 per cent) 'wins to rides' ratio for trainer C Dwyer - a figure far higher than the ratio for this trainer's son when riding stable runners. Thus, when at the start of the 1996 flat season, I noticed that Stack was due to partner Lloc (whose claims also came to my attention through Strategy 4, as previously described) I decided to get involved with this four-year-old in the second race at Folkestone on 26 February.

Stack's booking did prove significant and led me to a lucrative payout at 10-1!

This very same convergence of the strategy under current discussion and the fourth in this book (about siding with stablemates of handlers previously successful at the same, early season, meeting) pinpointed another 7-1 winner at this very same February 1996 Folkestone meeting! This was Green Gem (see also illustration for Strategy 4) whose jockey booking of K Darley by S Williams was shown as a statistically significant (since formerly a 45 per cent winning) one in my Superform table showing trainers' performances by jockeys.

S C WILLIAMS
K Darley 6-7-22
A Mackay 5-4-38
K Fallon 3-5-8
D Wright 2-4-21
J Tate 2-2-18
Miss K Wright 2-2-7
T Ives 2-1-6
A Daly 1-0-1
Dane O'Neill 1-1-2
G Carter 1-0-4
G Hind 1-2-9
J Carroll 1-0-2

Folkestone

Going: good to soft

1.50 (5f) 1, **Jennelle** (J Quinn, 5-2 fav); 2, Swift Refusal (11-4); 3, Caviar And Candy (25-1). 9 ran. NR: Mujadil Express. 6l, ¾l. C Dwyer. Tote: £2.40; £1.10, £1.40, £4.80. DF: £4.70. Trio: £107.90. CSF: £8.71. Sylvania Lights (12-1) was withdrawn, not unders orders — rule 4 applies to all bets, deduction 5p in pound.

2.20 (5f) 1, Lloc (J Stack, 10-1); 2, Malibu Man (10-1); 3, Bonny Melody (33-1); 4, Sonderise (13-2). Thai Morning 9-2 fav. 16 ran. 5l, ¾l. C Dwyer. Tote: £14.90; £4.70, £2.90, £8.50, £1.30. DF: £93.70. Trio: £348.00 (part won; pool of £196.08 carried forward to 4.00 at Huntingdon today). CSF: £99.17. Tricast: £2,983.76.

2.50 (6f) 1, **Beldray Park** (J Quinn, 25-1); 2, Blessed Spirit (5-1); 3, Pride Of Brixton (13-8 fav). 14 ran. ¾l, 1¾l. Mrs A King. Tote: £55.10; £11.40, £2.30, £1.20. DF: £198.90. Trio: £132.80. CSF: £156.88.

3.20 (6f 189yd) 1, **Green Gem** (K Darley, 7-1); 2, Basood (11-2); 3, Nakhal (100-30). Ciserano 3-1 fav. 9 ran. 2½l, 2½l. S Williams. Tote: £7.40; £2.60, £2.40, £2.00. DF: £11.00. Trio: £25.80. CSF: £42.33.

PART TWO

SIDING WITH JOCKEYS

STRATEGY 15

JOCKEYS FOR RACES

Apart from their much-coveted and keenly-contested annual championship, perhaps the ultimate accolade and achievement for jockeys must be the honour of having races named after them.

Interestingly, Chepstow is one particular racecourse whose executive is fond of commemorating riders of distinction. Thus, the staging of the Sir Gordon Richards Handicap at a Chepstow evening meeting in late July, recalls the feat of this peerless former champion jockey who went through the card on 4 October 1933 and then on the following day won the first five races.

In more modern times, the Italian, Frankie Dettori, has yet to come close to emulating Sir Gordon's remarkable feat. However, this young jockey's astonishing success since starting to ride in this country a few seasons ago and his particular achievement in 1990, of riding his hundredth winner at their track, led the Chepstow executive to stage the Frankie Dettori Ton Up Stakes in his honour.

To me, on 26 August 1991, it seemed odds-on that a grateful Frankie would make a most determined effort to boot home a winner in this, his own (and in possibly another) event at this Welsh track, once glowingly dubbed 'the Goodwood of the West'.

Since Frankie was due to partner two forecast favourites – Mata Cara in his commemorative race and the odds-on Mud Wrestling in the following race – I felt these were the contenders that might well make his day at Chepstow a truly red letter affair.

So I was not really surprised to see Mata Cara win his race for Frankie and for his fellow Italian – master trainer Luca Cumani–and then to see this success immediately supplemented by that of Mud Wresting, a worthy three-length winner at 4-7.

In case some readers imagine that these successes were just a flash in the pan, they should be aware that the even more recent (1997) running of the Frankie Dettori Ton Up Conditions Stakes resulted in yet another victory for a horse in this event partnered by this ebullient and most popular Italian.

As the horse in question was also the form selection, as shown in the *Daily Mail,* and I was aware that Dettori was putting himself out by dashing to Chepstow on August Bank Holiday Monday after, the day previously, having ridden in Chicago, prior to arriving rather breathlessly back in Britain, only hours before the Chepstow fixture, I decided on a major investment.

I was confident that Bin Rosie would prevail in Frankie's 'own' race and duly struck a hefty tax-free wager on course at Chepstow at the disappointingly rather short odds of 2-7!

When such an honoured rider (all too rarely) turns out to be a woman, one can guarantee she will be doing her utmost to make even further headway against the headwind of prejudice against lady jockeys that, until 1972, prevented them from even competing in races run over the flat!

Moreover, if such a jockey travels thousands of miles so as to take a ride in her own race, one is surely entitled to assume that she has a further good reason for making a most determined effort to win this.

Such indeed was the case, when, on 8 July 1992, America's most accomplished lady jockey, Julie Krone, jetted in to humble Redcar – principally to take the ride on Al Karnak in the 6.40, the Julie Krone Maiden Stakes.

Knowledgeable racegoers like Redcar supremo, Lord Zetland, were well aware that Julie was an even greater 'class act' than Al Karnak. After all, she arrived with a 17% wins to all rides ratio and had, by the Redcar meeting, booted home almost 2,500 winners in her native America. Moreover, she had left New York only days earlier as this city's leading rider.

In the event, Al Karnak was adjudged so superior to his three rivals that, on course at Redcar, I was forced to wager tax-free at 2-11 but the considerable sum I had to invest at this rate of odds was spectacularly augmented when Julie bought home the winner of her race by 20 lengths! This seemed to me to be the nearest thing to a racing certainty I'd seen in a long time.

Each season a number of races commemorating still-competing jockeys are staged and while I never, merely for sentiment's sake, support the mounts of these doubtless flattered individuals, I certainly do, if like Julie Krone's mount in her own race, they seem to stand out on form.

STRATEGY 16
JOCKEYS AS TIPSTERS

One rather suspect adage in racing is that jockeys are the world's worst tipsters - a belief that my experiences have often confounded.

One of these has involved my regular reading of *The Daily Telegraph* in which jockey Marcus Armytage (who won the 1990 Grand National on Mr Frisk) writes a very entertaining and well informed regular column.

Regular study of this particular part of *The Telegraph's* coverage of racing has alerted me to the fact that if, as Whistler (actually a *Sunday Telegraph* racing correspondent), Marcus gives, as his updated daily 'nap', a horse he is due to ride later that same afternoon or evening, a hint is being provided that is tantamount to privileged 'inside information'!

Such an insight into the usually well-guarded world of racing intelligence was provided quite recently which put those who gained this well into the black.

As it happens, my reading of *The Sunday Telegraph* always leads me to make a note of Whistler's advance selections for the coming racing week and then, in subsequent editions of *The Daily Telegraph*, I check to see if Armytage has had cause to revise any of his daily naps.

With no little excitement, on a recent Friday, I realised that Whistler himself was due to take the ride on a horse he had napped for Lingfield's one o'clock race.

Of course, I have always been aware that the blinkers of optimism can blind connections to the chances of rival horses but, knowing how level-headed is Whistler, both on a horse and on the page, I felt he might be very justified in being so bullish about his mount, Almuhtaram. When this handicapper ran out a ready one-and-three-quarter length winner at the appealing odds of 9-2, I resolved to also support any of his future naps that Whistler would actually partner!

> **Whistler (Marcus Armytage)**
> **of** *The Sunday Telegraph* **not**
> **only napped Almuhtaram but**
> **also rode the 9-2 shot to victory**
> **at Lingfield.**

Even more recently, on the eve of the 1996 Cheltenham Festival, the *Racing Post* printed a feature giving the naps of several leading racing professionals for this peerless three-day rite of spring. Again, as with my noting of Whistler's selections in *Telegraph* newspapers, I make it my habit to heed the occasional gems of inside information that can be passed on in print by some jockeys.

On 11 March I saw that Richard Dunwoody, as one of racing's prominente, was passing on his idea of a Cheltenham Festival 'good thing'. This was neither the likely favourite for the Champion Hurdle or the Gold Cup (both of which he was due to partner and eventually lose on) but an Irish runner in the Bumper that now concludes the second day's card.

The Irishman, Dunwoody (who increasingly rides in Ireland whenever he can free himself of his many English bookings) was tipping an Irish runner, for which, as a top flight jockey, he had been especially booked. I felt that here was an inspired tip, I had no hesitation in supporting Whither Or Witch and was delighted when this winner stormed home from 23 rivals at 11-4! Should any readers doubt the wisdom of heeding the advice of the only racing professionals who get really close to horses when they are in action on the racecourse, then they should study the following bullish, even magnanimous, recommendation of the eventual 7-1 1996 Grand National winner that was made by sidelined jockey, Jamie Osborne (who had previously been criticised by trainer Terry Casey for coming too soon in the Hennessy at Sandown and so losing that race on Rough Quest).

FROM *THE TIMES*

Rough justice as best-laid plans go awry at Aintree

Jamie Osborne, reduced to the role of spectator, offers advice on finding the big-race winner

Rough Quest will be racing for the seventh time. His latest run was his best when he finished runner-up to Imperial Call in the Cheltenham Gold Cup. This effort forced the handicapper to raise him a massive 19lb in future races, which makes him a handicap good thing today.

Having ridden this horse in the Hennessy at Newbury, I am well aware of his capabilities. By my own admission, he did not receive the best of rides that day and, with the benefit of hindsight, I would have ridden him differently.

Mick Fitzgerald will aim to hold this one up until past the elbow. If he strikes the front too soon he is likely to stop. He has been drifting in the market all week and I now think he represents the best value in the race.

When he won the Ritz Club Chase in 1995, he had had a hard race in defeat at Wincanton just five days earlier and I think he is tough enough to bounce back from his Cheltenham exertions. He is definitely the one I would like to swap for my armchair today.

When I read the above comment from Osborne on the morning of Grand National day 1996, I remembered that in my magazine rack I had a copy of *The Times* in which, three days earlier, Rough Quest's jockey, Mick Fitzgerald himself, had passed on his own decidedly bullish recommendation of his eventually thrillingly successful Aintree winner. This is what this jockey/tipster declared three days before the National:

"The National is still unique. It is not just an ordinary race and I don't care what anyone else says about the effect of modifying the fences. If Rough Quest gets round he's got a great chance. He'll get the trip - the biggest problem is the 30 fences."

STRATEGY 17

JOCKEYS' BIRTHDAY WINNERS

Having read through Strategy 10 in this book, readers should not imagine that it is only trainers amongst racing professionals who make really determined efforts to make their birthdays winning ones. Indeed, Kevin Darley is just one recent example of a rider who has benefited followers of the 'jockeys' birthdays plan'.

Interestingly, in the past, one racing diary, in the not unreasonable belief that someone on top who perhaps may well feel on top of the world is a person worth siding with, published a fairly comprehensive list of the birthdates of several leading jockeys.

As it happens, annual editions of *The Turf Directory* (Tel: 0171 351 7899) contain full lists of these dates, as well as those, when divulged, of owners and trainers. Another convenient way, on any particular racing day, of learning when jockeys came into the world is to purchase the *Racing Post* and to study its Birthday Greetings feature. Indeed, on the 5 August 1995, this led me, since this was his 35th birthday, to Kevin Darley and to his seemingly very well fancied mount in Redcar's opening seller.

When I noticed from the actual betting that the horse in question, Goretski, was being gambled on as a firm favourite, I decided to join in the (eventually winning) action.

My advice to any would-be follower of this particular strategy is not blindly to back all the qualifying mounts a jockey takes on his or her big day, but to concentrate on one that seems on form and betting interest to be able to help the man or woman riding it to have a real winner of a birthday and so gain a further reason for celebration!

> ☐ KEVIN Darley had extra cause to celebrate his 35th birthday when Goretski comfortably landed the Bedale Selling Stakes at Redcar.

STRATEGY 18

FLYING JOCKEYS

Jockey Gordon Richards' amazing annual tallies of winners (that brought him championship riding honours for no less than 26 flat racing seasons) were achieved before the widespread use of light aircraft and helicopters, so many of which now quite commonly transport jockeys from one race meeting to another in the course of a single racing day.

Indeed, in midsummer such is the number of fixtures held when the days are long that, during them, some jockeys spend more time in aircraft than they do either at home or on any one racecourse. As it happens, the idea of basing a winning strategy on these 'flying jockeys' first came to me not long ago. To be specific, it was the sight of jockey Richard Hills leaping from a helicopter that had rushed him to the centre of Warwick racecourse from Kempton where, on the same May Day bank holiday afternoon he had already been in action and the rewarding consequences of concluding that here was a man on a mission (he proceeded to ride three winners at 6-1, 9-1 and 7-1) that first alerted me to the wisdom of rowing in with any jockey whose breakneck journey (from one course to another in the course of the same afternoon or evening) involves any mount that can be fancied on form.

The identification of pointers provided by jockeys made even more breathless by dashing to racecourses than by riding on them involves a little homework and, at times, some sharp racecourse observation. However, it can often prove lucrative, even for stay-at-home backers who are recommended to study last-minute jockey bookings as indicated in the stop-press columns of racing dailies and display boards on racecourses.

As was noted with regard to Julie Krone in a previous chapter, on occasion some jockeys travel vast distances to take particular rides. Thus, after Julie, as the most successful of America's lady flat race riders, had won her 'own' race at Redcar, I decided to scrutinise the claims of the other four horses that she was due to partner at this particular meeting.

Reasoning that trainers who were more than merely hopeful of success might well have scrambled to engage such an accomplished rider, I noticed Down to Rio in the 7.40, Gant Bleu in the 8.10 and Cockerham Ranger in the 9.10.

Since the last mentioned of these was a dark horse of a debutante (even though forecast favourite in my *Daily Telegraph*) I decided it might well be invidious to leave any of Julie's mounts out of my wager. Thus I had a win Yankee on the four of them and was delighted when Gant Bleu at 9-1 and Cockham Ranger, in also winning at 3-1, furthered Julie's reputation as the world's best woman rider, nicely augmented my bank balance and reminded Redcar racegoers of the wisdom of rowing in with a flying jockey!

Obviously, jockeys seldom fly in, as did Julie Krone, after flights of thousands of miles but, during the long daylight hours of midsummer, many of Julie's British counterparts do dash by helicopter or light 'plane from an afternoon fixture to an evening one.

Indeed, I have often 'made hay' in June, July and August by carefully scrutinising the riding plans of jockeys to see if any are due to undertake breakneck journeys from one racecourse to another, far distant one.

Such homework, performed on 7 August 1995, indicated that jockey T Quinn, after taking a mount for the stable retaining his services - that of P Cole - in Windsor's 2.30 race on Special Beat, was then going to faraway Leicester to take two mounts for this same trainer. These were Mountain Valley in Leicester's first race and Persian Elite in the 7.30.

As the latter was the forecast favourite in my *Daily Telegraph*, I

FROM *THE DAILY TELEGRAPH*

Krone flies in for treble

TONY STAFFORD	FORM
6.40—Al Karnak	6.40—Al Karnak
7.10—Karinska	7.10—Karinska
7.40—Sweet Mignonette	7.40—Timurid
8.10—Johnston's Express	8.10—Royal Girl
8.40—Maji	8.40—Little Ivor
9.10—Arkendale Diamond	9.10—Scored Again

EFFECT OF DRAW: High numbers best in sprints
Advance official going: GOOD TO FIRM

6.40: JULIE KRONE MAIDEN STAKES 1m 3f £1,590

1	4/2-0	RAHIF (12) Mrs G Reveley 4 9 7 .... K Darley	2
2	1	TATHIR (CAN) (20) D Morley 4 9 7 .... M Birch	4
3	53	AL KARNAK (IRE) (9) M Moubarak 3 8 9 .... Julie Krone	3
4	0	WELL AHEAD (30) M Johnston 3 8 4 .... Dean McKeown	1

4 declared
S.P. FORECAST: 10-11 Al Karnak, 7-2 Tathir, 4-1 Rahif, 6-1 Well Ahead.

7.10: LISA CROPP CLAIMING STAKES 2YO 7f £1,688

1	3634	BOLDVILLE BASH (IRE) (6) T Barron 8 11 .... K Darley	9
2	06	SIMPLY A STAR (IRE) (6) M W Easterby 8 9 .... T Lucas	11
3	00	MORNING NEWS (IRE) (23) M Tompkins 8 7 Julie Krone	10
4	00	CYPRUS CREEK (5) N Tinkler 8 6 .... Susanne Berneklint	1
5	00000	JERSEY BOB (IRE) (21) J Wainwright 8 3 .... P Burke	3
6	5	KARINSKA (23) M Prescott 8 3 .... G Duffield	5
7	3602	KISS IN THE DARK (18) Mrs G Reveley 8 3 .... K Fallon	12
8		SAINTED SUE J Haldane 8 2 .... L Charnock	2
9		SEVINCH M W Easterby 8 2 .... J Marshall (7)	8
10	02	LETTERMORE (12) R Whitaker 8 1 .... A Culhane	7
11	0	SNUG SURPRISE (28) J Wainwright 8 1 .... A Mackay	4
12	06	TOUCH N' GLOW (23) J Spearing 8 1 .... J Lowe	13
13	5	FORTHEMOMENT (21) P Calver 8 0 .... J Fanning (3)	6

13 declared
S.P. FORECAST: 11-4 Karinska, 9-2 Kiss In The Dark, 6-1 Morning News, 8-1 Touch N' Glow, 10-1 Forthemoment, 12-1 others.

7.40: FAIRFIELD INDUSTRIES INTERNATIONAL CHALLENGE HANDICAP 1m 2f £3,002

1	140-000	NORTH ESK (USA) (18) J W Watts 3 10 0 .... J Lowe	4
2	6-00011	TIMURID (FR) (18) (C) J Dunlop 3 9 9 .... M Birch	3
3	000165	DAWN SUCCESS (12) (D) D Chapman 6 9 7 .... S Wood †	2
4	5/00U50-	EXPLOSIVE SPEED (USA) (406) M Hammond 4 9 5 .... Dean McKeown	1
5	2000-06	TANCRED GRANGE (18) Miss S Hall 3 9 2 . N Connorton	5
6	000521	KHAZAR (USA) (18) (C) M Prescott 3 9 0 .... G Duffield	9
7	061354	FLYING DOWN TO RIO (22) (BF) M Naughton 4 8 13 .... Julie Krone	6
8	50-1311	SWEET MIGNONETTE (9) (C) Mrs G Reveley 4 8 13 (5ex) .... K Darley	8
9	200120	SPANISH PERFORMER (6) T Fairhurst 3 8 1 .... J Fanning (3)	7

9 declared
S.P. FORECAST: 15-8 Sweet Mignonette, 3-1 Timurid, 5-1 Khazar, 8-1 Flying Down To Rio, 10-1 Dawn Success, Spanish Performer, 12-1 others.

8.10: REDCAR MOTOR MART HANDICAP 7f £1,674

1	461312	EUROBLAKE (6) (D) T Barron 5 10 0 .... Alex Greaves	18
2	330-000	VICTORIA ROAD (IRE) (22) (D) M N Easterby 4 9 13 .... M Birch	14
3	0-02001	ROYAL GIRL (21) Miss S Hall 5 9 9 .... N Connorton	11
4	625-245	CLAUDIA MISS (26) (D) W Haigh 5 9 5. Dean McKeown	4
5	800-030	ARABAT (6) (D) M Naughton 5 9 1 .... Susanne Berneklint †	15
6	325/0-30	LORD MAGESTER (FR) (19) Mrs G Reveley 5 8 11 .... J Lowe	3
7	303216	GANT BLEU (FR) (6) (D) R Whitaker 5 8 10 .... Julie Krone	16
8	233400/	IMHOTEP (683) Mrs G Reveley 5 8 10 .... L Charnock	17
9	364160	QUIET VICTORY (6) (D) Miss L Siddall 5 8 9 .... S Maloney (5) †	8
10	45020-0	SKY CAT (11) (D) C Tinkler 8 8 5 .... K Darley	13
11	500-063	BATTUTA (12) R Earnshaw 3 8 6 .... K Fallon	7
12	0U0-024	ALLEGRAMENTE (6) R O'Leary 3 8 5 .... T Lucas	1
13	505-800	FLASHY'S SON (16) M Hammond 4 8 5 .... G Duffield	5
14	0-04000	LOWLANDS BOY (18) (D) T Fairhurst 3 8 5 .... J Fanning (3)	10
15	000-402	APRIL SHADOW (7) C Thornton 3 8 2 .... A Culhane	9
16	000420	OYSTON'S LIFE (9) J Berry 3 8 0 .... Joanna Morgan	12
17	00044	JOHNSTON'S EXPRESS (IRE) (2) E Alston 4 7 9 .... J Quinn	2
18	5-06503	HIZEEM (9) (D) M Naughton 6 7 7 .... Jaki Houston	6

18 declared
S.P. FORECAST: 4-1 April Shadow, 9-2 Royal Girl, 6-1 Euroblake, Quiet Victory, 8-1 Battuta, Gant Bleu, 9-1 Claudia Miss, 12-1 Imhotep, 14-1 Lord Magestar, 16-1 others.

8.40: MIDDLESBROUGH FOOTBALL CLUB APPRENTICE HANDICAP 3YO 1m 3f £1,618

1	0-22236	MAJI (16) D Morley 9 7 .... E Bentley (5)	1
2	2016-00	LINGDALE LASS (20) Mrs G Reveley 8 5 .... S Copp (7)	5
3	0-4604	CHANTRY BELLINI (7) C Thornton 8 4 .... K Sked (7)	4
4	000-0	RAP UP FAST (USA) (90) C Thornton 8 2 .... J Marshall	2
5	0-00503	LITTLE IVOR (7) Denys Smith 7 9 .... C Teague (7)	1
6	000-	SING ANOTHER (315) Mrs G Reveley 7 9 .... Darren Moffett	6
7	00-000	TEES GAZETTE GIRL (18) Mrs G Reveley 7 8 .... Claire Balding (5)	3

7 declared
S.P. FORECAST: 5-2 Little Ivor, 7-2 Maji, 4-1 Chantry Bellini, 6-1 Lingdale Lass, 8-1 Rap Up Fast, 10-1 Sing Another, 14-1 Tees Gazette Girl.

9.10: SUSANNE BERNEKLINT MAIDEN STAKES 2YO 5f £1,520

1	034262	ARKENDALE DIAMOND (USA) (22) B Beasley 9 0 .... D Nicholls	2
2		BOLD PHILIP (42) B Beasley 9 0 .... S D Williams (7)	5
3	060	COCKERHAM RANGER J Berry 9 0 .... Julie Krone	1
4	04	MISSED THE BOAT (IRE) (9) T Barron 9 0 . Alex Greaves	4
5	3	SCORED AGAIN (18) R Whitaker 9 0 .... A Culhane	3

5 declared
S.P. FORECAST: 7-4 Cockerham Ranger, 3-1 Scored Again, 4-1 Arkendale Diamond, 5-1 Missed The Boat, 6-1 Bold Philip.

FROM *THE INDEPENDENT*

REDCAR

6.40: 1. AL KARNAK (Julie Krone) 2-11 fav; 2. Well Ahead 20-1; 3. Rahif 9-1. 4 ran. 20, 3½. (M Moubarak, Newmarket). **Tote:** £1.10. Dual Forecast: £3.70. Computer Straight Forecast: £3.75.

7.10: 1. BOLDVILLE BASH (K Darley) 9-2; 2. Touch N' Glow 7-1; 3. Kiss in The Dark 8-1. 13 ran. 5-2 fav Karinska (4th). nk, 1½. (T D Barron, Thirsk). **Tote:** £5.70; £1.40, £2.30, £1.80. DF: £24.20. CSF: £33.28.

7.40: 1. KHAZAR (G Duffield) 6-1; 2. Timurid 7-2; 3. Sweet Mignonette 11-4 fav. 9 ran. ½. (Sir Mark Prescott, Newmarket). **Tote:** £5.80; £1.90, £1.50, £1.30. DF: £6.10. CSF: £25.64. Tricast: £63.93.

8.10: 1. GANT BLEU (Julie Krone) 9-1; 2. Flashy's Son 16-1; 3. Johnston's Express 9-1; 4. Claudia Miss 10-1. 17 ran. 11-2 fav Euroblake. 1, nk. (R Whitaker, Wetherby). **Tote:** £8.80; £2.40, £3.80, £2.10, £2.10. DF: £1,022.40. CSF: £128.04. Tricast: £1,193.67. NR: Allegramente.

8.40: 1. TEES GAZETTE GIRL (Claire Balding) 10-1; 2. Little Ivor 9-2; 3. Chantry Bellini 6-1. 7 ran. 6-4 fav Maji (4th). 2½, 6. (Mrs G Reveley, Saltburn). **Tote:** £14.00; £2.50, £2.30. DF: £26.50. CSF: £47.31. Tricast: £47.31.

9.10: 1. COCKERHAM RANGER (Julie Krone) 3-1; 2. Scored Again 10-11 fav; 3. Bold Philip 33-1. 5 ran. 1½, ¾. (J Berry, Cockerham). **Tote:** £2.70; £1.40, £1.40. DF: £2.70. CSF: £5.74. Placepot: £140.30.

resolved to confine my interest in this four-year-old to win only wager and to place an each way bet on Mountain Valley, as the betting forecast did not have this filly listed as the likely favourite. Thankfully, this proved a sensible decision as Mountain Valley ran second at 8-1 and Persian Elite started, not at 9-4 as forecast, but at a much more acceptable 3-1!

I also noticed on the same day that, after riding in Windsor's 3.30, another well-known jockey, Paul Eddery, would be involved in an even longer flight (in the same time as T Quinn had to get to Leicester's much closer racecourse) so as to ride in Yorkshire.

Eddery thus seemed like a man on a definite mission and, as the first horse involved in this, Rock Sharp, was a forecast favourite, I also resolved to waste no time in being associated with this two-year-old. As expected, Rock Sharp won (at exactly his forecast odds of 5-2).

Even more recently, Paul Eddery's much better-known jockey brother, Pat, champion jockey on many occasions, also demonstrated the wisdom of confining one's attention to the jockey who, on a particular race day, is prepared, or required, to make the greatest dash (given the short time available and the length of the flight he or she faces, after having performed at an afternoon fixture) to get to an evening race meeting.

On 20 August 1997, After Pat Eddery had ridden at York (where he had gained a 16-1 success in a prestigious race) he made a rapid getaway so as to take three rides at faraway Kempton - on Secret Archive in the 6.30, Ridaiyama in the 7.30 and Drummer Golf Time in the last race.

As all three were made significant-looking favourites, I took the hint and was pleased to see this trio prevail at 11-10, 5-2 and 9-2 respectively!

On a particular race day some jockeys 'fly in' quite unexpectedly both to race meetings and on several horses. Such indeed was the case on 31 March 1997 when the fact that, rather than cool his heels waiting for a rained-off Dubai World Cup to be re-staged on 3 April,

Frankie Dettori, at considerable expense, flew back to Britain to ride at Newcastle, should have alerted backers to the horses concerned, especially those trained by one of his main stables - that of John Gosden. Not only did Dettori, on Minersville at 8-11 and Perfect Paradigm at 5-2, notch a double for the Gosden yard, he also brought home Stately Princess at 5-4 for Mick Channon and his fourth and fifth rides yielded a second and a third!

FROM *THE DAILY TELEGRAPH*

Busy Dettori lets fly with a treble

FRANKIE DETTORI, on a flying visit back to England while he awaits the rescheduled Dubai World Cup on Thursday, maintained his cracking start to the season with three winners, a second and third from five rides at Newcastle yesterday.

By Marcus Armytage

Two of his winners, Minersville and Perfect Paradigm, were for the in-form John Gosden, while the other, Stately Princess, was for Mick Channon. Tonight, Dettori flies back out to Dubai

NEWCASTLE
Going: GOOD TO FIRM

2.25 (1m): **MINERSVILLE** (L Dettori, 8-11F) 1; **Tigrello** (10-1) 2; **Final Trial** (10-1) 3. 10 ran. hd, 2. (J Gosden). Tote: win £1.70; places £1.40, £1.50, £2.80. Dual F'cast: £4.60. CSF: £9.12. Trio: £21.40.

2.55 (5f): **STATELY PRINCESS** (L Dettori, 5-4) 1; **Carambo** (12-1) 2; **Flower O'Cannie** (11-2) 3. 4 ran. Antonia's Double 11-10F. ¾, ½. (M Channon). Tote: win £2.30. Dual F'cast: £7.10. CSF: £12.48.

3.30 (1m3y sell h'cap): **GADGE** (T Siddall, 7-2F) 1; **Sandmoor Denim** (14-1) 2; **Seconds Away** (16-1) 3; **Sheraz** (10-1) 4. 20 ran. 3, hd. (A Bailey). Tote: win £5.10; places £1.80, £3.90, £7.10, £2.30. Dual F'cast: £55.00. CSF: £63.92. Tricast: £538.98. Trio: £322.00. **Winner bought in for 4,000gns.**

4.00 (5f h'cap): **SURPRISE MISSION** (J Fortune, 15-8F) 1; **Broadstairs Beauty** (16-1) 2; **Maiteamia** (9-1) 3. 11 ran. nk, ¾. (Mrs J Ramsden). Tote: win £2.60; places £1.50, £2.40, £2.00. Dual F'cast: £41.10. CSF: £33.13. Tricast: £203.14. Trio: £61.30.

4.35 (1m4f93y): **PERFECT PARADIGM** (L Dettori, 5-2) 1; **Dark Green** (11-10F) 1; **Lawahik** (5-2) 3. 8 ran. 1¼, 1¾. (J Gosden). Tote: win £3.00; places £1.40, £1.10, £1.10. Dual F'cast: £1.60. CSF: £5.21.

5.05 (7f h'cap): **THREE ARCH BRIDGE** (Dean McKeown, 14-1) 1; **Impulsive Air** (7-1) 2; **Foist** (11-4F) 3; **Be Warned** (20-1) 4. 18 ran. ¾, sh hd. (M Johnston). Tote: win £15.70; places £3.60, £2.00, £1.60, £5.40. Dual F'cast: £55.70. CSF: £108.88. Tricast: £342.91. Trio: £103.30.

QUADPOT: £8.80. PLACEPOT: £17.30.

STRATEGY 19
JOCKEY CHANGES

Going racing is an experience extolled by racing commentator John McCririck as likely to give the backer several major advantages. One of these is spotting any last-minute and significant changes of jockeys from those whose names appear in evening papers or in national or racing dailies.

One particular ploy I often enjoy implementing when I 'go racing', as McCririck recommends, is to see whether any 'unscheduled' rider who is eventually given the leg up in the paddock is a replacement, not for one previously listed 'pilot', but for two of these!

Such a development is uncommon but is often a potentially lucrative pointer, as was demonstrated at an evening meeting held at my once local course of Stratford-upon-Avon. The 'three way' change of riders that then attracted my attention concerned Castellani, trainer Malcolm Eckley's bottom weight in the Bishopton Novices Handicap, a two mile race for four-year-olds and upwards.

This particular contender had the name of jockey, Adrian Maguire by its own in a paper published the evening before it was due to take its chance. Then, on the morning of the race, I saw from *The Daily Telegraph* and my *Sporting Life* that David Bridgwater had replaced Maguire.

Fortunately, when on the racecourse, I spotted that top lady jockey Gee Armytage was replacing Bridgwater (and not through injury) I thought that trainer Eckley's extensive negotiations with three jockeys might prove significant.

To my delight the 'three jockeys and one horse' ploy paid off handsomely when Gee rode out Castellani to a three length victory at the most rewarding odds of 12-1.

FROM *THE COVENTRY EVENING TELEGRAPH*

8.00 BISHOPTON NOVICES' HANDICAP HURDLE. £1,800 Added. 2 miles. (4-y-o plus). Penalty Value £1,235. (11 declared).

(1) 0-30313 FUTURE KING 7 (D) A Jarvis 5-11-10 T Jarvis 94
(2) 43-0233 PEACEMAN 18 Mrs D Haine 6-11-6. E Murphy 95
(3) 001200 MAJOR IVOR 74 (D) Mrs G Reveley 7-10-11. – 96
(4) 053336 WINGS OF FREEDOM (IRE) 22 J Jenkins 4-10-10 . . . . – 94
(5) 000014 ERIC'S TRAIN 16 (D,BF) Mrs J Pitman 6-10-9 – 95
(6) 154606 BY FAR (USA) 53 (CD) O O'Neill 6-10-7 V Slattery (5) 95
(7) 00P FERN HEIGHTS 18 C Broad 5-10-5 . . . M Jones 94
(8) 055-505 TARTAR'S BOW 165 R Holder 5-10-3 . . . . – 93
(9) 03605 SMART REBAL (IRE) 20 J Akehurst 4-10-2 L Harvey 94
(10) 0U000P EMERALD RULER 44 J Webber 5-10-0 . . . . . – 94
(11) 06063 CASTELLANI (V) 7 M Eckley 7-10-0 A Maguire 95

FORECAST: 5-2 Eric's Train, 7-2 Future King, 5-1 Peaceman, 6-1 Castellani, 8-1 Wings of Freedom, Major Ivor, 12-1 Others.

FROM *THE DAILY TELEGRAPH*

8.00: BISHOPTON NOVICE HANDICAP HURDLE 2m £1,235

1 0-30313 FUTURE KING (7) (D) A Jarvis 5 11 10 . . . . T Jarvis
2 43-0233 PEACEMAN (18) Mrs D Haine 6 11 6 . . . . P Hide (7)
3 001200 MAJOR IVOR (74) (D) Mrs G Reveley 7 10 11 . . . . . . R Hodge (5)
4 053336 WINGS OF FREEDOM (IRE) (22) J Jenkins 4 10 10 . M Ahern
5 000014 ERIC'S TRAIN (16) (D) (BF) Mrs J Pitman 6 10 9 . . . M Bowlby
6 154606 BY FAR (USA) (53) (CD) O O'Neill 6 10 7 . . . . V Slattery (5)
7 00P FERN HEIGHTS (18) C Broad 5 10 5 . . . . M Jones
8 055-505 TARTAR'S BOW (165) R Holder 5 10 3 . . . . E Byrne
9 03605 SMART REBAL (IRE) (20) J Akehurst 4 10 2 . . . . L Harvey
10 0U000P EMERALD RULER (44) J Webber 5 10 0 . . . . A Webb
11 06063 CASTELLANI (7) M Eckley 7 10 0 . . . . D Bridgwater

11 declared

S.P. FORECAST: 7-2 Future King, 4-1 Eric's Train, 5-1 Smart Rebel, 6-1 Peaceman, 8-1 Wings of Freedom, 10-1 Major Ivor, Castellani, 12-1 others.

1991: Prime Warden 5 11 5 G McCourt 10-1 R Holder 8 ran.

8.00 (2m nov h'cap hdle): **CASTELLANI** (Gee Armytage, 12-1) 1; **Eric's Train** (9-2) 2; **Emerald Ruler** (16-1) 3. 11 ran. Major Ivor 4F. 2, 3½. (M Eckley). Tote: win £11.60;

STRATEGY 20

JOCKEYS WASTING TO WIN

Over the centuries jockeys have adopted some particular drastic methods of weight reduction which have varied from violent purgatives favoured by 19th century jockeys to potentially dangerous and debilitating 'pee pills'.

Still today a jockey, at least temporarily, may on occasion starve himself in order to make a weight that is lower than that at which he normally rides. For example, recently amateur William Hurst lost four stone in order to ride Mils Maj at 10st 11lb in the Ayrshire Agricultural Association Handicap Hurdle run over 2 miles and 4 furlongs at Ayr.

William, son of the owner of Mils Maj, certainly sweated to help land a bet of £3,500 to £500, made at 7-1 shortly before this gelding galloped away from his field, after opening in the course betting at 8-1.

FROM *THE RACING POST*

```
4.30   Ayrshire Agricultural Association
[OFF 4.34]  Handicap Hurdle          2m4f
For: four yrs old and upwards-Rated 0-130 1st £2,705 2nd £755 3rd
£365

1   MILS MIJ 7 10-13.........................................MrW Hurst
    br g by Slim Jim—Katie Grey (Pongee)
    led and soon clear, hit 6th, headed 7th and soon lost place,
    headway approaching 3 out, led after 2 out, ran on  bet of
    £3,500-£500                        [op 8/1] 7/1
2   3½ KANNDABIL 5 10-12b .......................... G Bradley
    gr h by Nishapour (FR)—Katana (FR) (Le Haar)
    chased leader, led 7th until after 2 out, one pace      [op
                                       8/1] 12/1
3   1½ GOSPEL ROCK (NZ) 8 10-03 §3 ....................T Reed
    br g by Church Parade—Leopard Rock (NZ) (Rocky
    Mountain (FR))
    chased leaders, disputed lead approaching 3 out, ridden and
    beaten 2 out  bet £3,000-£480     [op 6/1 tchd 11/2] 6/1
```

A much more widely known amateur jump jockey is Marcus Armytage who won the 1990 Grand National on Mr Frisk. He too has been known to diet hard to land a notable riding success, at such important 'showplace' meetings as the Cheltenham Festival.

According to my *Daily Telegraph,* he recently 'sweated long and hard' so he could ride there at 10st 2lb - around 5lb lower than his regular minimum.

Having noted this, I supported the horse concerned in Marcus's major sacrifice (that unusually he had been engaged to ride by trainer David Nicholson) in the Fulke Walwyn Kim Muir Challenge Cup.

"That's the lightest I've ever ridden," was Armytage's most significant comment, which he voiced after he had brought home Nicholson's Tug of Gold to a one-and-a-half length victory.

Such dieting, especially if it is undertaken rather drastically (and far more sportingly and generously by an unpaid amateur) can provide a major pointer to the chance of its equine beneficiary, and it can be detected if one knows at what weights jockeys customarily ride. Details of these 'natural' weights are documented in such annual publications as Raceform's *Horses in Training.*

FROM *THE DAILY TELEGRAPH*

4.40: FULKE WALWYN KIM MUIR CHALLENGE CUP H'CAP CH (AMATEUR RIDERS) £17,883 3m
TUG OF GOLD gr g Tug Of War — Grey Squirrell (Mrs J Mould) 7 10 2 ... Mr M Armytage **11 -1** 1
PACO'S BOY b g Good Rhyne (USA) — Jeremique (F K Roofing Ltd) 7 9 11 ... Mr N Moore **9-1** 2
LATENT TALENT b g Celtic Cone — Fra Mau (C Heath) 8 10 9 ... Mr J Durkan **7-1** 3
STRONG GOLD b g Strong Gale — Miss Goldiane (Mrs S Robins) 9 9 12 ... Mr G Lewis **20-1** 4

STRATEGY 21

JOCKEYS PUSHING THEMSELVES TO COMPETE

Wasting does not represent the only sacrifice that jockeys can make in doing their utmost to be associated with a particular racecourse victory.

National Hunt jockeys in particular sometimes make Herculean efforts to overcome physical barriers in order to be so associated, as was once demonstrated most impressively by one of their number.

When, in fact, jockey Jamie Osborne took some mounts at a Plumpton meeting not so very long ago, I realised that here was no ordinary jockey booking since Osborne, in very self-sacrificing style, had rushed back over the Atlantic to ride them! Indeed, I supported both Kaklanski and Scobie Boy, since I felt their sound claims on form were receiving a propitious pointer, not just in Osborne's impressive past Plumpton strike rate for Egerton, but, most significantly, in the shape of this jockey's clearly rather special booking. After all, Osborne had, only hours before, ridden in the Colonial Cup in South Carolina! Careful scrutiny of the racing press and thorough monitoring of jockeys' journeys from one racecourse to another far distant one will often alert the backer to the sacrifice of really rushed, stressful and expensive travelling that some riders are occasionally prepared to make. Indeed, the pointers provided by sacrifices on the part of jockeys who are clearly 'pushing themselves to win' can often be profitably exploited, as Osborne recently so impressively demonstrated.

FROM THE RACING POST

> JAMIE OSBORNE arrived early at Plumpton yesterday and immediately fell asleep. But he woke up in time to ride a short-priced double on Kalanski and Scobie Boy for trainer Charlie Egerton.
>
> The Lambourn jockey could be forgiven his bit of dossing as he had completed a hectic weekend, which took in six airports and two dramatic taxi rides in competing in the Colonial Cup in South Carolina over the weekend.
>
> Osborne explained: "I left Cheltenham after the fourth race on Saturday. After riding Flown in the Cup, we jumped in a taxi and just made the last plane out of Charlotte on Sunday evening. I got back to Heathrow at 8am this morning and came here to get a couple of hours sleep in the weighing-room!"

Even more recently, on 25 August 1997, when I read the following report in my *Daily Mail,* I resolved to support only those mounts of the very determined globetrotter involved - Frankie Dettori - that were also shown as form selections in this newspaper.

Gratifyingly, this prudent approach led me to support Monsajem in Chepstow's 2:45 and Bin Rosie in the following race that actually (and in a most propitious-looking manner) carried the name of its jockey!

FROM THE DAILY MAIL

FRANKIE DETTORI, banned for five days by the Goodwood stewards on Saturday for careless riding on demoted Cape Cross in the Celebration Mile, has six fancied rides at Chepstow this afternoon.

The Italian made history when riding all seven winners at Ascot last year — the question punters will be asking is can he go through the card again?

Yesterday he was in Chicago for three rides, principally Godolphin's Allied Forces in the Arlington Million. But he jets back this morning before heading on to Chepstow.

Dettori must also decide whether to appeal against his Goodwood ban (September 1-5). Yesterday his agent Matty Cowing said: 'I haven't got a clue whether Frankie will appeal. He will decide when he gets back from America.'

Even if he fails to make the magic six at Chepstow, Dettori will almost certainly take the lead in the jockey's title race by the end of the afternoon.

He is level with Kieren Fallon on 121 winners but would have been in front if the two winners he had a Goodwood on Saturday — Swiss Law and Cape Cross — had not been thrown out for riding infringments.

In the last few weeks, Dettori has piled up the winners. while, Fallon, who rides a

As it happened, these two horses figured in the near 8-1 treble that, despite his jetlag, the title-chasing Dettori achieved at Chepstow.

Thus was further confirmation of the wisdom of siding with a jockey who makes a Herculean effort to be at the races most acceptably provided.

FROM THE DAILY MAIL

FRANKIE DETTORI was cut to 4-1 on favourite (from 4-7) for the jockeys' championship by the Tote yesterday following a near 8-1 treble at Chepstow.

Any hope of the charismatic rider going through the Chepstow card disappeared in the opener when his mount Casino Ace proved no match for Gay Kelleway's impressive winner Admire.

But Monsajem, Eleventh Duke and Bin Rosie were all propelled to the winner's enclosure, the latter in the Frankie Dettori Ton-Up Conditions Stakes, the contest run to commemorate his 1990 feat of becoming the second teenager since Lester Piggott to ride a century of winners.

STRATEGY 22

POINT-TO-POINT JOCKEYS ON RACETRACKS

Such is the appeal of racing 'between the flags' and its attraction to those who savour its Corinthian flavour and truly sporting nature that it takes a powerful incentive to induce a rider who could ride several fancied 'pointers' to, instead, turn out at a National Hunt meeting, just to ride one racehorse.

Such a significant jockey booking can only be detected by diligent research or by recourse to such reports as the following that appeared during the 1996 Point-to-Point season under the heading 'Jones misses rides on family hopefuls'.

This *Times* report really took my interest, as I know from past research for my, as yet unpublished, book on ladies in racing, that trainer Nigel Tinkler is particularly keen on the 'Kim Muir' and on a lady rider winning it, as he helped Gee Armytage to do just this not so many seasons age.

However, on 24 February, my mind was not on this Cheltenham race, save that I felt that, with it at the back of her mind for the future, Pip Jones was about to make of her family's interests a present sacrifice of almost Puritan severity for a very good reason that had everything to do with the Finningley Handicap Chase at Doncaster!

Thus, denying myself any other self indulgence, I invested heavily on Puritan and then zealously cheered him home, as he ran out a decent priced winning favourite.

FROM *THE TIMES*

Jones misses rides on family hopefuls

POINT-TO-POINT BY CARL EVANS

PIP JONES, after her treble at Erw Lon last week, has had to give up another winning hand at today's **North Hereford-shire** meeting because Nigel Tinkler wants her to ride Puritan at Doncaster, prior to an attempt on the Fulke Walwyn-Kim Muir Chase at the Cheltenham Festival.

Pip's brother Tim, who rides and trains, wanted his sister to ride Linantic and Caracol at the North Herefordshire, but he cannot take over in her absence since he has been booked by Jayne Webber to partner Fresh Prince and Sandy Beau at the. **South Midlands Area Hunt Club.**

4.50 FINNINGLEY HANDICAP CHASE
(£3,171: 2m 3f 110yd) (8)

601	F221	PURITAN 25 (B,CD,F,G,S) N Tinkler 7-12-0.........	Miss P Jones
602	1331	REVE EN ROSE 12 (D,F,G,S) M McMillan 10-11-9	J R Kavanagh
603	UP65	STRONG SOUND 39 (F,G,S) P Cheesbrough 9-11-7 ..	R Supple
604	6F/	ISLAND GALE 668 (S) D McCune 11-10-9...................	F Perratt
605	F54P	BUCKS SURPRISE 38 (G) J Mackie 8-10-2...................	T Eley
606	4-03	CHARTERFORHARDWARE 38 (S) W Clay 10-10-0....	Guy Lewis (3)
607	0/P	NO MORE THE FOOL 10 (G) Mrs L Williamson 10-10-0.	S McNeill
608	34P0	MAGGOTS GREEN 7 (D,F,S) J Bradley 9-10-0	K Gaule (3)

7-4 Puritan, 2-1 Reve En Rose, 6-1 Strong Sound, 8-1 others.

JOCKEYS RESTORING THEIR REPUTATIONS

As I know only too well, any unjustified impugning of one's professional reputation can initially cause deep resentment but, subsequently, can spur one to a vigorous re-affirmation of one's worth and ability.

Clearly, any involvement with the turf, given all its vicissitudes (which feature so many high hopes, either dashed or realised) is a stern test of character and that of Keiron Fallon, first jockey to ten times champion trainer, Henry Cecil, was sorely tested in July 1997. Indeed, Fallon must have felt that the slings and arrows of outrageous fortune had unfairly wounded him.

What happened was that, after a successful start to his first season as the retained jockey to the most powerful stable in Britain, in Sandown's richest flat race, the Eclipse Stakes, Fallon took the ride on the apple of Cecil's very sharp eye - the 1996 One Thousand Guineas winner, Bosra Sham.

Unfortunately, his riding of this filly (that Cecil later revealed had never been better in her life) involved what Richard Evans of *The Times* described as 'an impossible run between Derby winner Benny the Dip and the far rail at a vital stage in the race. This sealed the jockey's fate since, after failing to get through on the inside of Benny the Dip, Fallon was forced to snatch up the filly before pulling to the outside, by which time the winner, Pilsudski, had flown'.

FROM *THE TIMES*

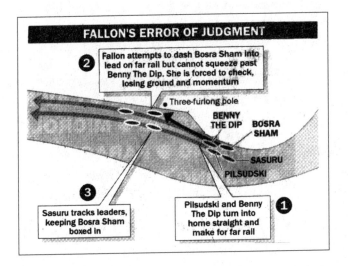

Uncharacteristically, a bitterly disappointed Henry Cecil cast aspersions on his jockey's ability by declaring that Bosra Sham had been abused. Fallon, in contrast, refrained from recrimination but defended himself by declaring: "I had to challenge when I did. There was no gallop and there was no point sitting any longer. Michael Hills (on Sasuru) was on my outside so I could not go out there. The only way to go was where there was a gap. Take a close look and see what else I could have done".

While interested in a diagrammatic newspaper representation of Fallon's riding of Bosra Sham and appreciating that this was not something the jockey would want to frame and hang on his wall, I surmised that he would immediately try to confound and silence his detractors with riding performances designed to eclipse his ill-starred one in Sandown's race of that name. As it happens, this prestigious contest is followed by Newmarket's important first July meeting and I reasoned that, from its opening on the following Tuesday, Fallon would do all he could to once again endear himself to his disgruntled 'guvnor'. Encouraged and enriched by Fallon's rapid post Eclipse 7-1 success on an outside Monday mount for the stable of I Williams, I could hardly wait to read the racing page of my *Times* to scan the Newmarket runners for 8 July!

Careful scrutiny soon revealed that Fallon's mounts for his 'home' Warren Place stable were the top form-rated Craigsteel in the opening race and Dushanytor in another televised contest. In accordance with the principle of only supporting a runner fancied on subjective, non-numerical criteria, if it is also the quite dispassionately top-rated form selection of the private handicapper *The Times* employs, I concluded that Craigsteel, rather than second rated Dushanytor, would help Fallon to 'clear his name' and so it proved.

FROM *THE TIMES*

2.05 STRUTT & PARKER MAIDEN STAKES   C4
(Div I: 2-Y-O: £4,753: 7f) (11 runners)

101	(10)	ARKADIAN HERO (M Tabor & Mrs J Magnier) L Cumani 9-0	Pat Eddery	--
102	(1)	CORNICHE (H H Prince Fahd Salman) P Cole 9-0	T Quinn	--
103	(11)	COURT SHAREEF (D & C Holder) R Dickin 9-0	M Roberts	--
104	(6)	2 CRAIGSTEEL 25 (Sir David Wills) H Cecil 9-0	K Fallon	99
105	(4)	INDIMAAJ (Kuwait Racing Syndicate) J Dunlop 9-0	M J Kinane	--
106	(8)	JALAAB (H al-Maktoum) R Armstrong 9-0	R Hills	--
107	(5)	MAAZOOM (Sheikh A al-Maktoum) J Gosden 9-0	L Dettori	--
108	(7)	RAINBOW HIGH (K Abdulla) B Hills 9-0	M Hills	--
109	(9)	RIVER BEAT (Grangewood (Sales & Marketing) Ltd) M Tompkins 9-0	R Cochrane	--
110	(2)	SURPRISE PRESENT (M Suhail) R Hannon 9-0	R Hughes	--
111	(3)	VICTORY NOTE (Mrs J Magnier & R Sangster) P Chapple-Hyam 9-0	J Reid	--

BETTING: 5-2 Craigsteel, 7-2 Arkadian Hero, 4-1 Victory Note, 6-1 Surprise Present, 8-1 Corniche, Jalaab, 10-1 Rainbow High. 14-1 Indimaaj. 16-1 Maazoom, 20-1 others.

1996: BAHHARE 9-0 W Carson (15-8 fav) J Dunlop 11 ran

FORM FOCUS

As it happened, this very same line of reasoning led me to support no less than three Cecil-Fallon runners on the following day at Newmarket. These - Light Programme, Bold Fact and Memorise - were all top-rated on form and, most gratifyingly, they all won to produce a lucrative treble.

2.05 MORE O'FERRALL STAKES `C4`
(3-Y-O: £5,481: 1m 2f) (12 runners)

101	(7)		DR MARTENS (R Griggs Group Limited) L Cumani 9-0	Pat Eddery	--
102	(1)	2	LIGHT PROGRAMME 19 (K Abdulla) H Cecil 9-0	K Fallon	99
103	(11)	0-	PRINCE DE LOIR 334 (J Wilson) D Cosgrove 9-0	W Ryan	--
104	(5)		RICARDO (K Abdulla) R Charlton 9-0	T Sprake	--
105	(10)	02	ROBBAN HENDI 36 (Sheikh A al-Maktoum) M Jarvis 9-0	R Cochrane	81
106	(8)	43	DOVEDON STAR 7 (BF) (M Whatley) P Kelleway 8-9	J Weaver	97
107	(12)		MARILAYA (H R H Aga Khan) L Cumani 8-9	K Darley	--
108	(2)	5	POLENISTA 27 (I Stewart-Brown) J Dunlop 8-9	T Quinn	76
109	(4)		PRADESH (Sheikh Mohammed) J Gosden 8-9	A Garth	--
110	(3)	3-	SAAFEYA 270 (Sheikh A al-Maktoum) J Gosden 8-9	L Dettori	82
111	(6)		SHASKA (Sheikh Mohammed) J Gosden 8-9	G Hind	--
112	(9)	0	WATER FLOWER 84 (W Gredley) J Fanshawe 8-9	M Hills	87

BETTING: 15-8 Light Programme, 4-1 Saafeya, 7-1 Marilaya, Polenista, 8-1 Dovedon Star, Shaska, 10-1 Dr Martens, Robban Hendi, 14-1 others.

1996: GREENSTEAD 9-0 J Carroll (16-1) J Gosden 13 ran

2.35 TNT INTERNATIONAL AVIATION JULY STAKES `C4`
(Group III: 2-Y-O: £15,924: 6f) (8 runners)

201	(7)	30511	TIPPITT BOY 20 (D,F,G) (Highgrove Developments Ltd) K McAuliffe 9-1	J Reid	95
202	(8)	115	POOL MUSIC 20 (BF,F) (Mrs C Parker) R Hannon 8-13	R Hughes	95
203	(4)	1	AIX EN PROVENCE 19 (D,G) (J Featherstone) M Johnston 8-10	J Weaver	90
204	(2)	1150	BLUERIDGE DANCER 22 (B,F) (A Cunliffe) B Meehan 8-10	K Darley	95
205	(6)	13	BOLD FACT 22 (D,F) (K Abdulla) H Cecil 8-10	K Fallon	99
206	(3)	11	CALCHAS 14 (D,S) (Sheikh A al-Maktoum) M Prescott 8-10	G Duffield	90
207	(1)	21	LINDEN HEIGHTS 12 (CD,S) (H Chung) L Cumani 8-10	Pat Eddery	83
208	(5)	010	SWIFT ALLIANCE 22 (D,F) (Bickerstaff Woolsey) R Akehurst 8-10	T Quinn	80

BETTING: 6-4 Bold Fact, 5-1 Calchas, 6-1 Tippitt Boy, Pool Music, 7-1 Linden Heights, 10-1 Aix En Provence, Blueridge Dancer, 25-1 Swift Alliance.

1996: RICH GROUND 8-10 J Reid (40-1) J Bethell 9 ran

3.10 INFLITE ENGINEERING DUKE OF CAMBRIDGE `C4`
HANDICAP (3-Y-O: £19,820: 1m 2f) (16 runners)

301	(7)	521-U51	MAYLANE 27 (G,S) (Sheikh A al-Maktoum) A Stewart 9-7	M Roberts	94
302	(15)	110-160	AMYAS 22 (F,G,S) (Mrs J Corbett) B Hills 9-7	M Hills	93
303	(10)	20-3501	CINEMA PARADISO 13 (F,S) (C Wright) P Cole 9-6	T Quinn	93
304	(6)	362-110	STANTON HARCOURT 45 (D,F) (C Humphris) J Dunlop 9-5	Pat Eddery	97
305	(14)	1-22	PRIENA 27 (F) (Cuadra Africa) D Loder 9-5	K Darley	93
306	(16)	015	RIVER PILOT 25 (D,S) (Lady Rothschild) R Charlton 9-4	T Sprake	98
307	(11)	5-52231	ATLANTIC DESIRE 12 (D,F,G) (Atlantic Racing Ltd) M Johnston 9-2	J Weaver	97
308	(5)	1-20	MERSEY BEAT 81 (D) (K Higson) G L Moore 8-13	A Clark	94
309	(12)	6-4414	MEMORISE 20 (D,G) (K Abdulla) H Cecil 8-12	K Fallon	99
310	(4)	4-00120	PARTY ROMANCE 20 (D,G) (A Ali) B Hanbury 8-12	W Ryan	98
311	(1)	31-0430	OVER TO YOU 22 (G) (M al-Maktoum) E Dunlop 8-9	J Reid	98
312	(3)	0013005	BOLD ORIENTAL 12 (D,F) (M Tabor & Mrs J Magnier) N Callaghan 8-9	L Dettori	96
313	(9)	1502	MANAZIL 14 (S) (H al-Maktoum) R Armstrong 8-7	R Hills	98
314	(8)	0600400	FOOT BATTALION 11 (G) (J Bigg) R Hollinshead 8-4	R Ffrench (5)	98
315	(13)	6010	BEVIER 22 (F) (Sheikh M al-Maktoum) C Brittain 8-2	A Munro	87
316	(2)	5-03	REGAL THUNDER 61 (Mrs R Savill) M Stoute 7-13	J Quinn	94

BETTING: 11-2 Priena, 6-1 Atlantic Desire, Memorise, 8-1 Bold Oriental, Maylane, Regal Thunder, Stanton Harcourt, 12-1 Amyas, Over To You, 14-1 Cinema Paradiso, 16-1 Party Romance, River Pilot, 20-1 others.

1996: FREEDOM FLAME 8-5 M Roberts (9-1) M Johnston 13 ran

So the principle of backing a jockey who is hell-bent on rapidly restoring his reputation and has a form horse under him was spectacularly vindicated.

Interestingly, Henry Cecil, with regard to Bosra Sham, when clearly still smarting from her shock eclipse at Sandown, had talked of 'pride having been dented'. At the time my thought was that this comment really applied to Kieron Fallon. Incidentally, had I needed any confirmation of the wisdom of supporting jockeys urgently seeking to retrieve their impugned reputations, this had been offered about a year earlier, when, on 24 September 1996, after riding a 140-1 treble for trainer Mark Johnston, on three horses sent on a 254 miles raid from Middleham to Epsom, jockey Jason Weaver commented: "Mark told me not to come back without a winner when I went to Newbury and Wolverhampton on Saturday and I felt I'd let him down when I turned in on Monday with no successes to report. But hopefully he'll be pleased with today's haul".

Epsom

Going: good to firm, good in places

2.15 (1m 114yd) 1 **ATLANTIC DESIRE** (J Weaver, 4-1); 2, **Tommy Tortoise** (T Quinn, 6-1); 3, **High Extreme** (J Reid, 13-8 fav). ALSO RAN: 10 Waterville Boy (4th), 12 Slightly Oliver (6th), 33 Mendoza (5th). 6 ran. 6l, 2½l, 4l, 4l, 8l. M Johnston at Middleham. Tote: £3.20; £1.40, £1.90. DF: £7.20. CSF: £18.32. Fruitie O'Flarety (7-1) withdrawn, not under orders — rule 4 applies to all bets, deduction 10p in the pound.

2.45 (6f) 1, **BALLADOOLE BAJAN** (J Weaver, 11-4 jt-fav); 2, **Mantles Prince** (R Hughes, 6-1); 3, **Petite Danseuse** (A Daly, 11-4 jt-fav). ALSO RAN: 11-2 Chingachgook (5th), Clara Bliss (4th), 9 Class Distinction, 25 Eaton Park (6th). 7 ran. ½l, 1½l, 1l, 6l, 2½l. M Johnston at Middleham. Tote: £3.00; £2.00, £2.40. DF: £16.60. CSF: £17.69.

3.20 (1m 2f 18yd) 1, **MAGELLAN** (T Quinn, 8-11 fav); 2, **Double Leaf** (R Cochrane, 6-4); 3, **Province** (R Hughes, 7-1). ALSO RAN: 100 Easy Choice (4th). 4 ran. 2l, 19l, dist. C Brittain at Newmarket. Tote: £1.90. DF: £1.40. CSF: £2.21.

3.50 (1m 114yd) 1, **STAR OF ZILZAL** (A Clark, 100-30 fav); 2, **Nagnagnag** (R Hughes, 4-1); 3, **April The Eighth** (R Cochrane, 6-1). ALSO RAN: 8 Civil Liberty (4th), 9 Herodian, 10 Blue Zulu, 11 Kamari (6th), 12 My Best Valentine, Night Wink (5th), 14 Lucky Archer. 10 ran. NR: Welton Arsenal. 1l, nk, hd, ½l, sh hd. M Stoute at Newmarket. Tote: £3.60; £2.00, £1.80, £2.80. DF: £5.80. Trio: £10.60. CSF: £16.43. Tricast: £68.78.

4.20 (1m 4f 10yd) 1, **MOUNT PLEASANT** (T Quinn, 10-11 fav; Richard Evans's nap); 2, **Matthias Mystique** (S Sanders, 66-1); 3, **Laazim Afooz** (R Hughes, 14-1). ALSO RAN: 15-8 Serenus (4th), 6 Gumair (6th), 66 Petros Pride (5th), Sliparis. 7 ran. NR: Amadour, Unassailable. 6l, ½l, 1l, 19l, ½l. P Cole at Whatcombe. Tote: £1.80; £1.30, £8.60. DF: £25.20. Trio: £19.80. CSF: £33.06.

4.50 (1m 114yd) 1, **MAID FOR BAILEYS** (J Weaver, 13-2); 2, **Don't Get Caught** (R Cochrane, 5-2 fav); 3, **Mr Nevermind** (S Whitworth, 10-1). ALSO RAN: 7-2 Balance Of Power (6th), 7 Superior Force, 10 North Reef (5th), 14 Helios, 16 Dancing Lawyer, 20 Sejaal, Typhoon Lad, 25 Absolute Utopia (4th), Bernard Seven. 12 ran. ¾l, ½l, 1l, ¾l, 3l. M Johnston at Middleham. Tote: £6.60; £1.80, £1.10, £2.60. DF: £8.80. Trio: £29.60. CSF: £23.05. Tricast: £154.00.

Placepot: £95.30.   **Quadpot:** £10.50.

STRATEGY 24

JOCKEYS KEEN TO WIN AFTER ABSENCES

As jockey Jamie Osborne suggested when he tipped the 1996 Grand National winner, Rough Quest, in an article he wrote when sidelined by injury, this particular situation leaves members of his profession desperate to resume the daily doing of a job they live for and really love to do.

As it happens, I have long exploited absent jockeys' very understandable longings to get back in the saddle and on a payroll, by supporting the first mounts they take on their return to race riding, provided I also fancy these on other non-emotional criteria such as their past form.

In my view there are no pluckier jockeys than the ladies who ride (often suspect) jumpers in point-to-points and, of these, five times women's champion, Alison Dare made a comeback at the third (10 January) meeting of the 1996 season, after breaking her leg on the racecourse the previous March.

I felt this resumption might well be a winning one on the part of a rider who has shown herself relentless and determined in her quest for winners and so decided to support Alison at the Barbury Castle meeting. I also knew from my study of MacKenzie and Selby's Annual Guide to pointing that, of her mounts, Down The Mine, despite his dangerous sounding name, was a safe conveyance and so made this seasoned performer my nap for this early fixture.

In the event Down the Mine gave Alison an armchair winning ride and so allowed her to get off the mark for the new season and resume her pursuit of the ladies' title.

FROM *THE TIMES*

Dare gives masterly display on comeback

POINT-TO-POINT
BY CARL EVANS

ALISON DARE, five times women's champion rider, celebrated a winning comeback on Down The Mine at Barbury Castle on Saturday. She had been out of action since breaking her leg in March.

Initial pain mellows, but there is a deeper anguish in being on the sidelines. After 19 seasons' riding without so much as breaking a finger, Dare's incapacitation was frustrating, particularly when other riders substituted on horses trained by her mentor, Dick Bainbridge.

"I wanted a good, safe horse for her return," Bainbridge said when the **Point-to-point Owners and Riders Club** meeting produced a competitive ladies' open race.

Fifteen went to post but 14 were just supporting players from the moment the flag fell as Down The Mine made all, his partner producing a masterly display in the saddle. Dare sat quietly until the final bend, where she simply coaxed Down The Mine with a rhythm that kept them ahead of Workingforpeanuts and Pamela's Lad.

"I'm not a positive person and I have had to force myself to be that way to get through," Dare said, after returning on her 201st winner

Similarly, when the much more widely-known champion jockey, Frankie Dettori, returned to action, not after an absence caused by injury but one occasioned by some globe trotting, I also reasoned that he would also be eager to resume riding in Britain with a winner. My feeling that Frankie would experience not beginner's luck but that of one beginning again was only strengthened when I read in my *Times* that Frankie had declared: "I'm bored stiff and can't wait to get back" and saw that one of this newspaper's racing correspondents felt his mount had a 'sound chance' on the basis of her victory last time out after her own 14 week break!

So it was that I decided to take a serious interest in Flirty Gertie which duly trotted up to put Frankie back on the winning trail and 'acclimatise' him to the 'winning in Britain' experience.

Readers who wish to gauge when sidelined or absent jockeys are due to, or are about to, return to possibly winning ways should study the On the Sidelines feature that appears towards the end of the *Racing Post*.

Obviously, National Hunt jockeys have to endure many more spells on the sidelines after injuries, since these are the daily hazards of their risky occupation.

Sometimes these injuries even happen away from racecourses, as was Jump jockey Jason Titley's unfortunate experience in mid-November 1996. He suffered internal injuries in a schooling fall and this caused him to be sidelined for six frustrating weeks.

However, when my *Racing Post* of 23 December indicated that Jason was to resume race riding at Ludlow, I decided to attempt to defray some of my Christmas expenses by backing his 'return' mount, if this was a fancied runner. As the horse in question proved to be both the form horse and the 15-8 favourite, I had a decent bet and was delighted to see Jason get the early Christmas present he must have wanted above all others!

FROM *THE DAILY TELEGRAPH*

LUDLOW RESULTS

Jason Titley, who resumed riding at Ludlow yesterday following six weeks on the sidelines following internal injuries in a schooling fall, received a couple of confidence boosters.

His first mount, Too Sharp, won for Henrietta Knight

Going: GOOD TO FIRM (firm in places)
1.00 (2m5f110y sell h'cap hdle): **SLEEPTITE** (J Power, 3-1F) 1; **Lovelark** (33-1) 2; **Bright Sapphire** (9-1) 3; Le Baron (15-2) 4. 16 ran. 4, 1½. (W Turner). Tote: win £3.80; places £1.10, £6.90, £2.40, £2.30. DF: £66.30. CSF: £92.83. TC: £779.85. Trio: £362.10. NR: Viscount Tully.

1.30 (3m h'cap ch): **ACT OF PARLIAMENT** (C O'Dwyer, 9-4) 1; **God Speed You** (8-13F) 2; **Harristown Lady** (10-1) 3. 6 ran. ½, 30. (K Bailey). Tote: win £3.30; places £2.90, £1.00. Dual F'cast: £2.00. CSF: £3.94. Tricast: £6.87. NRs: Imperial Vintage, Rectory Garden
2.00 (2m5f110y nov hdle): **MAID FOR ADVENTURE** (B Fenton, 9-4) 1; **Galatasori Jane** (11-4) 2; **Di's Last** (14-1) 3. 8 ran. Lucia Forte 11-10F. 10, ¾. (Miss H Knight). Tote: win £3.00; places £1.10, £1.10, £2.10. Dual F'cast: £6.20. CSF: £8.94. Trio: £7.50. NRs: Arioso, Sparkling Buck.
2.30 (2m nov ch): **SUPER COIN** (R Johnson, 4-11F) 1; **Eulogy** (10-1) 2; **Arabian Bold** (25-1) 3. 4 ran. 15, ½. (R Lee). Tote: win £1.30. DF: £3.00. CSF: £4.26. NR: Who Is Equiname.
3.00 (2m4f h'cap ch): **TOO SHARP** (J F Titley, 15-8F) 1; **Corrarder** (20-1) 2; **Spinning Steel** (10-1) 3. 6 ran. 1¾, 20. (Miss H Knight). Tote: win £2.70; places £1.20, £8.00. Dual F'cast: £14.10. CSF: £26.75. Tricast: £262.27. NRs: Blazer Morinière, Three Philosophers.
3.30 (2m nov hdle): **ULTIMATE SMOOTHIE** (A P McCoy, 5-4JF) 1; **Joshua's Vision** (6-1) 2; **Manvulane** (16-1) 3. 9 ran. Sounds Like Fun 1½, 2. (M Pipe). Tote: win £2.70; places £1.10, £1.20, £2.50. Dual F'cast: £7.10. CSF: £9.40. Trio: £13.50. NRs: Barton Scamp, Crimson King, Dark Orchard, Relaxed Lad, Shropshire Gale, Stormyfairweather. JACKPOT: £1,162.00. QUADPOT: £15.70. PLACEPOT: £38.90.
● KELSO.— Abandoned — frost.

Even more recently, on 19 February I read in my *Daily Telegraph* that champion jump jockey Tony McCoy, "having been sidelined for four weeks with a fractured left shoulder and broken collar bone, is making his comeback with two rides for Martin Pipe". I resolved to back these (on a 'retrieval' basis on the second horse, if necessary) to win £50. Such potentially quite costly staking should never involve a run of more than two selections (as, on this occasion with Theme Arena and Rare Spread in the first two races at Folkestone). My wager on the latter was a rare spread bet for me which was made necessary as the former, despite being made 3-1 favourite, ran unplaced. However, in winning the second race by 16 lengths as the 9-4 favourite, Rare Spread enabled McCoy to extend his lead as the season's champion jockey and brought me the profit I sought. Incidentally, the very same copy of *The Telegraph* that had alerted me to Tony McCoy's impending return to action, also contained the comment that "Dale Gibson is yet another jockey returning from injury and he is legged up for the first time for five months when he partners Puzzlement at Wolverhampton".

FROM *THE DAILY TELEGRAPH*

WOLVERHAMPTON

Going: STANDARD

2.00 (7f): MYSTERIUM (T G McLaughlin, 25-1) 1; **Sharpo Wassl** (8-13F) 2; **Qualitair Silver** (14-1) 3. 11 ran. nk, 2½. (N Littmoden). Tote: win £33.70; places £4.30, £1.50, £6.60. Dual F'cast: £37.20. CSF: £38.25. Trio: £140.20.

2.30 (7f): DUKE VALENTINO (D Griffiths, 10-11F) 1; **Jigsaw Boy** (9-2) 2; **Bogart** (14-1) 3. 8 ran. 3¼, 2½. (R Hollinshead). Tote: win £2.30; places £1.10, £2.10, £3.10. Dual F'cast: £6.70. CSF: £6.23.

3.00 (1m1f79y h'cap): PUZZLEMENT (Dale Gibson, 7-2) 1; **Globetrotter** (9-2) 2; **Pinchincha** (100-30) 3. 7 ran. Mardrew 3F. 2½, 3. (C Brittain). Tote: win £3.80; places £2.00, £2.20. Dual F'cast: £5.80. CSF: £20.31.

3.30 (1m4f h'cap): LEADING SPIRIT (D Holland, 13-8F) 1; **Nikita's Star** (4-1) 2; **Second Colours** (8-1) 3. 9 ran. 6, nk. (C Wall). Tote: win £2.90; places £1.10, £1.40, £3.40. DF: £7.90. CSF: £8.44. Tricast: £41.11. Trio: £29.30.

On finding Gibson's comeback mount in the third race was the forecast favourite, I needed no further encouragement and felt the puzzle of this seven runner contest had been solved. In the event I was delighted with the far better than forecast odds at which my selection prevailed.

Amazingly, only a week later, on 26 February I read in my *Telegraph* that, on what seemed something of an 'acclimatisation' ride on an unfancied outsider in a National Hunt, rather than a proper jump, race, jockey Lorcan Wyer (previously out of action since, in November 1996, sustaining serious facial injuries) had been run into by another horse at the start at Market Rasen! Sowhen, shortly afterwards, I also read in my paper that he was again back on the racecourse, but this time in a proper jump race and on a much better fancied prospect than at Market Rasen, I reasoned that this plucky jockey would do his utmost to prevent any more of the slings and arrows of outrageous fortune from again wounding him. Thus I had a sporting bet on Lorcan's mount, Cumbrian Maestro, in the opener at Catterick and was thrilled when this won for him by eight lengths at 6-1 for his 'home' stable of T Easterby.

FROM *THE DAILY TELEGRAPH*

Lorcan Wyer rode his first winner since returning from horrific injuries, which he sustained in a fall over hurdles at Aintree in November. He had to have his face rebuilt after sustaining multiple facial injuries, breaking his pelvis and collar-bone.

Then, on his return last week, he very nearly fractured his leg when run into at the start of a bumper. Yesterday, he brought Cumbrian Maestro home eight lengths clear in the Middleham Novice Hurdle at Catterick.

STRATEGY 25

JOCKEYS VYING FOR CHAMPIONSHIPS

As many a racing season enters its closing stages, the leading contenders for the jockeys' championship find themselves locked in a ding-dong battle for eventual supremacy.

In the 1997 flat racing season the struggle between the two leading contenders for championship riding honours was, however, fiercely fought out, not in November, but much earlier in the autumn.

During the second week of September, in fact, I was able to put the 'jockeys vying for championship honours' strategy into operation because leading jockeys, Frankie Dettori and Keiron Fallon had notched respective seasonal tallies of winners that had brought them very close to each other and hence suggested that each would do his utmost to try to edge ahead in the championship table.

In fact, Strategy 25 can only operated if this table's two leaders are shown as within five or fewer winners of each other. Such a situation certainly applied on 9 September since Dettori's tally of winners then stood at 130 to Fallon's 132.

As with many another winner-finding strategy presented in this book, I only support a qualifying horse if it is also the choice of the form expert in my daily newspaper.

On 9 September I determined to row in with only those mounts of arch rivals Dettori and Fallon that were also clear form choices.

This tried and tested ploy led me to the Dettori-ridden Sacho in the 3.45 at Leicester and to no less than five of Fallon's mounts at Lingfield - Jibe in the 2.30, Soft Touch in the 3.00, Wildcat in the 3.30, Darnaway in the 4.30 and Awesome Wells in the 5.30.

3.45 LEICESTERSHIRE MAIDEN STAKES (D) 1m 1f 218yds £4,283 (19)

401	4-0	**MUHASSIL (IRE) (162)** (R Walpole) K Morgan 4 9 7	**O Pears**	13
402	2/2-	**SACHO (IRE) (511) (BF)** (Sheikh Mohammed) J Gosden 4 9 7	**L Dettori**	3
403		**WATERWAVE (USA)** (Sheikh Mohammed) J Gosden 4 9 7	**M Hills**	2
404	0	**LADY OF GLENDOWAN (15)** (M Mitchell) Mrs B Waring 4 9 2	**E Byrne**	6
405	00-	**THATCHAM ISLAND (320)** (Berkshire Commercial Components Ltd) D Williams 4 9 2	**D Griffiths (3)**	18
406	5	**DUKHAN (USA) (104)** (Hamdan Al Maktoum) R Armstrong 3 9 0	**K Darley**	5
407	0	**KAYESAM (19)** (Mrs M Marston) J L Harris 3 9 0	**A Culhane**	14
408	3	**LONDON LIGHTS (162) (BF)** (Fahd Salman) P Cole 3 9 0	**T Quinn**	19
409	0	**QUIET VENTURE (10)** (Maktoum Al Maktoum) E Dunlop 3 9 0	**D O'Donohoe (3)**	17
410	0522	**TONIGHT'S PRIZE (IRE) (29)** (Shunya Seki) C Wall 3 9 0	**S Sanders**	8
411	0-	**TRIENTA MIL (313)** (Mrs J Robinson) P Dalton 3 9 0	**L Charnock**	11
412	02-	**TYROLEAN DREAM (IRE) (304)** (P Heath) M Tompkins 3 9 0	**M Henry (3)**	16
413	05	**BACK ROW (39)** (Lord Hartington) L Cumani 3 8 9	**Pat Eddery**	15
414	0-0	**BEGUINE (USA) (39)** (Lord Howard De Walden) W Jarvis 3 8 9	**J Reid**	1
415		**CHOICE LADY** (The Freddy Partnership) J L Harris 3 8 9	**Dean McKeown**	7
416	6	**FUWALA (10)** (A Wragg) D Shaw 3 8 9	**J Fanning**	4
417	030	**MINSTER STAR (41)** (R Rainbow) J Spearing 3 8 9	**J Fortune**	9
418	6	**PRILUKI (17)** (C Brittain) C Brittain 3 8 9	**M Roberts**	10
419	03	**SERPENTARA (27)** (Lady Howard de Walden) H Cecil 3 8 9	**W Ryan**	12

S.P. FORECAST: 5-2 Sacho, 5-1 London Lights, 6-1 Tonight's Prize, 7-1 Waterwave, Tyrolean Dream, 8-1 Back Row, Serpentara, 10-1 Dukhan, 12-1 others.

1996: Polar Champ 3 9 0 L Dettori 4-5F S Woods 8 ran

FORM

2.15—Oberon's Mistral
2.45—KITE (nap)
3.15—Bollin Dorothy
3.45—Sacho
4.15—Taverner Society
4.45—Brave Edge
5.15—Bear Hug
5.45—Canadian Puzzler

YESTERDAY'S RACING RESULTS

LEICESTER

Going: GOOD TO FIRM

2.15 (1m8y): **BRISTOL CHANNEL** (L Dettori, 6-1) 1; **Rambling Rose** (3-1) 2; **Oberon's Mistral** (5-1) 3. 10 ran. Bluewain Lady 7-4F. ⅓, 2⅓. (B Hills). Tote: win £7.30; places £1.50, £2.00, £2.30. Dual F'cast: £16.10. CSF: £22.27. Trio: £16.40.

2.45 (1m8y sell h'cap): **FRANCESCA'S FOLLY** (M Henry, 14-1) 1; **Constant Attention** (12-1) 2; **Arm And A Leg** (7-2F) 3. 15 ran. 2½, 2. (J Hills). Tote: win £15.80; places £4.30, £4.60, £1.80. Dual F'cast: £90.10. CSF: £161.83. Tricast: £685.31. Trio: £210.10.

3.15 (7f9y h'cap): **SAMARA SONG** (M Roberts, 7-1) 1; **Topton** (9-1) 2; **Alfahaal** (6-1F) 3; **Allinson's Mate** (16-1) 4. 20 ran. ½, 1. (I Williams). Tote: win £8.30; places £1.40, £2.00, £2.30, £4.30. Dual F'cast: £27.50. CSF: £69.12. Tricast: £391.25. Trio: £86.60.

3.45 (1m1f218y): **SACHO** (L Dettori, 3-1JF) 1; **Tonight's Prize** (3-1JF) 2; **Serpentara** (13-2) 3. 19 ran. 1¼, 2½. (J Gosden). Tote: win £3.90; places £1.30, £1.10, £2.50. Dual F'cast: £10.60. CSF: £10.69. Trio: £19.10.

4.15 (7f9y): **MUDEER** (L Dettori, 11-4) 1; **Close Up** (10-1) 2; **Last Christmas** (16-1) 3. 18 ran. Taverner Society 5-2F. 1¼, 1½. (Saeed bin Suroor). Tote: win £3.50; places £1.50, £4.80, £9.70. Dual F'cast: £59.90. CSF: £38.90. Trio: £115.20. NRs: Anemos, Be My Chance.

4.45 (5f2y): **BLUE IRIS** (M Roberts, 7-1) 1; **Crofters Ceilidh** (12-1) 2; **Rambling Bear** (9-4F) 3. 8 ran. ¾, 1¼. (M Jarvis). Tote: £6.30; pl £2.90, £2.00, £1.30. DF: £40.60. CSF: £71.68.

5.15 (1m1f218y h'cap): **EDAN HEIGHTS** (P Doe, 10-1) 1; **Cherokee Flight** (7-1) 2; **Secret Ballot** (14-1) 3; **Zamalek** (5-1F) 4. 18 ran. nk, 1¾. (S Dow). Tote: win £14.70; places £4.00, £3.30, £6.10, £1.80. Dual F'cast: £81.30. CSF: £84.64. Tricast: £959.15. Trio: £340.00. NR: Kissel.

5.45 (7f9y): **SENSORY** (Paul Eddery, 7-1) 1; **Shart** (11-8F) 2; **Fly By Night** (12-1) 3. 19 ran. ¾, 3. (B Hills). Tote: win £9.90; places £2.10, £1.70, £5.10. Dual F'cast: £11.60. CSF: £17.95. Trio: £111.50. NR: Mutafarij.

JACKPOT: Not won. Pool of £50,746.81 carried forward to Doncaster today.

QUADPOT: £14.50. PLACEPOT: £65.00.

LINGFIELD PARK

Going: turf, GOOD; a-w, STANDARD

2.00 (6f): **BAHAMIAN MELODY** (K Fallon, 5-2) 1; **Tightrope** (9-4F) 2; **Leofric** (20-1) 3. 12 ran. 1¼, 1¼. (D Loder). Tote: win £4.70; places £1.80, £2.10, £3.00. Dual F'cast: £5.20. CSF: £8.24. Trio: £76.00.

2.30 (7f): **JIBE** (K Fallon, 4-9F) 1; **Winsa** (4-1) 2; **Frond** (20-1) 3. 15 ran. 4, nk. (H Cecil). Tote: win £1.50; places £1.10, £1.10, £4.30. Dual forecast: £2.20. CSF: £2.60. Trio: £8.70. NRs: Alborada, Migrate.

3.00 (7f): **VOCATION** (Dane O'Neill, 33-1) 1; **Honey Storm** (10-1) 2; **Pride of Place** (4-1) 3. 16 ran. Muhaba 2F. nk, sh hd. (P Webber). Tote: win £44.40; places £7.90, £3.10, £2.40. Dual F'cast: £1,125.00. CSF: £318.15. Trio: £347.00. NR: Precision Finish.

3.30 (7f140y h'cap): **HOLY WINE** (R Cochrane, 4-1F) 1; **Simlet** (6-1) 2; **Short Romance** (20-1) 3; **Cosmic Countess** (11-2) 4. 17 ran. 3, 1. (D Loder). Tote: win £5.60; places £2.20, £2.00, £4.00, £1.50. Dual F'cast: £33.40. CSF: £25.19. Tricast: £441.61. Trio: £425.90. NR: Mystagogue.

4.00 (1m2f sell h'cap, a-w): **HARLEQUIN WALK** (J Quinn, 11-4JF) 1; **Magazine Gap** (20-1) 2; **Don't Drop Bombs** (8-1) 3. 14 ran. Father Dan 11-4JF. sh hd, 1½. (R O'Sullivan). Tote: £4.30; pl £2.00, £10.10, £2.70. DF: £110.80. CSF: £72.74. Tricast: £396.06. Trio: £344.60.

4.30 (7f): **DARNAWAY** (K Fallon, 4-6F) 1; **Floating Charge** (9-1) 2; **Blushing Desert** (25-1) 3. 15 ran. 6, 2½. (H Cecil). Tote: win £1.80; places £1.20, £2.60, £10.30. Dual F'cast: £11.10. CSF: £7.88. Trio: £284.30.

5.00 (7f h'cap): **SAFEY ANA** (K Fallon, 6-1) 1; **Delta Soleil** (7-1) 2; **Victory Team** (10-1) 3; **Pleading** (20-1) 4. 18 ran. Polish Romance 7-2F. 2, 1½. (B Hanbury). Tote: win £8.10; places £2.30, £2.00, £5.40, £8.40. Dual F'cast: £30.60. CSF: £47.68. Tricast: £412.97. Trio: £124.60.

5.30 (1m3f106y): **AWESOME WELLS** (K Fallon, Evens-F) 1; **Teme Valley** (5-1) 2; **Snow Partridge** (2-1) 3. 10 ran. 3½, 14. (H Cecil). Tote: win £2.30; pl £1.10, £2.10, £1.10. DF: £6.10. CSF: £6.33. Trio: £1.80. NR: Jester Minute.

QUADPOT: £35.60. PLACEPOT: £185.10.

LINGFIELD PARK

FORM
2.00—Poetto
2.30—Jibe
3.00—Soft Touch
3.30—Wildcat
4.00—Harlequin Walk
4.30—Darnaway
5.00—Northern Angel
5.30—Awesome Wells

I backed each of these six Strategy 25 qualifiers as win singles and was pleased to see Sacho win for Dettori at 3-1, while at more southerly Lingfield, Fallon had earlier won on Jibe at 4-9, before later scoring on Darnaway at 4-6 and Awesome Wells at evens!

As my *Daily Telegraph* duly reminded me the next morning, this brought Dettori's seasonal score to 133 and Fallon's to 137, thus allowing the 'contending jockeys' strategy to continue.

On 10 September I decided to again support any Dettori or Fallon partnered runner that was also the selection of the *Telegraph's* form expert. This led me to side with Fallon's mount, Bollin Joanne in the 2.35 at Doncaster and the Dettori-partnered Saafeya in the 4.40. Again I had a winning day and was left well satisfied, as Bollin Joanne first scored at 5-2 to provide me with some insulation against my later losing wager at 100-30 on the hard-ridden Saafeya who went down by only a neck!

Eventually, by 12 September, I found I was unable to find any strategy qualifiers as, by then, Keiron Fallon had extended his lead to seven over the soon-to-be suspended and, eventually decisively beaten, Frankie Dettori. As it happened, my last three wagers, according to the five or fewer separating winners rule of the 'contending jockeys' strategy, had been made a day earlier on 11 September, when I had supported the Dettori-ridden form horse, Monsajem in the 2.5 at Doncaster, and the Fallon-partnered Poteen in the 2.35.

Both proved most disappointing favourites but Fallon's success at

3-1 on a third qualifier, Midnight Line (also, most encouragingly, a Strategy 1 qualifier and thus entitled to 'daily nap' status) allowed me to break even on my day's wagering.

Fallon, incidentally, also scored on this same Doncaster raceday on 6-1 shot Canon Can and so lengthened his lead over his only rival for the season's riding honours.

PART THREE

SIDING WITH OWNERS

STRATEGY 26

OWNERS AND RACE MEETINGS

So high are the levels of taxation in Britain that many extremely rich owners of racehorses become tax exiles in financial havens. For a British national this ploy for avoiding high tax bills can, however, seriously curtail your lifestyle, through the restrictions placed on the number of days a year on which one can reside in this country.

Thus it seems something approaching an 'odds on' prospect that when a prominent racehorse-owning tax exile such as Robert Sangster does come back to his homeland (from, in his case, tax havens abroad) he will not wish to waste the rather limited time he has to avail himself of opportunities to win races.

Sangster is one of a mere handful of modern-day owners of racehorses who can mount a realistic challenge to mega-rich Middle-Eastern (mainly Arab) owners who, in recent seasons, have carried so much before them on the British turf.

Indeed, his resources, as perhaps befits a former owner of Vernon Pools, are so vast and his past record in major races so impressive that his runners in these should always command respect.

Many of the horses that run in the distinctive Sangster colours of blue and green are aimed at very valuable races that are staged at the season's most socially glamorous and prestigious race meetings and this is why, when I notice that he has a runner at one of these, I take particular notice and scrutinise its claims very thoroughly.

Naturally even Robert Sangster, like any other major owner, finds it difficult to register multiple wins, or gain just one, at really competitive race meetings like Royal Ascot, Goodwood or York. However, at still fashionable, but slightly less competitive, meetings like Ayr's four-day late September Festival, it is more easily achieved.

FROM *THE DAILY TELEGRAPH*

2.00: KEITH ASPLAND MEMORIAL STAKES 3YO 1m £3,047

1	0-10	BERLIN WALL (IRE) (25) (D) (BF) (R Sangster) P Chapple-Hyam 9 1......	Paul Eddery	2
2	01226	COOLEY'S VALVE (IRE) (31) (D) (Wafic Said) B Hills 9 1	D Holland	1
3	20-	ANGELO'S DOUBLE (IRE) (386) (J Mamakos) J Gosden 8 11	G Carter	3
4	6-	MARLEE LOCH (430) (Mrs M Stewart) G Moore 8 6	K Fallon	4

4 declared

S.P. FORECAST: 8-15 Cooley's Valve, 7-2 Berlin Wall, 6-1 Angelo's Double, 20-1 Marlee Loch.

1990: Arany 9 1 R Hills 9-2 M Tompkins 7 ran.

DICK PEACOCK SALVER GRADUATION STAKES 2YO 6f £4,077

	01	DARLING MISS DAISY (11) (J Lambton) G Pritchard-Gordon 8 13..............	W Hood	4
	331	PARFAIT AMOUR (10) (D) (Mrs G Wilkinson) R Whitaker 8 13................	A Culhane	6
		DENIM BLUE (G Reed) C Thornton 8 11................	B Raymond	14
		EL CORTES (USA) (R Sangster) P Chapple-Hyam 8 11	Paul Eddery	10
		HOB GREEN (Mrs A Sigsworth) Mrs J Ramsden 8 11	Dean McKeown	2
	5	ISAIAH (21) (Miss C Spurrier) M Johnston 8 11................	J Carroll	7
		LITHO BOLD FLASHER (Litho 2000 (Graphics) Ltd) W Pearce 8 11	L Charnock	8
		ODEON (USA) (K Higson) Denys Smith 8 11................	K Fallon	15
	2	PHILIDOR (38) (J Smith) J Eustace 8 11................	J Reid	1
	0	PREMIER MAJOR (IRE) (42) (Premier Properties Plc) W Pearce 8 11	D Nicholls	9
	0	TOUCH PAPER (USA) (14) (Sheikh Mohammed) B Hills 8 11	D Holland	12
		BREEZE AWAY (G Pemberton) R Whitaker 8 6	J Fortune	11
		FERROVIA (Lord Derby) J W Watts 8 6................	W R Swinburn	5
	2	OREO COOKIE (IRE) (34) (E Madden) G Richards 8 6	J Lowe	13
		PORTITE JANE (J Barry) M Brittain 8 6................	S Maloney (5)	3

15 declared

S.P. FORECAST: 3-1 Parfait Amour, 4-1 Darling Miss Daisy, 5-1 El Cortes, 8-1 Philidor, 10-1 Ferrovia, 2-1 Oreo Cookie, Odeon, Touch Paper, 14-1 others.

4.10: LADBROKE AID NURSERY HANDICAP 2YO 6f £7,960

1	215	COCHABAMBA (IRE) (41) (C) (R Sangster) P Chapple-Hyam 9 7	J Reid	4
2	441123	HEATHER BANK (27) (CD) (BF) (Mrs G Harper) J Barry 9 6	J Carroll † 10
3	02531	MILAGRO (27) (D) (Mrs D Hammerson) R Hannon 9 5................	R Perham (5)	7
4	011	BY HAND (20) (D) (Mrs M Heggas) W Haggas 9 2	J Weaver (7)	8
5	4221	VIVID CONCERT (IRE) (41) (H Steckmest) W Jarvis 8 11	M Tebbutt	1
6	341	LADY SABO (70) (Cronk Thoroughbred Racing Ltd) G Lewis 8 9........	Paul Eddery	5
7	311230	MELTONBY (60) (D) (J Hetherton) J Hetherton 8 5................	J Lowe	2
8	0150	NIL NISI NIXU (USA) (25) (Rt Aird) J Barry 8 4................	G Carter †	6
9	05060	LIFT BOY (USA) (74) (J Bianchi) Denys Smith 7 11	L Charnock	9
10	223640	PHIL-MAN (11) (Mrs M Morley) T Fairhurst 7 8	J Fenning (3)	3

10 declared

S.P. FORECAST: 3-1 By Hand, 9-2 Milagro, 5-1 Vivid Concert, 8-1 Heather Bank, Cochabamba, 10-1 Lady Sabo, 12-1 Nil Nisi Nixu, 14-1 others.

1990: Swingaway Lady 8 4 M Roberts 8-1 G Richards 13 ran

```
                    AYR
                Going: GOOD
     2.00 (1m): BERLIN WALL (Paul Eddery,
  11-2) 1; Cooley's Valve (4-11F) 2;
  Angelo's Double (6-1) 3. 4 ran. ¼, 6. (P
  Chapple-Hyam). Tote: win £4.20. Dual F'cast:
  £1.70. CSF: £7.51.
     2.35          (1m2f192y       h'cap):
  FRESCOBALDO (C Munday, 9-1) 1;
  Young George (12-1) 2; Canny Chronicle
  (11-1) 3. 11 ran. Vague Dancer 7-2F, ¼, 2. (M
  Naughton). Tote: win £8.10; places £3.00,
  £4.50, £3.80. Dual F'cast: £58.90. CSF:
  £91.29. Tricast: £978.04.
     3.10 (6f): EL CORTES (Paul Eddery, 4-1)
  1; Isaiah (11-1) 2; Darling Miss Daisy
  (10-1) 3. 14 ran. Touch Paper 15-8F. 2, hd.
  (P Chapple-Hyam). Tote: win £4.60; places
  £2.10, £3.40, £3.00. Dual F'cast: £60.30.
  CSF: £43.73. NR: Portito Jane.
     3.40 (Ladbrokes Ayr Gold Cup H'cap. 6f):
  SARCITA (B Doyle, 14-1) 1; Tbab (14-1) 2;
  Dominuet (40-1) 3; Gilt Throne (33-1) 4.
  28 ran. Bold Habit 6F. 3½, sh hd, nk. (D
  Elsworth). Tote: win £12.70; places £3.40,
  £3.50, £16.60, £14.40. Dual F'cast: £86.40.
  CSF: £168.00. Tricast: £6,685.93. Trio (Any
  two of the first three with any other): £19.30.
  NR: Paddy Chalk.
     4.10 (6f): COCHABAMBA (J Reid, 8-1)
  1; Vivid Concert (5-1) 2; Nil Nisi Nixu
  (20-1) 3. 10 ran. By Hand 3F. 1, nk. (P
  Chapple-Hyam). Tote: win £8.70; places
  £2.70, £1.80, £4.50. Dual F'cast: £38.60.
  CSF: £42.25. Tricast: £689.38.
     4.40 (7f): SUMONDA (W R Swinburn,
  11-4) 1; Katy Ann Bee (Evens-F) 2;
  Miranda Jay (11-4) 3. 4 ran. 1, 4. (G
  Wragg). Tote: win £3.20. Dual F'cast: £2.20.
  CSF: £5.72.
     5.10 (6f h'cap): STACK ROCK (K Fallon,
  17-2) 1; Darakah (11-2) 2; Forever
  Diamonds (12-1) 3; Dorking Lad (14-1) 4.
  18 ran. Catherines Well 5F. 1, ¼. (E Alston).
  Tote: win £9.60; places £2.60, £2.00, £1.80,
  £3.30. Dual F'cast: £31.70. CSF: £50.59.
  Tricast: £522.54. NRs: Sally Fay & Denaben.
     PLACEPOT: £6,122.
```

Interestingly, I always monitor the prospects and fates of the Sangster runners when this meeting is held and, when it was recently staged, having noted the early success there of Soiree, I reasoned that if even more runners went to post at Ayr sporting blue and green, their owner might put in an appearance at this pleasant seaside track.

Robert Sangster, in fact, had three runners on the final day of this particular meeting - sent to race there by his youngest trainer and his son-in-law, Peter Chapple-Hyam - all the way from Wiltshire. I felt that if I could spot this young man's major patron and chief employer in the paddock, this might be a most propitious pointer.

To my delight, my 'detective work' on a man on legitimate holiday as a tax exile paid rather a handsome dividend as his three runners on the third day of the Western meeting, Berlin Wall, El Cortes and Cochabamba - in winning at 11-2, 4-1 and 8-1 (the last mentioned after surviving a nail-biting stewards' enquiry) completed a 291-1 treble. As *The Daily Telegraph's* John Oaksey later remarked: "Ayr's final day was mostly Robert Sangster's who enjoyed every moment of his winning treble and magical day at the races".

As it happened, while this was being crowned by Cochabamba, Sangster let slip to some pressmen that he would be back in Britain to attend the early October meeting at Newmarket.

I noted this and made sure I attended this important professionals' meeting at which I weighed in heavily on Rodrigo De Triano - Sangster's even money hope for the group one Middle Park Stakes which he won in fluent style.

Even more recently, in 1996, at Chester's prestigious May meeting (which is a particular favourite since it is close to his own former stamping ground and the Tarporley base of his former trainer, the late Eric Cousins) Robert Sangster again demonstrated the wisdom of supporting his horses at fashionable race meetings. Indeed, in the mere three early Spring days the 1996 Chester fixture encompassed, horses owned by him won four races at 3-1, 11-4, 6-1 and 9-1!

Given Robert Sangster's by now self-evident fondness for success at Chester's Spring Meeting, I was particularly keen to assess the prospects of his runners there in 1997. Knowing of his owner's liking also for a tilt at the ring, I took a definite hint when, on the opening day of the three day meeting, Panama City was made the 6-5 favourite for the big race, the age-old Chester Vase.

As Richard Evans, racing correspondent of *The Times* later reported: 'given the slow early pace, the stamina-endowed Panama City did particularly well to prevail in the sprint to the line and justify favouritism'.

On Chester Cup day, the second of the 1997 meeting, knowing that, through being born just down the road from the Roodeye, Robert Sangster is passionate about the city and its tight oval racecourse, I reasoned that, as the Chester Cup is the track's best-known race and always attracts heavy betting interest, Top Cees, running in his multi-millionaire owner's famous blue and green colours, would be likely, not only to stay every yard of the marathon trip he had to run over, but also to be trained to the minute to land a gamble by Mrs Linda Ramsden.

In the event, I was reassured when Top Cees at a most acceptable 11-2, ran out a 10 length winner to delight and enrich Chester's most ardent race fan.

On the following final day of the Chester meeting, when I read the headline: 'Sangster aims to scoop Treble Chance' in my *Times,* I really sat up and took notice, and became quite excited to read under it the report of Richard Evans that, in relation to his next big race Chester runner - the well-fancied Royal Court in the meeting's final feature race, the Ormonde Stakes - Sangster had emphatically declared: "We will win!"

I resolved to take a major interest in this lightly-raced four-year-old and was thrilled to see him prevail, as befitted his significant status as a Sangster owned favourite (at 9-4). Thus it was that Robert Sangster's dream of capturing the feature race on each and every day of the Chester three day festival came true in almost fairytale fashion!

FROM *THE DAILY TELEGRAPH*

THE TIMES THURSDAY MAY 8 1997

RACING: OWNER BANKS ON ANOTHER ROODEYE DIVIDEND WITH ROYAL COURT IN ORMONDE STAKES

Sangster aims to scoop treble chance

ROBERT SANGSTER'S life-long love affair with Chester could reach historic proportions today as he attempts to complete a clean sweep of the main prizes at the three-day meeting.

The runaway success of Top Cees in the Tote Chester Cup, which came 24 hours after Panama City had carried the Sangster silks to success in the Chester Vase, tees up the possibility of a unique treble with the well fancied Royal Court lining up for today's feature race, the Ormonde Stakes.

Born just down the road from the Roodeye, Sangster is passionate about the city and its tight oval racecourse and he is confident about rewriting the record books. "We will win," he said after Top Cees became the first horse since Sea Pigeon to win the Chester Cup a second time.

Robert Sangster is not the only prominent owner who is fond of capturing prestigious races at certain socially fashionable race meetings. Indeed, this feat has often also been accomplished by Jeff Smith.

This wealthy enthusiast, like Robert Sangster, covets victory at meetings like Goodwood. In fact, at a recent midsummer meeting there two of his horses, quite remarkably, triumphed as they had done so exactly a year earlier, but in quite different races!

As John Oaksey put it at the time: "Philidor and Lochsong completed a brilliant double in Mr Smith's purple and light blue colours. Last year Philidor won the California Handicap and Lochsong the Stewards' Cup but now it was the Schweppes Golden Mile and the King George Stakes. Such a same horse - same day double-double may have happened before at Goodwood. But if so, I could find no one who claimed to remember the occasion."

What is certain is that Jeff Smith will certainly not forget his achievement from which I was fortunately also able to profit, because I remembered that, precisely 12 months before it, he had landed a major gamble, as well as won two classy races, with these same two horses. Indeed, it turned out that I almost staked as much on Philidor and Lochsong staging a repeat performance in their 1993 races as their owner since, as was later reported in *The Daily Telegraph*, mindful of having been badly stung a year earlier, the bookmakers at Goodwood limited the canny Mr Smith to a £50 double at 8-1 and 2-1 respectively - odds with which I was more than satisfied.

Interestingly, in typically determined style, less than a month after landing his seemingly unprecedented double at Goodwood, Jeff Smith sent Lochsong and Philidor to the season's next big festival meeting at York.

In fact, I can remember getting quite excited when I first noticed that Lochsong was quoted at a generous rate in the betting forecast for the Nunthorpe Stakes, as was Philidor for the Bradford & Bingley Handicap.

In the end, I felt that it might be asking too much of Jeff Smith's two most faithful servants to again land him a double at a major meeting and so decided to back Lochsong and Philidor in single each way wagers, as well as coupling them in a winning double. In the event, I was more than pleased when Lochsong won at 10-1 and Philidor came second at 8-1!

FROM *THE DAILY TELEGRAPH*

Smith makes layers see double again

THE WEATHER did its spoilsport best to pull a wet blanket over Goodwood yesterday — but for owner Jeff Smith and apprentice Neil Armstrong Kennedy, "Glorious" would surely have been an understatement.

For the second year running, the same two horses, Philidor and Lochsong, completed a brilliant double in Mr Smith's puple and light blue colours.

Last year, Philidor won him the Californian Handicap and Lochsong the Stewards' Cup — now it was the Schweppes Golden Mile and the King George Stakes.

Such a same-horse-same-day-double-double *may* have happened before at Goodwood. But if so I could find no one who claimed to remember the occasion.

Jeff Smith, who landed a big gamble on the Philidor-Lochsong double last year, rang one of the Big Three (he wouldn't say which) yesterday morning and was limited to a bet of £50 at 8-1 and 2-1 respectively. "Never mind" he said, "they have both been marvellous to me and perhaps one day we will arrange a marriage..."

The moral of all this is clear - it will often pay the backer to see which prominent owners, not only like to win races at particularly prestigious fixtures but, like Sangster and Smith, also like to 'tilt at the ring'. If one notices from one's newspaper that such an owner managed to win one, or occasionally more than one, race 12 months previously at the corresponding race meeting, any runners there that he or she is about to cheer on should be given careful consideration.

Even more recently, the Queen, as another prominent owner, has felt a particularly strong desire to win at a particular race meeting. This was staged on a veritable royal red letter day - that commemorating the fortieth anniversary of her 1953 Coronation.

Interestingly, the intention way back then was for Captain Boyd-Rochfort, then the royal trainer, to mark this momentous occasion by winning that year's Derby, but the Queen had to settle instead for congratulating Sir Gordon Richards on his first-ever victory in this peerless race.

As it happens on the 'ruby' anniversary of her enthronement, I paid particular attention (as did the royal party happily present at Epsom) to the Queen's only runner on what again was Derby Day. The horse in question was the Lord Huntingdon trained Enharmonic, ridden by the season's champion jockey, Frankie Dettori.

I was very tempted by the 12-1 freely on offer at Epsom and was almost as delighted as the Queen, a very involved Prince Charles and the rest of an enervated royal party, when Enharmonic captured the age old Diomed Stakes by a nail-biting head.

As it turned out, this was the second time in a year that I had capitalised on knowing that the Queen is a particularly ardent supporter of flat racing at famous race meetings.

One of these, of course, is Ascot's royal meeting in June. Indeed, so much does she enjoy this highlight of the social calendar that I always scrutinise any runner there that sports her famous colours of purple, gold braid and scarlet sleeves.

I do this especially keenly with regard to one particular race run at the royal meeting of which I'm fairly sure Her Majesty is rather fond. This is the Royal Hunt Cup - a cavalry charge of a one mile handicap in which, over 40 years ago, in the year before her Coronation, Her Majesty's Choir Boy was almost out of sight at the finish. Then, as he eventually came labouring past the stands there was an outburst of hearty laughter that it was soon realised could only have come from one unimpeachable source! The best part of this story is that Choir Boy won the very next running of the Hunt Cup at 100-6!

As a student of turf history I knew of all this, and since I was also well aware of the skill of the current royal trainer, Lord Huntingdon in getting a 'race rusty' runner into the winner's enclosure, I paid particular attention when, on a recent June Wednesday, I noticed that Colour Sergeant had been 'let into' the Hunt Cup with only 7st 13lb.

Undeterred by the fact that he had not raced for 228 days, I took all of the 20-1 available about this four-year-old before he registered a thrilling win from 30 rivals.

Another variation of the 'Owners for Race meetings' Strategy involves supporting any horse that is owned by the individual or concern that sponsors the race it contests at this meeting. The belief here is that it will be really trying to win its connections their own prize money. Such an outcome certainly came about when Wee River, at Ayr on 11 November 1995, landed the spoils for Irish sponsor (and bookmaker) Sean Graham in the 3.15 Sean Graham 'Barrhead' Chase Handicap.

STRATEGY 27

OWNERS AND INFORMATION

A petrol pump attendant who works close to a racecourse once told me that the racehorse owners who proudly introduce themselves to him all tip him their horses! Indeed, that this should be so is scarcely surprising as racehorse ownership should only be embarked upon by incurable optimists who are prepared to back their runners, if only so as to be able to reward all those connected with them if they just happen to 'oblige'.

However, passing on tips to an individual like a petrol pump attendant whom you are unlikely to see again and to whom you have in no way to subsequently account, is worlds away from making confident claims before millions of television viewers.

In fact, most of those who subject themselves to the potentially critical gaze and alert ears of this very large group of individuals take great pains to be coherent, grammatical and, above all, not to be in anyway embarrassing.

Indeed, as one who during a radio interview once unwittingly tipped a dead horse to win the Grand National, I feel I know all about the perils of speaking to mass audiences!

Mindful then of most interviewees' understandable circumspection and caution when faced with probing questions from programme presenters, I pricked up my ears when, well before a running of Kempton Park's Bic Lady Shaver Handicap Hurdle, during a Channel Four transmission, I heard Chester-based racehorse owner, Brian Oxton, being 'bullish' about the chance of Welshman - the bottom weight for this particular contest.

When I noticed that this owner's confident prediction that his six-year-old would win this two and a half mile affair seemed rather at odds with its rather lacklustre recent form, I felt that some longish odds were likely to be on offer.

Indeed, during his interview, it emerged that a 14-1 quote had led Oxton to make a £100 ante-post each way wager on Welshman and it was this knowledge that led me to take his very positive TV tip and join in the betting action.

In the event the issue was never in doubt as, thanks partly to an inspired ride by Dean Gallagher, Welshman came home clear of the 100-30 favourite, The Widget Man, and so fuelled Brian Oxton's subsequently expressed hopes of 'even greater things over the sticks and on the level in the marathon Chester Cup'.

As I wrote recently in my *Racegoers' Encyclopaedia* (Collins Willow), in responding to tips one has to be 'neither too gullible nor too cynical' but to adopt selective approaches (such as the one described above) which is based on the belief that, on occasion, owners can let slip what is privileged information.

Having had cause to so describe what Oxton had told me about his horse's chances at Kempton, I pencilled in the name 'Welshman' in my diary against the date in May on which the Chester Cup was scheduled to be staged. Amazingly, 167 days after Brian Oxton's prediction, Welshman won the Chester Cup by three lengths at 11-1!

Tough Welshman triumphs in Cup

By John Oaksey

THE LADBROKE Chester Cup was Welshman's 20th race in the last 12 months and, rain or shine, Flat or jumping, he has not run a single bad one. Yesterday's victory, won the hard way, was well-deserved.

Fortunately, now that the *Racing Post* includes the post-race comments of the connections of both winning and losing horses (in its Race Analysis feature that forms part of its unrivalled reporting of the preceding day's races), it has become far easier for the stay-at-home enthusiast to become privy to some potentially lucrative information that comes straight from the mouth of an individual so close to a racehorse as to be really 'in the know' as regards its future prospect.

STRATEGY 28

OWNERS FIELDING MANY RUNNERS

One strangely neglected aspect of horse racing which has hardly been mined as a potentially valuable source of profitable wagering is racehorse ownership. In view of this, I recently acquired the latest annual edition of Superform's excellent 1,296 page *Racehorses A to Z, Flat Racing*, since this is the only reasonably-priced regular publication I know of that gives the owners of all performers that have very recently been in action. Moreover, my close scrutiny of racing results over many seasons has often suggested that when owners who are not immensely wealthy ones from the Middle East send many representatives to a race meeting, or sometimes to more than one, particularly during the National Hunt season, then they often thereby signal that they are quite likely to land a rich haul of several winners.

Obviously, if an owner is far from mega rich they are not going to incur the heavy expenses of getting their trainer(s) to despatch many horses to the races, if there is not the belief that several have live chances of doing more than paying their fares.

Those who have studied the earlier strategy in this book on trainers who often land doubles and trebles may recall my point that they sometimes try to do so for their biggest patron, or even attempt to combine with one or more other racehorse handlers who are also employed by this 'major player' of an owner, so as to bring about a really red letter day at the races. R Ogden is just such an owner, for whom jump trainers Andy Turnell and Gordon Richards have combined to produce this very outcome. This, in fact, happened on 20 October 1995 at Newbury where Ogden's newly-signed jockey, Paul Carberry, partnered the Richards-trained Buckboard Bounce and General Command to respective victories at 4-1 and 6-4, before, in the penultimate race, he booted home the Turnell-trained Squire Silk at 11-2!

Carberry soon strikes

Yesterday at Newbury he demonstrated why Robert Ogden — who is in the process of expanding his jumping interests and has horses with Gordon Richards, Andy Turnell and Ferdy Murphy, has signed him up on a three-year contract — when he completed a treble with the owner's Buckboard Bounce, General Command and Squire Silk.

It is my daily habit to see if a trainer has sent many horses that are in the same (non Middle-Eastern) ownership in the consignment(s) of stable runners sent to one racecourse, or more than one, on any single racing day. For example, during the 1995/96 jumping season, my scrutiny of the names of the runners at a Newton Abbot meeting alerted me to the fact that, of the seven runners sent to race there by top trainer Martin Pipe, two were owned by D Johnson and, of these two, one, Seasonal Splendour, was the selection of the form expert of the *Daily Telegraph* and was also quoted in the first three in the betting forecast for its 12.45 race. Pipe's other runner for D Johnson, his most heavily represented patron at the meeting - Prerogative - seemed the stable's second string in the final race, as its stablemate, Sohrab, had a lower price in the betting forecast and so I resolved to make Seasonable Splendour my selection.

Interestingly, at this very same West Country meeting, I noticed that another trainer, Paul Nicholls (see Strategy 4) who often achieves more than one race win on one racing day for P Barber (who is a particularly prominent patron of his Shepton Mallet stable) had sent two horses to race that were due to carry this owner's green and white colours, and that thus this pair - Ottawa in the 2.45 and Bramblehill Buck in the 3.15 - made Barber the most strongly-represented of the six different Nicholls owners who were all trying to enter the winners' enclosure!

Using the same differentiation procedure as before to choose between these two runners, I went for Bramblehill Buck as both the forecast favourite and *Daily Telegraph* form selection and, again, the Gods were kind enough to agree with this reasoning, as this chaser (and not the disappointing Ottawa) won at 2-1!

NEWTON ABBOT JACKPOT CARD AND FORM

TONY STAFFORD

12.45 – Seasonal Splendour
12.45 – Seasonal Splendour (nb)
1.45 – Ferrufino
2.15 – Zajira (nb)
2.45 – NORTHERN SADDLER (nap)
2.45 – MONTAGNARD (nap)
3.15 – Bramblehill Buck
3.45 – Arctic Kinsman

COURSE CORRESPONDENT

1.15 – Court Melody
1.45 – DRESS DANCE (nap)

2.45 – Time For A Flutter
3.15 – Smiling Chief

Advance official going: SOFT (heavy in places)

12.45 PRE-CHRISTMAS MAIDEN HURDLE 2m 1f
£2.906 (16 declared)

1.15 LES SEWARD MEMORIAL TROPHY NOVICE CHASE
3m 2f 110yds £3.599 (13)

1.45 HORSERACE BETTING LEVY BOARD HANDICAP HURDLE 2m 1f £2.211 (7)

2.15 BEST IN THE WEST HANDICAP CHASE 2m 110yds £4,395 (5)

2.45 BULPIN CHALLENGE CUP (HANDICAP) HURDLE FOR AMATEUR RIDERS) 2m 6f £2,358 (15)

3.15 TOM HOLT AND REALITY HANDICAP CHASE 2m 5f 110yds £2,873 (10)

3.45 WILLIAM HILL 'GOLDEN OLDIES' STAKES (INVITATION RACE) RND 3 2m 1f £1,516 (9)

BLINKERS FIRST TIME

139

STRATEGY 29

OWNERS AND RACETRACKS

The entrepreneurial skills that so enrich some businessmen that they can afford to own racehorses are sometimes applied to the direct benefit of horse racing. Thus grandstands have been built by building magnates who have further supported their favourite sport by sponsoring races.

In very recent times, one such business benefactor of the turf has been Stan Clarke, the Chairman of Uttoxeter racecourse, whose imaginative development and promotion of this leisure amenity has placed it much more firmly on the racing map.

Stan, of course, achieved international notice when his Lord Gyllene won the Monday re-staging of the 1997 Grand National, after a terrorist bomb scare prevented the race from going ahead, as originally scheduled, on the previous Saturday. When Lord Gyllene ran out a ready winner at Aintree in the spring of 1997, this brought back vivid memories of how handsomely this fine stamp of a staying chaser had repaid me for supporting him on another racetrack.

This, appropriately enough, had been Uttoxeter where, knowing that the National was this chaser's long-term objective, I took particular notice when I saw that, as the representative of the course Chairman, he was due to line up in a full-blown four-and-a-quarter mile Aintree rehearsal.

Fifteen days earlier - and for the self-same two good reasons, that he was propitiously owned and the form selection in my newspaper (that now, once again, influenced me) I had profited from his win at Uttoxeter. Like the provider of the encouraging form summary in my *Daily Telegraph,* I was sure that he would repeat this feat over a further eight furlongs.

140

As readers by now may be well aware, one of my habitual ploys is only to take a betting interest in a horse whose connections seem well placed to win, if it has the form credentials to do so. As the form expert of *The Daily Telegraph* had also made Chairman Stan Clarke's horse his selection, I felt this nine-year-old had an outstanding 'trier's chance'. In winning by eight lengths at 11-8 Lord Gyllene impressively advertised his 1997 Grand National prospects.

UTTOXETER

TONY STAFFORD	FORM
1.40—Guinda	1.40 - Guinda
2.10—Bell Staffboy	2.10—Bell Staffboy
2.40—Nick The Beak	2.40—Arithmetic
3.10—Lord Gyllene (n b)	3.10—Lord Gyllene
3.40—Karar	3.40—Sir Leonard
4:10—Barton Ward	4.10—Mentmore Towers
4.40—Toulston Lady	4.40—Take Cover

3.10 SINGER & FRIEDLANDER NATIONAL TRIAL (HANDICAP CHASE) 4m 2f £24,137 (9) **CH4**

1 4444 P1 FLYER'S NAP (7) R Alner 11 12 0 .... P Henley (3)
2 22 2311 LORD GYLLENE (NZ) (15) (C) S Brookshaw 9 11 9 .... R Johnson
3 00013 4 MUDAHIM (21) Mrs J Pitman 11 11 2 .... W Marston
4 241 325 BETTY'S BOY (IRE) (14) K Bailey 8 11 1 .... J Railton
5 1FP 241 COURT MELODY (IRE) (15) P Nicholls 9 10 11 .... J Culloty †
6 113U12 SAMLEE (IRE) (15) (C) (BF) P Hobbs 8 10 6 .... J R Kavanagh
7 2 1P220 CHURCH LAW (15) Mrs L Taylor 10 10 0 .... Sophie Mitchell (5)
8 213 20U ANDROS PRINCE (77) Miss A Embiricos 12 10 0 .... Mr R Thornton (5)
9 5 60041 WOODLANDS GENHIRE (23) (D) P Pritchard 12 10 0 .... R Bellamy †

S.P. FORECAST: 15 8 Lord Gyllene. 9 4 Flyer's Nap, 6 1 Mudahim, Samlee, 7 1 Court Melody. 12 1 Betty's Boy. 16 1 Woodlands Genhire. 20 1 others.

FORM GUIDE. **Flyer's Nap** returned to his best form with an emphatic 8l victory over Sunley Bay at Chepstow and won with plenty in hand. **Lord Gyllene** made it a real test of stamina when, after going clear 3 out he stayed on strongly to beat **Samlee** (rec 10lb) 15l, with Church Law (rec 20lb) well behind in 9th over 3¼m of today's course and is progressing well. **Court Melody** appreciated the easier going when opening his seasonal account at Folkestone last time. **Woodlands Genhire** faces a stiff task from 32lb out of the Handicap. **Mudahim**, 4th of 5 in a Grade 2 hurdle at Haydock, will be all the better for that first run of the season and his first for his new trainer and this staying chaser should go well.

LORD GYLLENE to complete hat-trick. **Flyer's Nap** next best.

Gyllene to lord it in stamina test

3.10 Stamina is the requisite here, and **LORD GYLLENE**, twice successful by a wide margin here, can make it three for his owner, the course chairman. **Samlee** was a remote second to my selection last time, but the extra mile may help.

UTTOXETER   **Good**

1.40 (2m4f nov ch): HARVEST VIEW (M Berry, 8-1) 1; **Guinda** (8-11F) 2; **Jasilu** (10-1) 3. 11 ran. 2½, 13. (C Brooks). Tote: win £8.00; places £1.70, £1.20, £2.00. Dual F'cast: £8.60. CSF: £13.55. Trio: £14.20.

2.10 (2m5f h'cap ch): BELL STAFFBOY (Michael Brennan, 2-1JF) 1; **Noyan** (2-1JF) 2; **Who Is Equiname** (8-1) 3. 6 ran. 9, 11. (J O'Shea). Tote: win £3.20; places £1.80, £1.90. Dual F'cast: £3.10. CSF: £6.23. NR: Oban.

2.40 (2m6f110y h'cap hdle): SUPREME LADY (J Culloty, 5-1) 1; **House Captain** (7-2F) 2; **Freddie Muck** (13-2) 3. 11 ran. 3½, hd. (Miss H Knight). Tote: win £6.60; places £1.80, £1.50, £1.90. Dual F'cast: £10.20. CSF: £19.36. Tricast: £102.36. Trio: £21.50.

3.10 (4m2f h'cap ch): LORD GYLLENE (R Johnson, 11-8F) 1; **Mudahim** (6-1) 2; **Court Melody** (10-1) 3. 9 ran. 8, 1½. (S Brookshaw). Tote: win £2.40; places £1.20, £2.50, £2.80. Dual F'cast: £7.10. CSF: £9.68. Tricast: £55.41. Trio £76.20.

3.40 (3m2f h'cap ch): GENERAL PONGO (R Farrant, 8-1) 1; **Lord of The West** (25-1) 2; **What's Your Story** (14-1) 3. 13 ran. Little Martina 5F. 1½, 6. (T George). Tote: win £11.10; places £3.10, £6.60, £3.80. Dual F'cast: £114.10. CSF: £165.77. Tricast: £2,513.03. Trio: £576.70.

4.10 (3m110y nov hdle): MENTMORE TOWERS (R Farrant, 9-4F) 1; **Barton Ward** (3-1) 2; **Banny Hill Lad** (25-1) 3. 14 ran. 12, 20. (Mrs J Pitman). Tote: win £3.60; places £1.60, £1.60, £9.60. Dual F'cast: £3.90. CSF: £8.69. Trio: £238.10. NR: Flashman, Forest Mill.

4.40 (2m h'cap hdle): GLOBE RUNNER (A Roche, 6-1) 1; **Samanid** (14-1) 2; **Take Cover** (4-1) 3. 11 ran. Arabian Heights 5-2F. 2½, 7. (J O'Neill). Tote: win £8.80; £2.60, £3.50, £1.60. DF: £48.00. CSF: £77.61. Tc: £346.23. Trio: 48.70.

PLACEPOT: £53.70. QUADPOT: £29.50.

As well as (the admittedly rare) individuals who own racecourses as well as having runners on them, there are some other payers of racing's feed bills that one should note on particular courses. I refer here not to the runners of stewards at the meetings at which they officiate or those of 'lords and ladies' who have cast-off runners in plebeian sellers at their local meetings (both ideas for rather fanciful system that I've come across), but to the directors of companies who arrange for the names of these to be advertised in the names of races. Any public library will show who these individuals are and, if one of them is seen to be bidding (via the form selection for his company's 'own race') to win back the prize money donated, then one may have found another owner's horse to really bet on at a particular race meeting!

PART FOUR

SIDING WITH HORSES

STRATEGY 30

GETTING VALUE ON FOREIGN RAIDERS

In earlier chapters mention has been made of xenophobia on the part of home-based bookmakers that can cause them to offer high-value odds on horses that come from other countries to race in Britain and of the wisdom of thus supporting these foreign raiders where they race.

For example, the two Irish-trained runners in the 1996 Midlands Grand National at Uttoxeter - Another Excuse and Feathered Gale - finished first and second to provide excellent forecast dividends, while only 11 days later, in Dubai, the only three American-trained raiders - Cigar, Soul of the Matter and L'Carriere - produced exactly the same outcome for backers when occupying the first three places in the four million dollar World Cup!

There is a clear lesson to be learnt from such results in that one should wager with those making and calling the odds in whatever countries foreign raiders have travelled to from their far distant home stables.

The one exception to this rule concerns the many Irish raiders at a fixture that, by a few days, precedes the Midlands Grand National - the Cheltenham Festival of mid-March.

Here such have been the past successes of Irish raiders that the odds now offered against their successors are invariably cramped and thus represent very poor value.

In Ireland, however, one can occasionally profit from the fact that, given the past, rather poor, but now quite rapidly improving, record of English raiders in major races, good value on such contenders can often be obtained.

Interestingly, in the 1995 season, in which Godolphin's Dubaiwintered runners carried nearly all before them, Wizard King was described by his trainer Mark Prescott as 'the only horse in the world not to have thrived in Dubai!'

For this reason he was sent back by Sheikh Mohammed to be trained at Newmarket by Prescott who, through feeling Wizard King's problem was not visiting foreign shores but really warm ones, sent him to contest the Platinum Stakes - a £15,000 event at Ireland's Fairyhouse racecourse. Here Wizard King for once produced some magic in making all under especially booked 'job jockey', the Irish champion, Michael Kinane.

Wizard King's attractive odds, accorded him by Irish bookmakers and tote patrons, again underlined the soundness of the belief that value can be obtained by supporting foreign trained horses with local odds makers.

STRATEGY 31

COURSES FOR HORSES

Interestingly, former steeplechase jockey and writer, Dick Francis, who is best known for his racing thrillers, in his non-fiction book, *The Sport of Queens,* has provided a very useful set of separate categories into which Britain's many National Hunt courses can be placed. These are 'flat and easy', 'flat and difficult', 'hilly and easy' and 'hilly and difficult'.

Francis himself does not indicate whether the courses he groups together under these separate headings are left- or right-handed and neither does his particular analysis of differences in racecourses' topography also include an analysis of their class.

However, when these two considerations are also applied courses can be categorised in even more refined ways that can be of considerable interest and value to the backer.

One result of this process is that some courses can be classified as right-handed, hilly and testing, as regards their terrain and the fences found on them. If such courses, whose negotiation involves many contenders having to run in a clockwise direction, were ranked according to class in the form of a list, this would be headed by Ascot and Sandown and would end with Towcester and Carlisle.

Thus any Sandown contender with winning Ascot form or vice versa would be one to consider, while any past winner on these tracks that lines up at humbler Towcester or Carlisle should have its credentials closely examined. Similarly, a Towcester winner running in a race run over Carlisle's less testing track should be accorded definite respect.

Should readers have any doubt about the wisdom of supporting horses that have previously won on Britain's very few testing tracks that run the 'wrong way', when such performers again run on one or other of these, they might like to consider, not only the vast number of Sandown and Ascot victories achieved by Desert Orchid, but also the fact that another classy 'chaser, Artifice, won four steeplechases on the former track and six on the latter!

Other National Hunt tracks on which the 'courses for horses' ploy can often be profitably exploited are those whose topographical idiosyncrasies make them true specialists' tracks. These are Fontwell, with its tricky 'figure of eight' 'chase course that is only a mile round, its counterpart at Windsor that is less tricky and far less tight, and two steeplechasing circuits that have 'drop' fences - Aintree and Haydock.

In general, tracks with highly distinctive configuration or demanding fences (such as those at Wetherby, by way of further example) are those on which past course winners should be greatly respected.

Another configurational feature which Dick Francis does not discuss in *The Sport of Queens* is the tightness of some courses which naturally confers an advantage on handy speedsters, rather than long-striding gallopers that need extensive straights on which to really stretch out.

As it happens, none too many horses are sufficiently nippy and well-balanced to really relish running on a track that seems to be forever turning, especially if it does so to the right, and, for this reason, I pay particular attention to jumpers that have notched more than one victory on right-handed tracks with a circumference of one mile three furlongs or less and short run-ins from their final fences of no more than 350 yards (that tend to suit front-running speedsters that have forged clear of their rivals). Taunton, Market Rasen and Perth are three such right-handed tracks and here previous course winners top-rated on time for their impending races should be seriously considered.

Front runners that are also well rated by watch-holders should enter calculations in races run on tracks whose configuration suits their enterprising style of running. Such performers are identified in the form guide *Superform* or *Timeform* and those tracks on which they enjoy a pronounced 'edge', apart from Perth, Taunton and Market Rasen, are left-handed Bangor, Cartmel, Catterick, Fakenham, Kelso, Lingfield (both on the turf and the all weather circuits) Liverpool (on the Mildmay course), as well as Newton Abbot, Southwell and what was once my local course at Stratford-on-Avon.

As for course and distance winners on flat racecourses, a recent reviewer of Patrick Kilgallon's *How to Beat the Handicapper* re-iterated his point that Newmarket produces the highest strike rate, as regards past course and distance winners of handicaps that again run in these.

Indeed, profits can be made if winners over course and distance, sometimes in the previous runnings of the races they are again due to contest, are supported, if the going corresponds to that which prevailed when they succeeded exactly 12 months previously.

Some other courses on which, for fairly easily discernible configurational reasons, the 'courses for horses' approach ought to work out well over longish distances on the flat, are idiosyncratic Windsor, badminton racquet-shaped Hamilton Park, Bath with its high altitude and rather bizarre 'make and shape', circuitous Chester, taxing Beverley and Newcastle, right-handed Ripon and Leicester, gloriously singular Goodwood and rather peculiarly put together Pontefract!

In Ireland, two courses where it should pay the backer to favour past winners if the going suits them, are Galway with its tightness and Tralee for also being undulating!

STRATEGY 32
RACES FOR HORSES

The fact that such events as Kempton's King George VI Steeplechase, the Queen Mother Champion Chase at Cheltenham and the Champion Hurdle (run at the same venue) are regularly won by horses that have previously prevailed in them, does rather suggest that when at precisely the same point, in the racing season some runners re-encounter conditions that were conducive to their past successes, they are likely to do themselves full justice and so should receive more than a passing glance.

Indeed, 'knowing the ropes', or rather the way to the winner's enclosure, via at least one course and distance win in the very race in which they are again due to compete, can confer a distinct advantage on certain runners.

Since so many races run on the flat are confined to horses of a particular age, backers should look out for past winners of National Hunt races.

The best known of these is, of course, the Grand National in which Red Rum's three epic wins in 1973, 1974 and 1977 (at odds of 9-1, 11-1 and 9-1) and two seconds (in 1975 and 1976, at 7-2 and 10-1) point to the wisdom of seeking out proven performers in races unconfined to horses of any one particular age.

Quite often the 'races for previous winners' plan will indicate horses that go to post at odds that are quite as long as those (above) that were quoted against Red Rum's chances of winning a Grand National on five separate occasions.

Interestingly, the belief that such runners can be winners was corroborated recently when an aged hunter called Eastern Destiny lined up for a far more modest steeplechase than the Grand National.

This, the Town of Warwick's Foxhunters' Trophy Hunter Chase, provided the 'most popular result' of any seen at this meeting (as John Oaksey put it) as its winner was registering his third successive victory in this contest. Having, before going to Warwick, delved into my collection of the past 10 years' form books that I always arrange on the back seat of my car, I was well aware of this veteran 14-year-old hunter's two previous 'Town of Warwick' wins and so helped myself to the 14-1 that was freely available in the ring. Naturally, I was thrilled when Eastern Destiny's hat-trick of 'one race' wins allowed him to rank alongside Red Rum in one respect at least.

Those who seek to capitalise on the definite potential for profit that past winners of particular races can represent might do well to remember that previous winners of jumping races run the 'wrong way round' on right-handed tracks (like Sandown, for example) often go in again.

Indeed, this was rather spectacularly demonstrated when no less than two races run on one day at Sandown - the three mile Punch Bowl Amateur Riders' Handicap Chase and the Racecall Hurdle were both won by market leaders that most significantly had captured these particular events exactly 12 months previously.

Indeed, I find a past winner of a race again taking its chance, I always support it if it heads the market.

Incidentally, it is often possible to profit from another variation of the 'races for horses' strategy. This I discovered, almost by accident, but then refined after some considerable subsequent thought, when researching the past form of winners of some of the top races at Cheltenham's National Hunt Festival in March.

This research into past runnings of the Queen Mother two mile Champion 'Chase revealed the none-too-surprising fact that horses that, at the previous Festival meeting, had won or been placed in the Arkle Challenge Trophy over course and distance, frequently prevailed, or made the frame, in the race that celebrates the love of jump racing of perhaps the best-loved member of the royal family.

When the 'Queen Mother' was recently run in March 1996, the 1995 Arkle winner, and thus the 'strategy qualifier', Klairon Davies, despite having subsequently, when away from Cheltenham, lost his form, stormed home to take this meeting's second day highlight at 9-1!

Another 'graduation' from one festival race in one year to another in the next involves progressing from the Supreme Novices Hurdle, always the meeting's opening event, to the Arkle 'chase itself.

Since in 1996, the winner of the former contest did not contest the latter, the strategy qualifier became the horse it defeated over the lesser obstacles, Ventana Canyon that, exactly a year following this disappointment, atoned in the Arkle at 7-1! As it happened, another Irish horse completed a successful Cheltenham 'retrieval mission' at the 1996 festival to illustrate yet another variation of the 'races for graduating horses' strategy. This was the hunter, Elegant Lord, whose 3-1 success in the four mile Foxhunters' chase was expected by those who know how sensible it is to support any contestant in this that, when it was less strong and experienced, made the frame in the last running of this gruelling marathon contest.

Interestingly, this approach of supporting horses placed in the last running of the very same race in which they are again due to compete, often produces good returns in another long distance Festival slog, the 3 mile 1 furlong Stayers' Hurdle. Cyborgo, second at 3-1 in 1995, ran out a ready winner of its 1996 running at a most acceptable 8-1!

Readers keen to examine possibly propitious graduations from certain flat races to others are advised to try to get hold of Malcolm Howard's Raceform publication, The Winning Trail. Some useful information on some of these graduations also sometimes appears in the retrospective analyses of the last 10 years' runnings of important races that appear regularly in both The Racing Post and The Sporting Life.

HORSES COMING RIGHT AT PARTICULAR TIMES

To racing professionals, one particularly useful service is a feature known as Index to Winners that forms part of *Chaseform* and *Raceform* Notebooks. In this the circumstances involving a horse's past victories and, just as crucially, the dates on which these occurred, are precisely recorded.

Study of the past wins of seasonal campaigners over several seasons will show that many of them strike winning form at a particular time of year. Indeed, there seem to be 'spring' horses, those that bloom in the summer, autumn specialists and jumpers who come to hand during certain winter months.

In fact, this is why on any racing day, I always check to see if any horse which won, when 12 months previously a current meeting was staged on a racecourse, is again due to race upon it - whether in the same contest or not.

This particular approach can produce handsome returns, as was rather spectacularly demonstrated at Catterick one December, (as described in Strategy 5). On this occasion, my daily newspaper alerted me to the claims of Cavalier Crossett, as it showed this versatile jumper had exactly 12 months previously run away with the Zetland Chase. Thus, I decided to support this star of trainer Red Caine's Billsdale stable, as he was due to compete in the far humbler Strand Novices Hurdle.

This he won so readily (at 33-1 by many lengths) that, when I read that his canny trainer felt he ought to be again allowed to run at his favourite time of Hogmanay - in another Catterick race due to be run on the following day of 1 January I decided to see if pig farmer Caine's 'turn of the year' performer could again bring home the bacon.

To my delight, Cavalier Crossett duly did so - this time winning a two-mile handicap chase at 4-1!

STRATEGY 34

SUPPORTING PULLED-UP HORSES

Scrutiny of the form lines of jumpers will reveal the understandable fact that on some occasions in the almost 11 month National Hunt season, several such performers are pulled up during some of their races.

This proceeding is often made necessary by a physical problem encountered in running; some horses swallow their tongues or suffer muscle problems, experience discomfort on particular types of going, make a hash of their jumping or get knocked about by rival contenders.

At least by retiring early as a result of being hurt, exhausted or discomfited, or through exhibiting lacklustre form, the jumper is saved further distress or embarrassment.

Just as a broken down car is sent to a garage so it can be made to again run as well as possible, so a pulled up racehorse invariably receives a course of fairly intensive care based on a diagnosis of what prevented it from completing the course last time out.

On occasion, in fact, so effective is this treatment - it can extend far beyond rest by involving such horse doctors as Ronnie Longford - that on their return to the racecourse many runners with the letter 'P' as the last entry in their formlines run away with their 'comeback' races.

This rather anomalous fact can rapidly be confirmed if the results from any past jumping season are analysed. Moreover, backing previously pulled up jumpers next time out can prove remarkably profitable if confining your interests to those whose full recovery and total well-being are being suggested, if not signalled, by the fact that they receive support in the betting market - either by figuring as first, second or third favourites or by starting at prices that are shorter than those at which they opened.

Incredibly, as was pointed out in a letter sent to *The Sporting Life,* over a matter of days in a recent spring, the winners Oriel Dream, Laura's Beau, Deep Colonist, Topsham Bay, Tildebo, All Welcome, Mic Mac Express, Trojan Call and Granny Pray On, had all been pulled up a few days previously! Indeed, in returning to, and winning on, a racecourse so quickly, they clearly suggested that nothing too drastic had caused their previous 'early retirement'.

FROM *THE SPORTING LIFE*

Pulled-up horses

I WRITE with regard to Mr Rodgers' letter of March 26, about the number of horses who win after having been pulled up in their previous race.

May I suggest he follows the market rather than the form.

I backed the following in the last fortnight purely from market moves and they were all pulled up in their previous race — Oriel Dream, Laura's Beau, Deep Colonist, Topsham Bay, Tildebo, All Welcome, Mic Mac Express, Trojan Call, Granny Pray On.

In fact, I would say it's a very good system, provided they were pulled up in the last 10 days.

Those horses tailed off in their previous race are not quite so lucrative, but worth noting when running again within seven days.

A WHITE

Belmont, Surrey.

Laura's Beau even managed to win the Midlands' Grand National at Uttoxeter at 16-1, after having only days earlier at the Cheltenham Festival proved so disappointing that his jockey decided to pull him up!

As is perhaps better known, Laura's Beau subsequently showed his well-being by running third at 12-1 in the Grand National proper.

STRATEGY 35

HORSES THAT ADVERTISE THEIR PROSPECTS

Many successful salesmen rely on the persuasive power of a demonstration as a means of clinching a sale and so do some shrewd trainers of racehorses who, within the 'classified advertisements' section of either *The Sporting Life* or the *Racing Post* occasionally announce that they have horses for sale that are due to race on the very day these newspapers appear or on an impending one.

Clearly, such handlers are more than merely hopeful that the horses in these advertisements will acquit themselves so well that they will attract interest from several potential buyers.

One such trainer is Flat and National Hunt handler, Simon Dow, whose Wendover stable is to be found in Burgh Heath Road in Epsom.

FROM *THE SPORTING LIFE*

When I noticed that Simon had placed the above advertisement in *The Sporting Life,* so confident did I feel that his gallant gamble, in so confidently resorting to a 'shop window' approach to selling his three-year-old novice hurdler, would prove inspired, that I decided to make a sizeable each-way bet at 33-1 - the rate of odds at which Gallant Effort was allowed to go to post for the Toll House Novices' Hurdle, despite his top-class breeding and the (to me) significant-looking fact that a leading jump jockey had been engaged to ride him.

When, first time out, Gallant Effort ran a most commendable second to hot favourite and previous scorer, The Blue Boy, I felt he had most aptly lived up to his name and decided (since the advertisement in which I had taken such interest expressly stated he would stay with his trainer) that he was likely to go on to even better things, when more experienced and opposed by less formidable opposition.

FROM *THE SPORTING LIFE*

3.25	**Toll House Novices' Hurdle**	**2m**

£4000 added to stakes **for 3-y-o only which, at the start of the current season, have not won a hurdle** £30 to enter Wts: 11st each Fillies allwd 5lb Pen, a winner of a hurdle 4lb Of 2 hurdles, or of one value £3000 7lb Allowances: Horses which have not run in a flat race 3lb This race will not be divided at entry a surcharge will be levied on this race Closed on Oct 28

Penalty value £2,843; 2nd £854, 3rd £412, 4th £191

1 111111 **THE BLUE BOY (Ire)**(10) (D3) (T M Few)
M C Pipe   11 7 ... P Scudamore ★
Yellow, red disc, red and yellow halved sleeves, red cap..

2   1 **DOMAIN**(9) (D) (Richard Brooks)
R J Weaver   11 4 ..Dale McKeown ★
Purple, red chevrons, striped cap. .

3 5126 **FIERCE**(14) (D) (Miss Tina Wyndham)
J R Jenkins   11 4 ...... R Dunwoody
Emerald green, Royal blue spots, red cap..

4   1 **KEEN VISION (Ire)**(14) (D) (Allendale Racing) .... D W P Arbuthnot   11 4 ....B de Haan
Dark green, white chevron and star on cap. .

5   13 **TROJAN ENVOY**(17) (D Khan).. W Carter   11 4 .... D Murphy
Grey, black epaulets, black cap. .

6   **CURRENT EDITION (Ire)**(107F) (Miss B Swire) .... G B Balding   11 0 ......A Maguire (5)
Lilac, rose quartered cap. .

7   0 **GALLANT EFFORT (Ire)**(14) (T R Pearson) .... S Dow   11 0 .... H Davies
Dark green, light green sleeves, dark green and light green check cap..

8   **GOTTA BE JOKING**(46F) (Mrs P Scott-Dunn) .... T M Jones   11 0 .... T Grantham
Black, amber hooped sleeves, amber cap. .

Eight runners

FORECAST: 11-8 The Blue Boy, 4 Keen Vision, 11-2 Current Edition, 10 Trojan Envoy, 12 Fierce, 16 Domain, Gotta Be Joking, 20 Gallant Effort.

FROM THE RACING POST

The wisdom of this view was vindicated when, later, Gallant Effort visited the winner's enclosure on several occasions!

Even more recently, another horse advertised for sale in *The Sporting Life* just before it ran on a racecourse made such a gallant effort when it did so that it really endeared itself to prospective buyers. This was the sprinter To The Roof whose assets were so glowingly 'shop-windowed' in the following advertisement that appeared in the sporting press two days before he was due to race at Leicester on 17 April 1996 that I was persuaded he was, like Gallant Effort, worthy of at least each way support.

I was understandably disappointed, but not left out of pocket, when To The Roof's own gallant effort saw him beaten a neck into second place at 6-1!

STRATEGY 36

SELECTING TWO-YEAR-OLDS

Two-year-olds have always appealed to professional backers since they are seldom soured by racing and their form is often reliable - the reason why racing annuals often include features that consist of collations of prestigious first season form with such titles as *Tell-Tale Classic Form*.

The problem with these particular racehorses is that during their first racing season they tend, like human beings when in infancy, to grow, mature and develop rapidly but at varying rates and that is why a method of assessing their chances, especially if they are debutantes or dark, unexposed horses, needs to be described.

The one I have used successfully for several seasons involves finding a two-year-old that has had plenty of time to mature, is well-bred, well suited to the distance of an impending race and is well backed.

As for breeding, when faced with any field of two-year-olds (some of them often unraced or inexperienced), I always start by consulting a list, often published in racing annuals or specialist publications that details those currently at stud according to the amounts of prize money their progeny have captured in the previous season. Part of such a list appears overleaf:

	Sire Colour Born Grandsire	Rnrs	Wars	Wins	Value £	Pls	Value £	Total £
1	NUREYEV (b. 1977) Northern Dancer	6	4	8	537777	5	10516	548293
2	NEVER SO BOLD (b. 1980) Bold Lad (IRE)	19	6	8	263489	18	21234	284723
3	PERSIAN BOLD (br. 1975) Bold Lad (IRE)	25	5	8	56492	24	205927	262419
4	ALZAO (b. 1980) Lyphard	22	2	8	217701	22	14937	232638
5	CAERLEON (b. 1980) Nijinsky	18	7	10	154191	23	56570	210761
6	IMP SOCIETY (ch. 1981) Barrera	2	2	8	189637	4	10006	199643
7	DOULAB (ch. 1982) Topsider	24	11	14	174145	34	23771	197916
8	STORM BIRD (b. 1978) Northern Dancer	12	4	8	76705	19	116621	193326
9	THE MINSTREL (ch. 1974) Northern Dancer	19	8	11	69176	16	122466	191642
10	GREEN DESERT (b. 1983) Danzig	24	15	21	101837	34	80572	182409
11	BERING (ch. 1983) Arctic Tern	4	2	4	179121	2	860	179981
12	LAW SOCIETY (br. 1982) Alleged	20	10	11	91895	17	84383	176278
13	NORDICO (b. 1981) Northern Dancer	16	8	16	104215	29	63770	167985
14	MINSHAANSHU AMAD (br. 1979) Northern Dancer	1	1	3	34121	5	116563	150684
15	KRIS (ch. 1976) Sharpen Up	13	3	4	111161	13	34554	145715
16	NORTHERN PROSPECT (b. 1976) Mr Prospector	5	4	8	122838	8	10038	132876
17	KING OF CLUBS (ch. 1981) Mill Reef	13	4	6	23635	9	101353	124988
18	GLINT OF GOLD (b. 1978) Mill Reef	12	4	5	111423	5	1870	113293
19	MR PROSPECTOR (b. 1970) Raise a Native	8	4	5	91484	8	14992	106476
20	SAYF EL ARAB (b. 1980) Drone	19	7	16	58100	25	45580	103680
21	MISWAKI (ch. 1978) Mr Prospector	15	11	14	43096	19	58873	101969
22	TATE GALLERY (b. 1983) Northern Dancer	29	10	13	41546	41	55733	97279
23	ALYDAR (ch. 1975) Raise A Native	6	3	4	79381	5	14736	94117
24	NIGHT SHIFT (b. 1980) Northern Dancer	17	5	8	74475	16	18685	93160
25	IRISH RIVER (ch. 1976) Riverman	6	1	1	40230	4	50594	90824
26	WOODMAN (ch. 1983) Mr Prospector	5	2	5	78050	6	11395	89445
27	PRINCE SABO (b. 1982) Young Generation	15	9	14	55626	25	32523	88149
28	RIVERMAN (b. 1969) Never Bend	8	4	4	31751	6	44141	75892
29	DANZIO (b. 1977) Northern Dancer	10	6	10	50489	11	23444	73933
30	ARAGON (b. 1980) Mummy's Pet	18	2	3	50051	24	23168	73219
31	FORZANDO (b. 1981) Formidable	11	2	6	42828	14	25073	67901
32	PETORIUS (b. 1981) Mummy's Pet	26	7	10	50587	29	15225	65812
33	LAST TYCOON (b. 1983) Try My Best	22	7	10	48396	14	15147	63543
34	TIMELESS MOMENT (ch. 1970) Damascus	2	2	18	55857	8	7003	62860
35	NOMINATION (b. 1983) Dominion	16	8	13	48656	21	13998	62654
36	ABSALOM (gr. 1975) Abwah	37	10	12	38391	41	23980	62371
37	MAZAAD (b. 1983) Auction Ring	30	5	7	25093	29	37020	62113
38	SADLER'S WELLS (b. 1981) Northern Dancer	19	7	7	22281	13	39878	62059
39	SHAREEF DANCER (b. 1980) Northern Dancer	18	6	8	53090	6	8125	61215
40	PRIMO DOMINIE (b. 1982) Dominion	26	8	11	35978	28	21408	57386
41	EL GRAN SENOR (b. 1981) Northern Dancer	13	6	7	43362	13	12900	56262
42	BAIRN (b. 1982) Northern Baby	20	5	7	29459	19	26671	56130
43	SHIRLEY HEIGHTS (b. 1975) Mill Reef	12	4	4	16766	4	39107	55873
44	MUMMY'S GAME (b. 1979) Mummy's Pet	21	7	12	47629	12	7691	55320
45	RAINBOW QUEST (b. 1981) Blushing Groom	10	2	3	9658	15	44589	54247
46	DIESIS (ch. 1980) Sharpen Up	15	9	10	27046	20	26333	53379
47	KAFU (b. 1980) African Sky	22	7	10	36050	23	17108	53158
48	HATIM (ch. 1981) Exclusive Native	17	5	7	29427	19	22667	52094
49	THATCHING (b. 1975) Thatch	27	9	10	27324	19	23730	51054
50	GODSWALK (gr. 1974) Dancer's Image	31	8	12	31685	37	17978	49663
51	DOMYNSKY (ch. 1980) Dominion	11	3	6	34784	13	14577	49361
52	PRECOCIOUS (b. 1981) Mummy's Pet	18	7	10	31438	28	17292	48730
53	HORAGE (b. 1980) Tumble Wind	22	5	10	29302	21	18718	48020
54	SIMPLY GREAT (b. 1979) Mill Reef	16	7	11	39068	11	6626	45694
55	LOMOND (b. 1980) Northern Dancer	17	8	8	28792	13	16847	45639
56	BLUSHING GROOM (ch. 1974) Red God	13	8	8	31007	12	14603	45610
57	DANCING BRAVE (b. 1983) Lyphard	10	4	6	36766	5	8015	44781
58	NIJINSKY (b. 1967) Northern Dancer	8	4	6	38266	6	5988	44254
59	AHONOORA (ch. 1975) Lorenzaccio	13	6	7	32734	7	10823	43557
60	SOVEREIGN DANCER (b. 1975) Northern Dancer	5	2	3	14232	3	28445	42677
61	FLASH OF STEEL (b. 1983) Kris	15	3	4	8849	20	33399	42248
62	TAUFAN (b. 1977) Stop the Music	25	6	7	26000	25	14618	40618
63	WASSL (b. 1980) Mill Reef	13	3	6	23360	16	17215	40575
64	FAUSTUS (b. 1983) Robellino	21	6	8	26718	22	13847	40565
65	GOOD TIMES (b. 1976) Great Nephew	16	2	2	25513	12	14666	40179
66	ELEGANT AIR (b. 1981) Shirley Heights	17	5	8	27666	14	10842	38508
67	MUSIC BOY (b. 1973) Jukebox	20	5	7	19166	24	19290	38456
68	HIGH LINE (ch. 1966) High Hat	5	1	2	26294	5	11831	38125
69	BALLAD ROCK (ch. 1974) Bold Lad (IRE)	19	5	7	22395	20	13974	36369

LEADING SIRES OF 2-YEAR-OLDS
(by Prize Money Won)

I initially turned to this list when I wanted to make a systematic selection for the following seven furlong race at Southwell:

FROM *THE RACING POST*

SOUTHWELL

2.35 *Timeform Race Card Opportunities Stakes. Winner £2,488*   **7f(AW)**

£2,900 added **For** two yrs old only which, before July 1st, had not won a race **Weights** Colts and geldings.8st 11lb; fillies. 8st 6lb **Penalties** a winner 5lb. Of 2 races 10lb **Entries** 24 pay £29 **Penalty Value** 1st £2,488 **2nd** £690 3rd £331   **POSTMARK**

1 (1)	4111	**CHICMOND (IRE)**[27]	Sir M Prescott 2 9-07	G Duffield (108)
		P G Goulandris *em green and r blue (halved horizontally), blue slvse. qtd cap.*		
2 (7)	8	**COMMON COUNCIL**[109]	G A Pritchard-Gordon 2 8-11	K Fallon
		Lord Derby *black, white cap.*		
3 (4)	696	**COOL SOCIETY (USA)**[46]	C R Nelson 2 8-11	T Rogers
		John W Mitchell *em green. red sash, em green slvs, red seams, em green cap. red star.*		
4 (5)	8	**KIND OF LUCK**[18]	G A Pritchard-Gordon 2 8-11	W Hood
		Broadstone Stud Ltd *dark blue and light blue check, grey sleeves*		
5 (3)	8	**MACLAINES PRIDE(USA)**[12]	W A O'Gorman 2 8-11	A S Cruz
		Maclaine Racing *yellow, light blue star and sleeves*		
6 (6)	06	**MR NEWS (IRE)**[42]	W J Pearce 2 8-11	G Husband (5)
		The Northern Echo Racing Club Ltd *r blue, yllw chevrons, halved slvs, yllw cap*		
7 (2)	6	**SILK TAPESTRY (USA)**[26]	M R Stoute 2 8-06	P D'Arcy
		Kennet Valley Thoroughbreds Ltd *yellow, dark blue chevron and armlets.*		

LAST YEAR: **No corresponding race**

BETTING FORECAST: 10-11 Chicmond, 10-3 Silk Tapestry, 7 Maclaines Pride, 8 Common Council, 14 Cool Society, 25 Kind of Luck, Mr News

≡ SPOTLIGHT ≡

CHICMOND could be fancied here on his debut last of 4 to Sir Boudle at Brighton—a race in which useful subsequent winners Providence and Mystical Dancer took the minor honours—so the fact he has since progressed to win his last three races gives him an outstanding chance, even giving upwards of 10lb away to some unexposed rivals. This tough colt has been off the track since beating Master Planner 1½l over Catterick's sharp 6f last month but that rest was well-deserved and today's extra furlong promises to bring about further improvement in him.

He looks sure to start a short-priced favourite but **Silk Tapestry** will not be without her supporters. This $85,000 half-sister to a Grade 1 winner in the States showed a fair degree of promise behind Mystery Play in a newcomers' race at Newmarket and is probably capable of better but it should be noted that Michael Stoute's record at Southwell is not an enviable one —he has yet to saddle a winner in 10 attempts.

Cool Society has yet to display the ability his $58,000 price tag suggested he may possess and the once-raced pair of **Common Council** and **Maclaines Pride** make more appeal. Preference is for the latter.

DIOMED Chicmond	**TOPSPEED** Chicmond

The *Racing Post's* detailed summaries of the form of the contestants for this race provided very useful information on the runners' breeding, namely the sire of each runner, an index of its stamina and a foaling date.

As regards the sire of Chicmond (the first runner listed in Southwell's 2.00 race), I noticed from the very comprehensive *Racing Post* form summaries that this was Lomond whose name appeared in 55th place in my long list of sires by prize money gained by their progeny during the previous season. This meant that Chicmond was given an initially (ideally quite low) score of 55 which I then subtracted from a second score provided by the number of days (the more the better) that I saw had elapsed since Chicmond's actual birthday on 12 February, and his impending race at Southwell on 11 August.

Thus, I took 55 from $16 + 31 + 30 + 31 + 30 + 31 + 14 = 183$ to get a score of 128.

Next I wanted to assess the suitability, or otherwise, to Chicmond of the seven furlong race distance he was due to tackle at Southwell in specific terms of how close or otherwise this came to the average distance of the victories gained by his sire's previous offspring (as given by the figure shown after his sire Lomond's name in his form summary).

So as the difference between this figure of 10.1 and the race distance of 7.0 furlongs worked out as 3.1 I added 31 points to his existing score of 128 which gave him 159 points.

Finally, I wanted to take account of any indications or otherwise that the market might provide as to Chicmond's chances - often, as far as two-year-olds are concerned, this is a more than usually important consideration. This process was facilitated by the *Post's* forecast of starting prices (see above Southwell race details from the *Racing Post*).

Having decided to give the likely favourite an optimum low score of 20, the forecast second favourite 40, the predicted further points which meant that his final overall rating (for maturity, breeding, suitability of race distance and position in the betting market) worked out at 179 points.

None of his rivals that could be assessed on all these criteria and whose ratings did not produce unworkable minus figures received such a low score. Significantly, Chicmond was also top-rated on speed and time in the *Racing Post*.

Chicmond, as expected, won by nearly three lengths at 4-5 - form which he impressively franked two weeks later by capturing Sandown's far more prestigious Solario Stakes at 16-1!

Chicmond

b c Lomond (10.1f) – Chicobin (J O Tobin)
12Feb89 first foal; dam unraced.
Placings: -4111

Sir M Prescott   **2 9-7**

	Starts	1st	2nd	3rd	Win & Pl
	4	3	–	–	£11,832
7/91 Catt	6f 2yo firm				£3,581
7/91 Ayr	6f 2yo soft				£5,640
7/91 Nott	6f Mdn 2yo gd-fm				£2,611
				Total win prizemoney £11,832	

18 Jul Catterick 6f   2yo £3,581
3 ran   FIRM   Time 1m13.0s (slw1.8s)
1 CHICMOND 2 9-7 ⅓ .... G Duffield 3 1/2F
slowly into stride, soon·recovered, shaken
up to lead 2f out, ran on strongly
                              [op 1/2 tchd 4/7]
2 Master Planner 2 9-4 .. Dean McKeown 4 7/2
3 My Jersey Pearl 2 8-13 ...... L Charnock 2 9/2
Dist: 1½-1   Postmark: 101/93/84

16 Jul Ayr 6f   2yo £5,640
4 ran   SOFT   Time 1m15.16s (slw3.9s)
1 CHICMOND 2 8-11 .... G Carter 3 11/8F
raced stands' side, prominent, led well over
1f out, ridden and ran on final furlong
                              [op 11/10 tchd 6/4]
2 Sylvan Sabre 2 9-3 .... W Newnes 4 9/4
3 She's Special 2 8-6 v' .... M Roberts 2 14/1
Dist: 1½-1½-15   Postmark: 97/99/-

6 Jul Nottingham 6f   Mdn 2yo £2,611
9 ran   GD-FM   Time 1m14.1s (slw2.3s)
1 CHICMOND 2 9-0 .... G Duffield 10 9/1
prominent, led after 2f, ridden and ran on
final furlong   [op 7/1]
2 Red Slippers 2 8-9 .... L Dettori 7 11/8F
3 Daaris 2 9-0 .... W Carson 5 6/1
Dist: 2-12-2-8-1½   Postmark: 85/74/-

STRATEGY 37

FINDING PENALISED HORSES TO SUPPORT

Recently a winner of a relatively short sprint race of seven furlongs at Warwick won by such a large margin as to prompt several observers to remark that it would need a heavy penalty to prevent him from again winning readily.

As it happened, this runner's most impressive winning margin provided me with a graphic reminder of a principle that I had applied very profitably two days previously at Goodwood. This involved the fact that the sizes of penalties are seldom commensurate with, or reflective of, the margins of victory that produce them.

Naturally, there have always been backers attracted to runners in handicaps whose last time out victories are so recent that they carry penalties for prevailing after the weights for these competitive events were published. The reasoning here is that such contestants are in winning form, have yet to be properly assessed by the handicapper, may well be capable of further improvement and are readily identifiable from their formlines which carry precise details of the penalties they carry.

As the racing results of any week will readily demonstrate, the extra weight that the imposition of penalties involves is often insufficient to 'peg back' a runner that ran out a ready winner of a handicap last time out.

However, the would-be backer of all penalised last time out winners in handicaps will find the road to fortune made up of some losing distances!

Nevertheless, certain criteria can be applied so as to discriminate between horses whose penalties are likely to preclude further victories and those that are likely to penalise bookmakers. In essence, these standards of judgement reflect the following rather self-evident, but seldom heeded, facts that, in general:

1   The winner of a handicap that has attracted a sizeable field has shown itself to be a better performer than many other handicappers, whereas the winner of a race that only involved a handful of contestants has shown itself superior to relatively few rivals.

2   Victory by two lengths is better than winning by a head as is winning by two lengths and three lengths, as opposed to two lengths and a head.

3   Winning a sprint race by two lengths (or a seven furlong one by a 'street', as in the example from Warwick initially discussed in this chapter) is more impressive than winning a two mile race by the same margin.

4   The value or significance of winning margins depends on the number of runners. This is because being fourth in a four horse race is likely (unless the runners finished extremely close up) to be far less significant than finishing fourth in a field with 14 or more runners.

With the above principles in mind, the backer should consult a newspaper and first make a note of runners in handicaps that carry penalties for winning first time out.

For example, one Thursday in May, my *Daily Telegraph* indicated that for winning his previous (eight runner) race (10 days earlier at Windsor), Landowner had to shoulder a 6lb penalty in the one mile, 4 furlong Royal Sussex Regiment Handicap at Goodwood. As I always keep past copies of my *Daily Telegraph* so these cover the previous month's racing, I was able to discover that Landowner had previously raced and won at Windsor by two lengths and three lengths. Thus, I was in a position to calculate precisely whether this classy three-year-old might prove a penalty carrier to side with.

The first step (in deference to principle 3 above) was to determine how many rivals Landowner had left behind last time out. In fact, my *Daily Telegraph* of 21 May indicated that Landowner's previous race at Windsor had involved an eight-strong field and to assess a point (or placing from among these finishers) from which to take account of his winning margin, I consulted the following table. Most usefully this indicates how far down the placings one should go in making one's calculation of this crucial margin:

No. of Runnners	Placing to Extend to	
4 or 5	1st / 2nd	i.e. Mid point of lengths dividing these
6 or 7	2nd	- ditto -
8 or 9	2nd / 3rd	- ditto -
10 or 11	3rd	- ditto -
12 or 13	3rd / 4th	- ditto -
14 plus	4th	- ditto -

As Landowner had last time out won an eight runner handicap, I worked out how many lengths he had finished in front of the 'finisher' that would have exactly divided the actual 2nd and 3rd placed horse.

This calculation of Landowner's winning margin based on the above table, worked out as $2 + 1\frac{1}{2} = 3\frac{1}{2}$ lengths which was rounded up to four lengths.

The next stage was to convert this margin to pounds by dividing 20 by the distance of the race in furlongs. In the case of Landowner, as his last race had involved twelve of these (to the nearest furlong) he was given a lb/lengths rating of 1.67. As Landowner's previously calculated winning margin was four lengths, $4 \times 1.67 = 6.68$ lbs. was the calculation necessary to give a measure of his 'superiority' to his actual handicap weight in Goodwood's Royal Sussex Regiment Handicap.

Since in this race he has been given a 6 lb penalty, I adjudged this insufficient by 0.68 lb to peg him back and so took all of the 7-4 quoted against his chance of proving a successful Goodwood favourite. In the event Landowner prevailed by a decisive (if fairly narrow) margin of three-quarters of a length, as my calculations had rather suggested he might!

Race distance	lbs/length
5f	4.00
6f	3.33
7f	2.86
8f	2.50
9f	2.22
10f	2.00
11f	1.82
12f	1.67
13f	1.54
14f	1.43
15f	1.33
16f	1.25
17f	1.18
18f	1.11
19f	1.05
20f	1.00

STRATEGY 38

SUPPORTING HORSES WELL CLEAR ON RATINGS

Readers of the first 'companion' edition of this book may recall how high is my opinion of those experts who supply newspapers like the *Racing Post* and *The Sporting Life* with ratings based on complete private handicaps that involve horses' form against either each other or the clock.

Sometimes these ratings, as well as similar ones, that appear in many national dailies, indicate that a particular runner is so well clear of its rivals as to represent an outstanding wager.

Interestingly, this was the case, according to the very accurate form ratings of the private handicapper of horses' form who works for *The Times*, in relation to Rough Quest, the favourite for the 1996 Grand National, whose strong claims also came to my attention via my application of several other strategies already presented in this book. Indeed, on 30 April, I felt certain that I had never before seen a National contender rated 18 pts clear on form of his nearest rival!

In fact, this should not really have been possible, but the handicapper had no way of knowing, when he framed his weights for the 1996 race that, after this point, Rough Quest would run a blinder by finishing second to Imperial Call, the most impressive and really top class winner of the Cheltenham Gold Cup!

Elsewhere in its runner-by-runner guide to the National, *The Times* described Rough Quest as 'very well handicapped' which was abundantly clear from his top form rating of 99 - 18 points clear of Encore Un Peu on 81.

Amazingly, the race itself went exactly as *The Times* private handicapper had predicted, as Rough Quest defeated the French-sounding first string of the Martin Pipe stable!

There will not be many occasions when such 'stand out' bets on ratings appear in handicaps, or any other races for that matter, but, when they do, I always make it my habit to be heavily involved with them, as with Rough Quest who actually drifted in the late betting to start as a price of 7-1 that was definitely a 'value' one, given his outstanding chance on form.

3.00 MARTELL GRAND NATIONAL CHASE   **BBC1**
(Handicap: grade III: £142,534: 4m 4f) (28 runners)

301	1U53P5	YOUNG HUSTLER 16 (C,F,G,S) (G MacEchern) N Twiston-Davies 9-11-7	C Maude	80
302	6-1111P	LIFE OF A LORD 48 (F,G,S) (M Clancy) A O'Brien (Ire) 10-11-6	C Swan	77
303	011P0-4	DEEP BRAMBLE 35 (G,S) (P Barber) P Nicholls 9-11-5..........................	A P McCoy	79
304	1-45F42	SON OF WAR 34 (G,S) (Mrs V O'Brien) P McCreery (Ire) 9-11-0............	C O'Dwyer	77
305	1PF-P43	LUSTY LIGHT 42 (BF,F,G,S) (B Burrough) Mrs J Pitman 10-10-11	W Marston	73
306	1/23P2-P	PARTY POLITICS 35 (CD,F,G,S) (Mrs D Thompson) N Gaselee 12-10-11	C Llewellyn	77
307	F22F12	ROUGH QUEST 16 (G,S) (A Wates) T Casey 10-10-7	M A Fitzgerald	99
308	F0-20P3	CHATAM 18 (F,G,S) (A Nolan) M Pipe 12-10-3	J Lower	76
309	U0-3315	SUPERIOR FINISH 42 (BF,G,S) (P McGrane) Mrs J Pitman 10-10-2	R Dunwoody	79
310	/21P0-U	CAPTAIN DIBBLE 42 (F,G,S) (Mrs R Vaughan) N Twiston-Davies 11-10-0	T Jenks	80
311	P421-45	RUST NEVER SLEEPS 35 (G,S) (D Murphy) D Hassett (Ire) 12-10-0...........	T Horgan	77
312	0344P2	BISHOPS HALL 21 (F,G,S) (T Carroll) R Alner 10-10-0....................	Mr M Armytage	80
313	10-0411	WYLDE HIDE 20 (G,S) (J McManus) A Moore (Ire) 9-10-0..................	F Woods	73
314	P-P0603	ANTONIN 29 (F,G,S) (Baileys Horse Feeds) Mrs S Bramall 8-10-0	J Burke	80
315	P0-40P5	RIVERSIDE BOY 35 (B,G,S) (Bisgrove Partners) M Pipe 13-10-0..........	--	--
316	443644	BAVARD DIEU 21 (F,G,S) (Saguaro Stables) N Gaselee 8-10-0....................	J F Titley	70
317	0-40222	ENCORE UN PEU 18 (G,S) (V Nally) M Pipe 9-10-0	D Bridgwater	81
318	4P-52PF	SIR PETER LELY 28 (V,F,G,S) (J Doyle Ltd) M Hammond 9-10-0.........	Mr C Bonner	65
319	1-FP345	BRACKENFIELD 14 (B,F,G,S) (T and J Curry) P Nicholls 10-10-0............	Guy Lewis	64
320	3-35304	OVER THE DEEL 29 (F,G,S) (D Davies) H Johnson 10-10-0..............	Mr T McCarthy	80
321	45-FP0F	INTO THE RED 42 (C,G,S) (J Huckle) J White 12-10-0	R Guest	79
322	F21-F40	GREENHILL RAFFLES 105 (F,G,S) (P Russell) Miss L Russell 10-10-0	M Foster	57
323	P-36236	VICOMPT DE VALMONT 42 (G,S) (J Blackwell) P Nicholls 11-10-0............	P Hide	62
324	04PU22	PLASTIC SPACEAGE 21 (BF,G,S) (Spaceage Plastics) J Old 13-10-0	G Upton	64
325	P-11134	OVER THE STREAM 115 (F,G) (J & E Gordon) K Bailey 10-10-0	A Thornton	58
326	21406P	THREE BROWNIES 14 (B,G,S) (Mrs A Daly) M Morris (Ire) 9-10-0............	P Carberry	56
327	2-41134	FAR SENIOR 112 (F,G) (P Wegmann) P Wegmann 10-10-0......................	T Eley	54
328	225/4-5	SURE METAL 26 (F,G,S) (L Morgan) D McCain 13-10-0..................	D McCain	--

Long handicap: Captain Dibble 9-12, Rust Never Sleeps 9-12, Bishops Hall 9-11, Wylde Hide 9-8, Antonin 9-7, Riverside Boy 9-7, Bavard Dieu 9-5, Encore Un Peu 9-5, Sir Peter Lely 9-2, Brackenfield 8-13, Over The Deel 8-11, Into The Red 8-9, Greenhill Raffles 8-8, Vicompt De Valmont 8-8, Plastic Spaceage 8-6, Over The Stream 8-6, Three Brownies 8-6, Far Senior 8-6, Sure Metal 8-6.

BETTING: 7-1 Rough Quest, Superior Finish, Young Hustler, Son Of War, 8-1 Life Of A Lord, Party Politics, 10-1 Deep Bramble, 14-1 Lusty Light, 16-1 Wylde Hide, 20-1 Bishops Hall, 22-1 Rust Never Sleeps, 25-1 Chatam, 33-1 others.

1995: ROYAL ATHLETE 12-10-6 J Titley (40-1) Mrs J Pitman 35 ran

171

STRATEGY 39

SUPPORTING HORSES FAVOURED IN THE MARKET

When formerly acting as the author of a regular betting market report for *Racing Monthly* and undertaking research for my booklet, the *Backers Guide to the Betting Market* (obtainable for £5 from 14 Erisey Terrace, Falmouth, Cornwall TR11 2AP) I made the discovery that, perhaps despite the belief of many, only a minority of downward moves in the betting augur well for the chances of the horses concerned!

If readers of this book can attend the races, or be present in betting shops when they take place, then they are in a position to apply a strategy-based on movements in the market. What they should look for, as they monitor any changes in the odds of the runners for a race, is a situation (not a very common one) whereby both a first and second favourite drift in the pre-race betting shows and one other horse is the only one that has its odds cut to a rate lower than it received in the first show.

Races with this particular betting pattern can be well worth waiting for, as the following example should make clear.

In fact, in the Dove Selling Handicap Hurdle, the 5-1 favourite, Side Bar, drifted out from its opening rate of 9-2, as did the second favourite, Doman that opened at 4-1. Significantly, the 'strategy qualifier', the 6-1 winner Lofty Deed, was backed down to this price from its longer opening rate of 7-1, as the following detailed race and betting return from *The Racing Post* clearly shows.

1.45 Dove Selling Handicap Hurdle

[OFF 1.45] **(Class G)** 2m

For: 4yo+ Rated 0-90 1st £2,372.50 2nd £660.00 3rd £317.50

1   **LOFTY DEED** (USA) 5 10-8.................................G Bradley
b g by Shadeed (USA)—Soar Aloft (USA) (Avatar (USA))
held up, headway approaching 6th, led 2 out, driven out bet
of £4,200-£600 each way[op 7/1 tchd 8/1, 9/1 in a place] **6/1**

2   1½ **WILL SOON** 6 11-2...A Maguire
ch g by Nicholas Bill—Henceforth (Full of Hope)
always prominent, led 3 out, headed next, ridden approaching
last, no extra flat   [op 6/1] **7/1**

3   1¼ **ROCKY BAY** 6 10-5...J A McCarthy
ch m by Bold Owl—Overseas (Sea Hawk II)
chased leaders, led 5th, headed 3 out, hard ridden
approaching last, no extra flat **8/1**

4   2½ **WADADA** 4 10-0...A S Smith
b/br g by Adbass (USA)—No Rejection (Mummy's Pet)
prominent, ridden 2 out, stayed on same pace   [op
25/1] **33/1**

5   20 **GARDA'S GOLD** 12 10-0b ....D Meredith (3)
held up, headway 5th, weakened 3 out **10/1**

6   8 **MUST BE MAGICAL** (USA) 7 10-13.............A Thornton
mid-division, effort approaching 6th, soon beaten   [op 10/1
after 12/1 in a place, tchd 7/1] **8/1**

7   ¾ **DOMAN** 6 10-13..M Dwyer
prominent, ridden 6th, weakened next   [op 4/1 tchd 6/1 in a
place] **11/2**

8   ¾ **MILLIE** (USA) 7 10-0..M Robinson
behind and ridden 3rd, stayed on from 2 out, nearest
finish **50/1**

9   3 **SIDE BAR** 5 10-10v'...J Ryan
soon prominent, weakened 5th   [op 9/2] **5/1F**

10   15 **SCHWEPPES TONIC** 9 11-10h ....D J Burchell
led to 5th, gradually weakened   [op 10/1 tchd 12/1 in
places] **11/1**

11   13 **TYNRON DOON** 6 10-12b...........................N Williamson
chased leaders to 5th   [op 4/1] **6/1**

12   13 **BURN BRIDGE** (USA) 9 11-1.................M A Fitzgerald
always in rear **33/1**

13   9 **ALMOST A PRINCESS** 7 9-7....................M J Griffiths (7)
prominent to 4th, soon behind [op 16/1 after 33/1 in a place,
tchd 20/1] **16/1**

P   **EMERALD VENTURE** 8 11-4 ....Pat Caldwell
always in rear, tailed off when pulled up before last   [op
14/1] **20/1**

F   **BY FAR** (USA) 9 11-0...D Gallagher
fell 3rd   [tchd 33/1 in a place] **25/1**

P   **VALE OF YORK** 7 9-7.....................................Miss R Clark (7)
headway 4th, weakened approaching 6th, tailed off when
pulled up before last **100/1**

16 ran   **TIME:** 4m 19.10s (slow by 27.30s)   **SP TOTAL PERCENT** 136
1st OWNER: Mrs P A Linton TRAINER: W J Musson (Newmarket, Suffolk)
BRED: Longleaf Pine Farm
2nd OWNER: Park Racing Partnership TRAINER: W Bentley
3rd OWNER: Lodge Cross Partnership TRAINER: B J Llewellyn
4th OWNER: A E Blee TRAINER: S W Campion
TOTE: WIN £9.20 PL £2.60,£1.30,£3.70,£3.30 DF: £45.20 CSF: £48.96
TRICAST : £325.50

Selling details: The winner was bought in for 4,880gns
TOTE TRIO £125.40 - 3.02 winning units, pool £533.69

PART FIVE

SIDING WITH THE BIZARRE

STRATEGY 40

'DOUBLING UP' FOR SUCCESS

The type of 'doubling up' involved in some forms of multiple betting and retrieval staking normally makes little appeal to me, but there is one strange and essentially 'fun' variation of this procedure that, on occasion, and quite inexplicably, produces some very handsome returns.

As it happens, I came across the inspiration for this in 1995 when, in *The Paddock Book* by R Rodrigo I read an article by *Sunstar* with the intriguing title of *Four letter words come third*. This, rather than a plea for clean speech in public, was actually part of a system of racehorse selection originally devised by a Mr Searle of Ludgate Circus. This, rather oddly, involves supporting horses with names - for example Freebooter - in which the same letters follow each other. In Mr Searle's original, very complicated, rules (which I do not totally apply in my 'fun' and far simpler adaptation of his plan) four lettered qualifiers - like Loot for example - came third in an order of preference which explains the title of Sunstar's entertaining article!

Four Letter Words Come Third

'Sunstar'

MOST SYSTEMS are naturally somewhat intricate, but the careful man should not go astray. The majority of systems, too, cannot be properly worked by stay-at-home backers, although these are the people to whom a really good system would prove most acceptable. Many backers work systems on newspaper tips, betting forecasts, etc., but these are hardly systems in the ordinary sense of the word. Newspaper correspondents, as a rule, are sound and reliable, but they have their runs of bad luck. Racing men are now very well served with information, and the proprietors of the daily and evening papers spend large sums for the benefit of their racing patrons. The evening papers give a pretty accurate list of the day's runners, and this will considerably help the stay-at-home backers to profitably follow the system now put before them.

The system is to follow horses which have double letters in their names.

To my astonishment, my delight and, occasionally, my financial benefit, there were several occasions in 1995 (and there are many each season) when the backing of double lettered horses on their own in win singles, or in combinations that involve forecasts and such bets as trios and placepots and even six horse accumulators, produces quite spectacular dividends! Indeed, my personal, rather 'loose' interpretation of the strategy's original rules (which, on busy racing days I find too involved to work through), would have pinpointed six out of six double-lettered strategy qualifiers at Salisbury, on 11 August 1995!

SALISBURY

Going: FIRM

2.00 (6f212y): **POLAR QUEEN** (G Hind, 5-1) 1; **Fresh Fruit Daily** (5-1) 2; **Azdihaar** (2-1F) 3. 13 ran. hd, 1. (J Gosden). Tote: win £6.20; places £1.90, £1.80, £1.20. Dual F'cast: £25.70. CSF: £31.19. Trio: £12.90.

2.30 (1m6f h'cap): **DISPUTED CALL** (M Henry, 6-1) 1; **Supreme Star** (7-4F) 2; **Wottashambles** (5-1) 3. 8 ran. 8, 3½. (J Ffitch-Heyes). Tote: £6.50; pl £1.40, £1.30, £1.90. DF: £8.10. CSF: £16.30. Tcast £49.67.

3.00 (6f): **HURTLEBERRY** (M Henry, 7-2) 1; **Lucky Revenge** (50-1) 2; **Fond Embrace** (4-6F) 3. 10 ran. hd, 3½. (Lord Huntingdon). Tote: win £6.40; places £1.60, £5.60, £1.20. Dual F'cast: £194.40. CSF: £117.11. Trio: £77.90.

3.30 (1m h'cap): **FIONN DE COOL** (T Quinn, 9-2) 1; **Almond Rock** (7-2F) 2; **Weaver Bird** (4-1) 3. 8 ran. ¾, ½. (R Akehurst). Tote: win £5.90; places £1.30, £1.80, £1.60. Dual F'cast: £15.30. CSF: £18.83. Tricast: £59.64.

4.00 (6f212y): **KNIGHT COMMANDER** (M Roberts, 100-30) 1; **Muktabas** (15-8F) 2; **Hindaawee** (16-2) 3. 6 ran. 1¼, 1¾. (R Hannon). Tote: win £3.20; places £2.10, £1.60. Dual F'cast: £4.70. CSF: £9.88.

4.30 (6f h'cap): **LAW COMMISSION** (M Roberts, 14-1) 1; **Double Bounce** (7-4F) 2; **Norling** (16-1) 3. 12 ran. nk, nk. (D Elsworth). Tote: win £13.70; places £3.50, £1.70, £3.50. Dual F'cast: £12.10. CSF: £40.98. Tricast: £405.47. Trio: £44.60.

JACKPOT: Not won. Pool of £14,079.77 carried forward to Newbury today.

QUADPOT: £8.60. PLACEPOT: £16.80.

These, as can be seen from the following full set of results from this meeting, went in at 5-1, 6-1, 7-2, 9-2, 100-30 and 14-1! Indeed, the unclaimed jackpot involving them amounted to £14,079.77p!

Again, only 12 days later, at Ascot's evening meeting on 25 July 1995, only Rock Sharp, victorious in the 7.20, prevented a six-timer from again being landed by horses with letters in their names that were not just repeated but doubled. On this occasion, among the five strategy qualifiers, three won at prices as high at 14-1, 8-1 and 5-1!

If any readers feel that these two spectacularly successful days for this zany strategy were mere flashes in the pan in the baking hot summer of 1995, then they should ponder the fact that both followed hard on the heels of the four out of seven successes that were achieved at Pontefract by the double lettered brigade on 3 August 1995!

As for strategy qualifiers coupled in forecast bets, two of these, the 100-1 winner, Qattara and runner-up, Decent Penny, produced forecast payments of £713.10 (dual) and £779.11 (straight) when these runners dominated an Ayr race, also run in the 1995 season, during which in December, to my still greater amazement, something even more implausible happened, as the year of 'double-double' lettered Lammtarra's 14-1 success in the Derby drew to a close! What happened was that, at perhaps significantly 'double lettered' Nottingham, I found that, in the six races out of seven in which it was possible to make forecast bets, first and second places were duly achieved by double lettered strategy qualifiers!

The respective forecasts on:

NOTTINGHAM

Going: ch, GOOD; hdle, GOOD TO SOFT

12.30 (2m5f110y h'cap hdle): **BARRY-BEN** (R Massey, 7-2) 1; **Trevveerhan** (11-2) 2; **Its Grand** (10-1) 3. 7 ran. Wakt 9-4F. 2¼, 3. (W Brisbourne). Tote: win £4.80; places £2.80, £2.20. DF: £18.00. CSF: £21.66.

1.00 (2m nov hdle): **MILL THYME** (G Lee, 5-1JF) 1; **Daily Boy** (8-1) 2; **Wisdom** (7-1) 3. 25 ran. Nordic Breeze 5JF. 1¼, 3½. (Mrs M Reveley). Tote: win £5.10; places £2.00, £3.90, £4.00. Dual F'cast: £20.20. CSF: £53.78. Trio: £18.10.

1.30 (3m3f110y h'cap ch): **STUNNING STUFF** (R Johnson, 33-1) 1; **Columcille** (15-8F) 2; **Paper Star** (7-1) 3. 7 ran. dist, dist. (T George). Tote: win £26.00; places £4.20, £1.50. CSF: £30.00. CSF: £88.18.

2.00 (2m nov hdle): **CASTLE SWEEP** (P Niven, 4-7F) 1; **Keep It Zipped** (100-30) 2; **Macgeorge** (20-1) 3. 12 ran. 5, 5. (D Nicholson). Tote: win £1.80; places £1.00, £1.40, £4.80. Dual F'cast: £1.60. CSF: £3.73. Trio: £29.50. NR: Zitas Son.

2.30 (2m h'cap hdle): **FOX SPARROW** (A S Smith, 7-1) 1; **Zaitoon** (2-1) 2; **Suivez** (3-1) 3. 4 ran. Keep Your Distance 6-4F. 8, 2. (N Tinkler). Tote: win £6.80. Dual F'cast: £9.00. CSF: £19.19. NR: Saint Ciel.

3.00 (2m nov ch): **ASK TOM** (R Garritty, 5-1) 1; **Nagobelia** (10-1) 2; **Callisoe Bay** (1-5F) fell, remtd 3. 4 ran. dist, dist. (T Tate). Tote: win £4.30. DF: £12.80. CSF: £31.18.

3.30 (2m NH flat): **ST MELLION DRIVE** (O Burrows, 5-2F) 1; **Euphoric Illusion** (7-2) 2; **Riding Crop** (11-2) 3. 13 ran. ¾, nk. (M Pipe). Tote: win £2.00; places £1.00, £1.80, £2.70. Dual F'cast: £10.10. CSF: £13.24. Trio: £35.70. NR: Supreme Norman.

PLACEPOT: £4,879.60. QUADPOT: £20.70.

- paid dividends totalling £199.78 (straight) and £88.90 (dual) to prove that, if one wants to be accommodated as a winning horseplayer, it can, on occasion, pay to 'double up'!

Incidentally, had the only double-lettered runner in Nottingham's 3.00 race not fallen at the last fence, when in the lead, this rather bizarre, but oddly often successful, strategy would have produced a magnificent seven successive forecasts and landed a handsome placepot dividend!

Should readers imagine that 'doubling up for success' is a very rare possibility, then they might care to study the following letter, sent in 1997 to *The Racing Times* magazine.

DOUBLE OR NOTHING!

Dear Saddle Bag

I have discovered a system which has provided a steady stream of Grand National winners over the years and has now located 4 out of the last 5 Derby winners.

Using this simple method - back horses which contain the same 3rd and 4th letters in their name. Listed below are some of the winners it has flung up in the past.

Commander In Chief '93

Lammtarra '95

Shaamit '96

and now Benny The Dip '97.

Grand National winners have been:-

Well To Do, Hallo Dandy, Little Polveir, Freebooter, Merry Man II, Ben Nevis, Russian Hero etc

Good luck with the Racing Times I have never seen a magazine improve so much.

Mr C Jones Nottingham.

STRATEGY 41

ASSESSING ASTROLOGICAL SELECTIONS

Horse racing advisers can sometimes seem like seers; indeed once a phenomenally successful run of Peter O'Sullevan led his press room colleagues to style him 'Peter the Great'! As it happens, I take an open-minded and passing interest in the predictions of gurus, sages and clairvoyants and others who claim to be able to divine the future. I have even purchased the tips of a racecourse tipster in monk's robes called Hully Gully who claimed to have the ear of the Almighty!

Old Moore, of course, whose world famous Almanac went into its 300th edition in 1997, is one of the best known and most widely read prophets and it can so happen that his predictions as regards jockeys can prove spectacularly successful!

As with any other selection method based on non-scientific and non-numerical assessments of horses' chances, I only take its claims seriously if they are supported by the dispassionate evaluations of a private handicapper.

Interestingly, this was the case on 11 August 1997 when, on consulting Old Moore's assessments of the winning prospects of leading jockeys, I read the following: 'between August 11th and the end of the racing season Dettori will have an outstanding run of good fortune'.

I knew that in the case of this peerless young Italian such a run was not unprecedented, as towards the end of the previous season at Ascot, he had ridden a record seven consecutive winners and so gone right through the card!

Naturally then, on 11 August I was very keen to assess the chances of Dettori's eight mounts that were spread over two meetings - at Windsor and, later, at Leicester. The only one of these eight that was shown as the clear form selection in my *Times* was Dr Martens, Dettori's first mount at Windsor. This was why I decided to pull on my betting boots and was pleased to see Frankie boot home the first of five winners on this red letter racing day. Sadly, as one of too little astrological faith, I let his other four winners go unbacked, even though two were also favourites and another the forecast favourite!

Thus Frankie ended the day with five winners from eight rides and I did so, quite content with my 6-4 winner!

As a 'fun' strategy 'Jockeys predicted to succeed' thus seemed to have more to it than was dreamt of in my rather sceptical philosophy as a hard-bitten and hard to convince systems guru!

WINDSOR Good to firm

2.00 (1m 3f 135yds 'S') — BRIGH-
STONE (A McGlone) 1-4 **Fav** 1;
Foleys Quest (P Cleary) 12-1 2;
Northern Drums (T Sprake) 10-1 3.
5 ran. (M Pipe, Wellington). nk, 1½.
Tote: £1.10; £1.10, £3.20. **DF:**
£2.70. **CSF:** £4.53. **NR:** High Desire.
  2.30 (1m 67yds) — DR MARTENS
(L Dettori) 6-4 **Fav** 1; **Tonight's
Prize** (S Sanders) 4-1 2;
Slipstream Star (Martin Dwyer) 11-
1 3. 17 ran. (L Cumani,
Newmarket). hd, 8. **Tote:** £2.10;
£1.40, £1.40, £3.20. **DF:** £4.00.
CSF: £6.50. **NR:** Bright Fountain.
  3.00 (5f 217yds 2yo) — MIJANA (L
Dettori) 7-4 **Fav** 1; **Speedfit Too** (G
Carter) 13-2 2; **Halmahera** (S
Whitworth) 11-4 (**2ndFav**) 3. 6 ran.
(J Gosden, Newmarket). hd, 2.
Tote: £3.90; £1.50, £3.30. **DF:**
£15.20. **CSF:** £12.97.
  3.30 (1m 67yds Hcap) — GOLD
LANCE (L Dettori) 4-1 **Fav** 1;
Queen's Insignia (C Rutter) 10-1 2;
Multi Franchise (Dane O'Neill) 16-1
3; **Vanborough Lad** (R Ffrench) 11-
2 (**2ndFav**) 4. 18 ran. (R O'Sullivan,
Whitcombe). 1, hd, 1¼. **Tote:** £5.60;
£1.90, £1.70, £4.70, £1.60. **DF:**
£31.80. **CSF:** £43.59. **Tricast:**
£593.18.
  4.00 (1m 2f 7yds Hcap) — SEAT-
TLE SWING (G Milligan) 8-1 1;
Ocean Park (P Doe) 6-1 2; **Monte
Cavo** (P Roberts) 3-1 (**2ndFav**) 3. 6
ran. 6-4 Fav Monument. (Mrs A J
Perrett, Pulborough). 1¼, 1¾. **Tote:**
£11.20; £3.20, £2.40. **DF:** £26.00.
CSF: £48.87.
  4.30 (1m 3f 135yds Hcap) — FAR-
RINGDON HILL (C Ranson) 7-1 1;
Tarxien (Mr O McPhail) 5-1 2; **Mad
Militant** (Mr A Wintle) 11-2 3. 11
ran. 5-2 Fav Dauphin. (J Gosden,
Newmarket). shd, 2. **Tote:** £7.50;
£2.20, £2.40, £2.00. **DF:** £20.30.
CSF: £41.19. **Tricast:** £197.57. **NR:**
Mr Speculator.
  5.00 (5f 217yds 2yo Hcap) —
REGAL REVOLUTION (J Lowe) 4-1
(Jt2ndFav) 1; **Shalad'or** (T Sprake)
4-1 2; **Muftumenuf** (A McGlone) 14-
1 3. 8 ran. 7-4 Fav Zena. (P
Walwyn, Lambourn). 1½, hd. **Tote:**
£3.80; £1.60, £1.40, £2.50. **DF:**
£11.20. **CSF:** £20.52. **Tricast:**
£194.57. **NR:** Balance The Books.
  Jackpot £14,485.00.
  Placepot £111.00.
  Quadpot £79.20.

Fav Fleet Cadet. (C Brooks). 26, 1¼.
Tote: £3.40; £1.50, £2.70. **DF:**
£7.80. **CSF:** £21.89.
  4.45 (2m 3yo Hdle) — RUNNING
DE CERISY (A McCoy) 4-7 **Fav** 1;
Stoned Imaculate 20-1 2; **Silema
Creek** 25-1 3. 8 ran. (M Pipe). 3,
shd. **Tote:** £1.50; £1.20, £1.20,
£3.20. **DF:** £14.70. **CSF:** £16.08.
  Placepot £398.70.
  Quadpot £26.20.

LEICESTER   **Good**

5.50 (7f 9yds 2yo) — COLLEVILLE
(R Cochrane) 20-1 1; **Mustique
Dream** 4-1 2; **Saeedah** 4-5 **Fav** 3 20
ran (M Jarvis). 3, shd. **Tote:** £23.90;
£9.40, £1.60, £1.10. **DF:** £444.90.
CSF: £98.06.
  6.20 (5f 218yds 2yo Hcap) —
MARSKE MACHINE (R Cochrane)
7-1 1; **Bermuda Triangle** 7-2 **Fav** 2;
Maedaley 16-1 3. 14 ran (N Tinkler).
nk, 2½. **Tote:** £7.90; £2.00, £2.30,
£8.30. **DF:** £10.00. **CSF:** £32.41.
Tricast: £382.46.
  6.50 (1m 8yds Hcap) — CITY
GAMBLER (M Rimmer) 12-1 1;
Rocky Dance 5-1 2; **Inclination** 8-1
3. 11 ran 5-2 Fav Racing Heart (G
Bravery). 1½, ½. **Tote:** £10.40;
£3.30, £2.60, £1.70. **DF:** £24.60.
CSF: £88.04. **Tricast:** £371.64.
  7.20 (1m 1f 218yds Hcap) —
CORETTA (L Dettori) 11-4 1; **Pekay**
6-1 2; **Boss Lady** 15-8 **Fav** 3. 8 ran
(L Cumani). 2, 4. **Tote:** £4.20; £1.80,
£2.10, £1.10. **DF:** £14.30. **CSF:**
£18.14. **Tricast:** £34.09.
  7.50 (7f 9yds) — PETITE
DANSEUSE (L Dettori) 7-2 1; **Davis
Rock** 6-1 2; **Oxbane** 9-1 3. 12 ran 2-
1 Fav Secret Combe (C Dwyer). 3,
1½. **Tote:** £4.80; £1.90, £2.00,
£2.30. **DF:** £15.00. **CSF:** £25.29.
NR: Feel A Line.
  8.20 (1m 3f 183yds) — LOOKOUT
(M Hills) 7-2 1; **Harmony Hall** 9-1 2;
Arriving 6-4 **Fav** 3. 9 ran (B Hills).
½, 3. **Tote:** £4.80; £1.50, £4.30,
£1.10. **DF:** £21.60. **CSF:** £38.71.